BRAVE RIDER

Also by Harvey Goodman

Along the Fortune Trail

Winds of Redemption

So Too My Love

In the Event Of

The Secret of El Salto

BRAVE RIDER

HARVEY GOODMAN

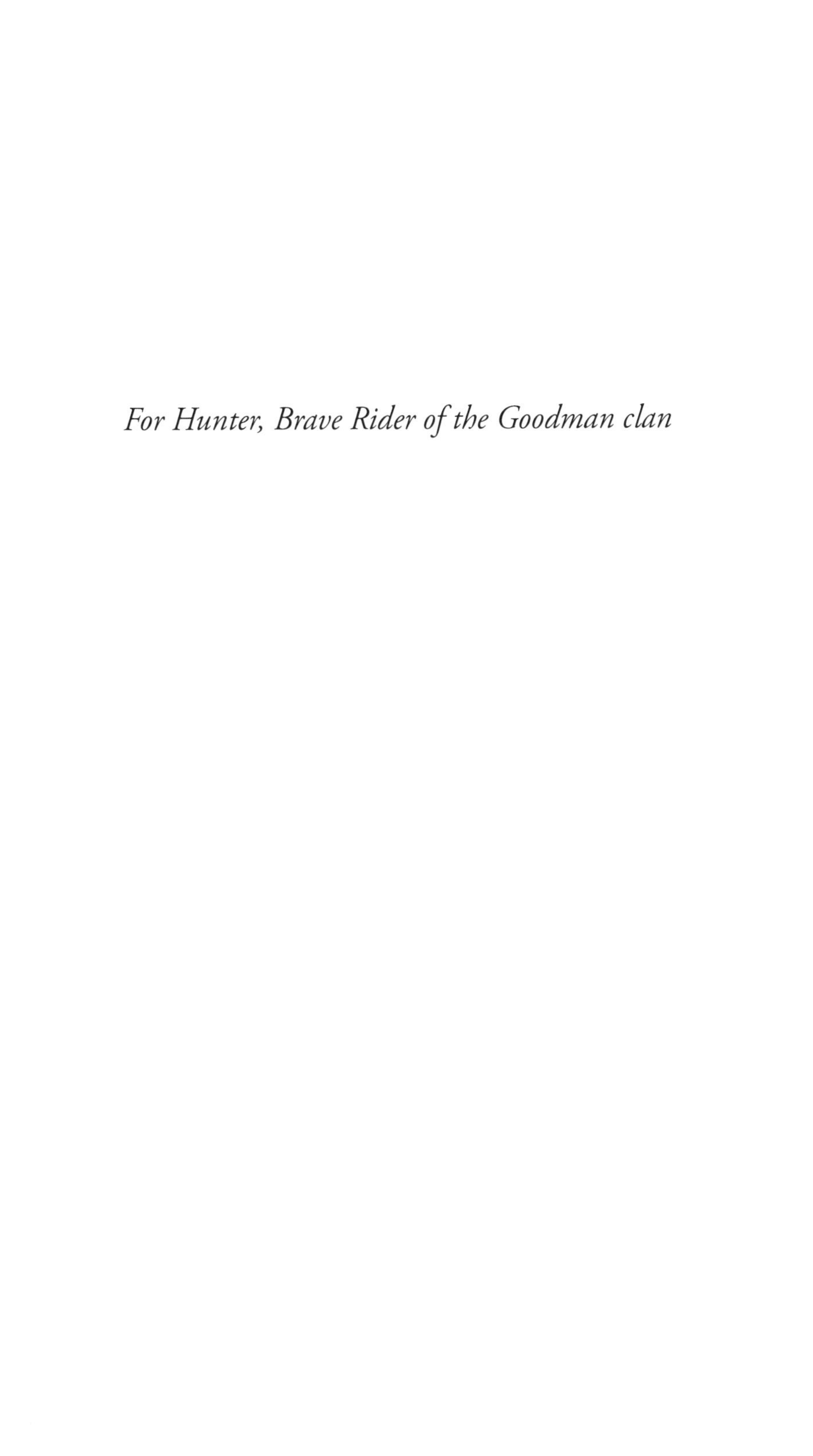

For Hunter, Brave Rider of the Goodman clan

Published by
Jupiter Sky Publishing LLC
Westcliffe, Colorado

ISBN 9798686283619

Cover design by Shelley Savoy
Print layout and ebook conversion by booknook.biz

1

The stagecoach rumbled over a partially washed out trail on the high plain, pulled by four big mules who were working harder now, loping at a good speed as the butte pass drew closer. A scent of sage wafted lightly as rays of searing white afternoon sun stretched through dark, broken clouds. On the driver's seat, Ollie held the reins. A tough young man named Jericho sat shotgun next to him, peering about at the countryside as he cradled the short double-barrel. An urge hit Ollie.

"You think you can roll a smoke right now?" Ollie asked, keeping his eyes fixed on the trail ahead.

The stage dipped hard left and jolted rough as Ollie took the best of the water-cut ravine that was unavoidable. Five people inside slammed to the seat and then lifted to the air, momentarily drifting in suspense of how long they might remain there. They rammed their seats again with a high-pitched whoop from a few.

"Sorry, folks!" Ollie called out. But Ollie wasn't really sorry. It was just a verbal nod to their endurance. Ollie wouldn't be slowing down and everybody knew it.

"Well, kid? What about it?" Ollie said as he handed his makings over.

Jericho gave a last quick appraisal of the trail and slipped the shotgun into the scabbard spiked to the end of the bench.

"I can sure roll it just as good as you could ever imagine!" Jericho said, taking the makings pouch from Ollie. "Might end up usin' a little more tobacco is all."

Jericho opened the pouch and fished for a paper and stick match. Ollie's eyes alternated between the trail and Jericho's progress. As Jericho tapped out tobacco to the paper, the stage caught another violent bump, causing half the pouch to suddenly empty onto the paper, and then into the wind.

"Whup!" Jericho exclaimed with a half laugh. "Better get it twisted 'fore you got nothin' left!"

He deftly pulled the drawstring on the pouch with his thumb and forefinger while his other hand pinched the top of the paper, preserving the trough of tobacco that remained.

"Well, I need the one you got started so don't lose it!" Ollie said.

"Nope, nope… won't do it," Jericho said as he handed the pouch back. Then he quickly rolled the smoke tight and held it out to Ollie.

"Hey, light it, would you," Ollie said, suddenly attentive to the reins to avoid the worst of the trail.

Jericho slipped the smoke to his lips then fired the match off the mahogany grip of his holstered pistol, expertly cupping his hand to shield the flame as he lit the smoke. He took one deep drag and exhaled with satisfaction.

"Here ya go," he said, handing the smoke to Ollie.

"Obliged. Say, did you want one too?"

"Ya know that's a fine notion. I believe I will."

Ollie started to hand his makings pouch over to Jericho.

"No, no… I got my own. Thanks just the same."

Jericho reached in his top pocket and pulled out a rolled smoke and match, quickly firing it and lighting his smoke.

Ollie looked over with disgust. "You got more of those rolled ones?"

"Eight or so," Jericho said.

"Peckerweed! Could have just given me one of yours and saved some time."

Jericho exhaled a drag and gave a nonchalant shrug. "You never asked. Figured you were partial to your own brand. Most are."

"You ain't smoked one since we met three hours ago. Didn't know you had any!" Ollie chimed then dragged on his smoke.

Jericho reached in his shirt pocket and pulled out three rolled smokes. "Here's a few… case ya want another soon. I reckon you'll like my tobacco better."

Ollie one-handed the reins and accepted the cigarettes, quickly slipping them into his coat pocket with a wry smile. "Say, what the hell is your name again, kid?"

"Jericho Buck."

"Buck? Ain't heard that one before. Where you from?"

"Here in the territory, over to the junction of the Colorado and the Seedskeedee Rivers… little town called Elsie."

"Colorado and the Seedskeedee?" Ollie recollected. "I was over that way once… before you were born, likely. Not much more than canyons, I recollect."

Jericho dragged on his smoke. "Some good farmland in spots, but I ain't one for farmin'."

"No?" Ollie quipped. "What are you one for?"

"Well… since I left home at fourteen… mostly wanderin'. Worked at freightin' on barge and land, cowboyin', bartendin', construction, buildings and layin' rails, paintin', stockyards, livery hand… hell, I even took up with a militia patrol for a couple months when there was trouble with Indians back in Abilene."

Ollie held the reins and dragged on his smoke. "You don't look much older'n fourteen now."

"Twenty-two, come November."

Ollie gave a slight nod of his head, his eyes remaining fixed on the trail as the stage bumped and rumbled. "Damn be, Jericho Buck, if I'd known you had such a colorful past, I'd'a taken up conversation with you a couple hours back when we started."

"Happy to oblige now," Jericho said. "My ma always told me not to go yappin' at my elders lest they was speakin' to me first. You wasn't speakin'... so I wasn't yappin'."

"Good counsel your ma gave you," Ollie said with a laugh. "I'm just glad you were in town and heard our regular was bad sick. We're half a day late and only getting one leg of the round-trip... but that's something... better'n none. And you'll get a free night's lodging and meals along with your pay, compliments of the Butterfield Stage Line. Good hotel too! Nice featherbeds."

"I'm game," Jericho said, taking another drag. "Pretty country in here. Never seen it."

Jericho looked off to his right where a half mile away a mild slope of hillside sat covered with ponderosa pine, the tips of the highest trees ablaze with the setting sun not far above.

"Say, you reckon I could get a few more runs if your sick man is down for a spell?" Jericho asked.

"I don't see why not... if he's down for a spell, and you're stickin' around for a while."

A voice boomed from the side of the stage where one of the occupants had his head out the door. "Hey! I'm gonna be sick out both ends! Stop the stage!"

Ollie pulled on the reins and slowed the team to a stop, yelling at the moment the wheels ceased rolling. "You got one minute, mister! So get rid of whatever ails you quick or you'll be walking the last six miles to town!"

The man speedily hopped down from the coach, doubled over at the waist and groaning. The trees to the west were too far away, and the butte wall fifty yards to the east offered no trees or brush for privacy. He quickly moved around to the back of the stage.

"We'll make it before dark," Ollie said.

Jericho took a last drag and flicked his smoke down to the dirt. Then he caught the movement from the corner of his eye and squinted into the sun at the treed hillside just over a mile away.

"Riders comin' out of them trees... three of 'em," Jericho stated with calm intent as he began to retrieve the shotgun from the scabbard.

Ollie was squinting where Jericho looked but could see nothing in the glare.

"Get yer hand off that shotgun or I'll blow you outta yer seat! Hands up!" said the man who'd claimed he was sick. He'd exited on Ollie's side then gone around the back of the stage and snuck up low and tight on Jericho's side before jumping into sight with a Colt Root .31 in each hand, one aimed at the stage door and the other at Ollie and Jericho.

Ollie and Jericho raised their hands into plain sight. "Why, you lowdown snake!" Ollie said in disgust.

"We'll have that payroll up there. I know you got it," the man said.

The man's eyes shifted to the stage door as he yelled, "You folks get out here now!"

Ollie saw the instant the man's eyes looked to the stage door. He grabbed the reins and gave a quick "yip" to get the stage moving again. But the big boom brought flame from the barrel as the man fired, hitting Ollie in the high chest and knocking him to the side. Ollie toppled off the seat and hit the ground with a thud. The mules held steady. The stage door had begun to open for the remaining folks to exit but slammed shut again when the gunshot exploded from just feet away.

"I said get out here!" the man barked, looking to the stage door once again.

Jericho saw his chance and took it, slamming down to his left shoulder flat along the stage bench as his right hand flashed like keg powder to his pistol, pulling it in a hot blur and firing from his side at the same instant the man fired. The man's bullet missed and he jerked back, his legs no longer under him when Jericho's bullet took him through the forehead.

"He's done, I got 'im!" Jericho yelled to the passengers. He instantly leapt down to the dirt next to Ollie and grabbed him under both arms. "Open the door… help me get 'im in! Quick now… they're comin'!"

A man of medium build in his forties came out the door like a shot with his husky wife right behind him. They were dressed proper, like townsfolk. "We'll get his legs," the man said.

Jericho lifted Ollie's torso to the floor of the coach and set him down, half in and half out, with the man and his wife each holding a leg. In a flash, Jericho climbed in over Ollie and then pulled Ollie all the way into the coach on the floor while two women inside pulled their feet up to make room.

Ollie grunted. He was bleeding bad but still alive. His eyes came wide open and fixed on Jericho. "You got that skunk that shot me?"

"Yep. Forgot to tell you I worked in a wild-west show for a spell, too. Fast-draw trick shooter I was."

"Would'a been more of a trick if you'd shot him before he shot me," Ollie said with a faint smile.

"Yep, not my best figurin', Ollie. I'm truly sorry. You just hold on."

Jericho pulled a handkerchief from his pants pocket and pressed it on Ollie's wound. "Keep pressure on that… you ladies help 'im." The women nodded.

"Either one of you have a gun?" Jericho asked.

The older woman answered, "I have a derringer in my purse."

"Get it ready," Jericho said, then handed his pistol to the

younger girl who was pretty and looked about his own age. "You got five shots here. Just cock the hammer and pull the trigger for each shot. Be ready!"

She nodded at Jericho who suddenly bolted outside like a scalded cat.

Jericho looked the older man in the eye as if they were partners in survival. "My name's Jericho. Can you drive a team?"

"You bet I can. I'm George… my wife is Sybil. Let's get going!" he answered.

"Get in the coach, ma'am," Jericho said to the man's wife. She looked at her husband, who reached inside his coat and handed her a pistol.

"Go on, Sybil," he told her.

"If they get close, start shootin'," Jericho said to all of them. "But not till they're close… real close! All right, we're gonna roll hard and fast!"

Jericho jumped up to the bench and lifted the top of the box seat. He pulled out a Sharp's .52 rifle and then grabbed the shotgun from its scabbard and handed it to George, who had climbed to the driver's seat.

"Keep this handy," Jericho said as he eyed the three men coming on at a gallop less than a quarter mile away and closing fast.

"Right across my lap," George replied as he sat down and took the reins.

Jericho spoke as he crawled up, lying flat across the baggage on the roof: "Hold steady a minute… till I say go. See if I can whittle 'em down one 'fore we're bumpin' crazy."

Jericho rested the rifle across a bag, then cocked it and sighted on the man in the middle just as gunfire began to erupt from their pistols, landing errantly short. Jericho exhaled and squeezed easy. The big Sharps bucked, and the desperado in the middle looked like he'd been lassoed from behind and ripped from his saddle.

The remaining two men began zigzagging as they kept firing, their bullets spitting up dirt near the mule team.

"Go!" Jericho yelled as he began to work another cap into place and reload.

"Heeyahh!" George yelled, snapping the reins over and over.

The mules jumped and quickly worked to a gallop, pounding over the uneven and pitted trail with an urgency that George was reinforcing as he continued snapping the reins and yelling, "Heeyahh! Heeyahh!"

The two desperadoes chased on, having fallen in behind the stage. They were unable to close as quickly now, evasively veering back and forth to avoid being an easy target for the man laid out up top with a rifle.

Jericho tried to sight for a shot but the stage jolted wildly as the team snorted at a full gallop over the rough terrain. The stage settled for an instant of calm, giving Jericho a chance. He immediately drew a bead and squeezed the trigger just as the stage took a nasty bump. His shot missed and he began to go airborne over the side. Jericho's left hand struck out for the cargo strap in a last desperate attempt to stay aboard. He grabbed it as his torso flopped over the side, his feet dangling by the stage window and his right hand still grasping the Sharps rifle in open space. He hung one-armed over the side for a moment and then felt one of the women collecting his feet as if she was going to try and pull him in through the stage window.

"No!" Jericho yelled. "I'm goin' back up!"

Jericho saw one of the desperadoes putting spurs to his horse and closing rapidly, seeing the chance to take the stage. Jericho guessed the second man would be coming up the other side, and he knew what they'd go for.

"Get your guns ready! Out both sides! They're comin' up from behind! Don't let 'em by… they'll shoot at the mule team and wreck us!"

Jericho slung the rifle up on the roof then quickly grabbed hold with his right hand and pulled himself back up on top. There was no time to reload. He wedged the rifle in tight with the cargo and yelled to George.

"You still got that shotgun?"

George turned his head as he held the shotgun back for Jericho. George's hand was blood-covered and his nose was still pouring. Jericho grabbed the gun, knowing that George had been hit in the face by it when they'd hit the bad bump.

Gunfire cracked from each side of the stage as George's wife Sybil fired from one window and the pretty girl with Jericho's pistol fired from the other. The desperadoes were working wider and coming up fast, only seconds away from being in position to hit the mules. Jericho swung around low in a prone position atop the stage cargo, praying there wouldn't be another bad jolt to send him flying. He had never fired a short barrel before but knew the pattern would be wide and brutal inside of fifty feet, and his aim only needed to be close.

The desperado who was closest brought up a new pistol in aim as the pretty young woman futilely fired her last round in his direction. Then Jericho sighted and squeezed the trigger. The shotgun roared, belching flame and causing the desperado's horse to buckle at the front legs as a few buckshot took it in the head and neck. Yet most of the shot found the rider's body, sending him to a wild tumble as he and his horse rolled up in a dust cloud. Jericho immediately swung the shotgun toward the other man, knowing the remaining barrel was all he had left till he could reload the Sharps. There was no need. The last desperado had caught sight of his partner done badly. He quit the chase, knowing the same would be for him.

"Keep 'em runnin', George," Jericho yelled.

2

The sheriff walked in the front door of the hotel lobby and strode toward the side counter of the desk where the sign hanging above read "Stagecoach Tickets." He was tall and tough looking with a full beard and two tie-downs that rode at his hips. Sheriff Joe eyeballed the desk clerk and spoke in a tone of official business. "Well, Carter, where's the man that rode shotgun with Ollie?"

"Still in the dining room," Carter answered. "Ought to be finished up by now. The young gal that checked in said he saved their bacon. That right, Joe?"

Sheriff Joe nodded. "That's what they all say. Fast movin'… fast thinkin'." Sheriff Joe turned and began walking toward the dining room.

"What about Ollie?" Carter quickly asked.

"He's banged up but he'll make it," Sheriff Joe answered without looking back.

Sheriff Joe walked to the table that had the only person he didn't know in the dining room, a lone young man in the corner. Jericho took a drag and exhaled as he watched the man with the star approach.

"You like the food?" Sheriff Joe asked.

"Damn fine eatin'," Jericho answered as he stood up.

Sheriff Joe nodded. "Five plates empty… appears you ate enough to form such an opinion."

"I was plenty hungry, Sheriff. Ain't et since last evenin'. I'm Jericho Buck."

Jericho held out his hand to shake.

"Joe Crawford," the sheriff said, shaking hands. "I'm the sheriff here in Pasco. Happy to make your acquaintance."

"And yours," Jericho offered with a genial gaze as he looked up at the sheriff who had six inches and twenty years on him. "Reckon you want to ask me about that try at a holdup?"

Sheriff Joe shook his head once. "Nope, not really. I already got that story from everyone else, including Ollie. Mostly just wanted to say thanks and make sure you can ride shotgun on the return trip to Leibert in the morning."

"Hope so. My horse is waitin' on me at the livery. How's Ollie?"

"All right. Doc got the bullet out. It tore up some muscle but nothing vital. He's in no shape to travel, though. Lost a lot of blood and Doc thinks he broke two ribs when he fell off the stage. Ribs might prove to be the worst of it."

Jericho took a last drag then stubbed the butt into a copper ashtray on the table. "Glad to hear he'll be all right. Could'a worked out a whole lot worse for all of us, but George kept them mules goin' and blowin'… and them gals kept enough lead in the air to afford me the right timin'."

Sheriff Joe nodded. "Well, Ollie believes the stage being four hours late gave them the wrong timing. He thinks they were ready for an hour or two, but then got sloppy. Maybe eating or napping… playing cards, no telling… but they weren't ready or in position like they should have been."

"Yeah, I reckon he's right," Jericho agreed. "They should have been in front of us. Ended up chasin' us. No tellin' if their partner in the stage was supposed to get us stopped or just be a man on the inside. Seems like those three other fellers should'a been hidin' 'round the corner of that butte… Butte Pass Ollie called it… the best place for an ambush."

"Yep, that's it," Sheriff Joe said. "Of course we won't know unless we catch 'em. George said you killed the one that was in the coach, and likely two of them that was chasing… one with a rifle and another with a shotgun, same shotgun that bounced up and hit George in the face. Eight stitches doc gave him. So there might be only one left alive. My deputy will drive the coach with you tomorrow, and I'll ride along to where it happened. See if we can find some bodies, and maybe some clues to who these no-goods were."

"Okay, Sheriff. I'll be ready to go in the morning."

Sheriff Joe gave a nod. "Stage leaves at 8:30. Maybe you could drop in my office at 7:00 or so. My wife'll be cooking up some biscuits and gravy. The way you eat, you won't want to miss it… the best you'll ever get. And you could tell me what you remember about the men, their horses and such. I won't bother you now. Give you some time to think on it. That sound good?"

Jericho smiled. "Like a full belly and the wind at my back. I'll be there."

3

The horse lay dead under the bright morning sun, stripped of its saddle and tack just thirty feet from the trail where it had gone down.

Sheriff Joe stood over the dead animal. "Dislocated knee from the fall. Then your man shot it right there in the forehead. That hole ain't buckshot," Sheriff Joe said.

Jericho nodded from a few feet away. "No, sir."

A livery worker driving a buckboard sat nearby, having accompanied Joe out to haul back any evidence the sheriff deemed important, namely corpses. Joe's deputy remained atop the driver's bench of the stage, which had momentarily stopped to examine the scene. The stage's occupants, three men and a woman, milled around, keeping their distance, just happy to stretch their legs amid the crisp, beautiful day.

"This blood over here must be the rider's," Jericho said as he began walking the blood trail leading away from the horse. "Pretty good size feller… big boot prints. His partner picked him up over here, looks like. I hit him with some double ought buck… got to be tore up."

"Yeah, well, he ain't here so nothing more to see," Sheriff Joe said. "I trust the one you shot in the forehead close range is done for. Let's go see if he's still around."

Jericho looked north up the trail. "He should be 'bout a mile or so up, directly on the west side of the trail. The one I shot with the Sharps should be a few hundred feet west of him… and maybe four perches north."

"All right," Sheriff Joe said, then walked to his horse and mounted up as the stage passengers hastily re-boarded and Jericho climbed up to the shotgun seat. The weird procession started north up the trail again at a brisk trot with the stage leading and Sheriff Joe riding his appaloosa off to the side. The buckboard pulled up the rear.

Ten minutes later, they arrived at the spot where Jericho was sure the dead outlaw should have been. "Stop 'er right here for a minute," Jericho said. The deputy reined up.

Jericho hopped down off the stage and walked to the spot. "Lot'a blood in the dirt here. Looks like they tied on and dragged 'im," Jericho opined.

Sheriff Joe dismounted and began inspecting the site. "Yep, lot of blood to be sure," Joe agreed, his eyes naturally following the trail of where the body had been dragged away. "Well, I suppose they could have collected the horse of the man you shot with the Sharps. Wouldn't have to ride double then. Where'd he go down?"

Jericho pointed west. "Out somewhere near that lone saguaro. They came out of them trees yonder on the slope… three of 'em."

Sheriff Joe nodded. "I'll go take a look for a body out there, though I don't suspect I'll find anything. They went to some trouble to cover this up. Likely one of the stiffs could have been identified. That payroll they were after doesn't normally move by stage, so somebody had some inside information… a local, I'm thinking." Joe abruptly stuck his hand out to shake Jericho's. "I want to thank you again for what you did, son. You're one of the breed. Hope to see you again. But for now you get that stage rolling for Leibert."

Jericho nodded as he shook Joe's hand. "Down the trail, Sheriff."

****

The stage rolled up Leibert Main Street at half past noon, having covered the thirty miles from Pasco in four hours, which held more to the usual time the run took. Wagons, horses, and buggies lined the street, tied up at the assorted storefronts as people strode the boardwalk pursuing commerce in the bustling frontier town. The general store had two benches and a few barrels where a group of older local men sat, some smoking pipes, cigarettes, or cigars as they surveyed the day's action and offered speculative commentary to each other about the observed comings and goings. They all perked up when the stage rolled by, peering with curiosity at the man who rode shotgun. Jericho looked their way, feeling the collection of eyes examining him with aloof respect. One of the men tipped his hat as Jericho met their stares. Jericho quickly turned his head to the deputy driving the stage, thinking the gesture must have been for him. But the deputy's eyes were on the street, navigating toward the stage stop at the hotel, another half a block away.

The stage pulled up and stopped in front of the hotel. Jericho turned around to the gear on top and began loosening the straps.

"I'll hand down the bags," he said.

"Right," the deputy replied and began to climb down.

The deputy helped the only woman disembark, then took the luggage and gear from Jericho as he handed it down.

"I'll take 'er on down to the livery and help get the team changed out," Jericho said. "Got'a check on my horse anyways. Tell the agent we'll be ready to roll in half an hour."

"You want me to order you a plate? I'm gettin' one for myself. You'd have to eat fast."

Jericho didn't hesitate. "Yes, sir! Them biscuits and gravy done wore off already. I'll be back directly."

Jericho sat down and reined the team to a trot down to the

livery. He pulled the hand brake on and jumped down as the livery owner and two boys came out. The boys were about fourteen and knew their business as they expertly began unhitching the heavily lathered animals.

"Looks like they don't need any help with this," Jericho said to the livery operator.

"No," the man replied. "You best go get yourself a cup of coffee. Rusty and Cole will park it right out front of the hotel. They'd have come got it too! I'm surprised Ollie didn't tell you."

Jericho didn't want to tell the whole story there and then, so he just nodded his head. "Obliged. Hey, you got a stall for my horse another night?"

"Sure do… as long as you need. Two bits a day."

Jericho gave him a quarter. "I'll go get that coffee and a bite."

A few of the passengers for the return trip to Pasco sat on benches just outside the hotel's front door with bags or personals at hand. As Jericho came up the hotel steps, one of the waiting men who'd watched him walk from the livery asked, "Are we still on schedule to leave at one o'clock?"

"Yes, sir… should be right on the button. We'll be loadin' up in a quarter hour."

The man checked his pocket watch as Jericho continued on into the hotel and made for the ticket desk. Zeb Purnell, the ticket agent, saw him coming and suddenly became very animated raising his arms for emphasis.

"Heard all about it! Heard all about it!" Zeb declared in tone of reverent newsworthiness. Zeb quickly stood up and extended his hand to shake Jericho's. "On behalf of the Butterfield Stage Line, I offer hearty gratitude and congratulations for your heroic actions!"

Jericho glanced about and waxed a bit embarrassed, knowing other people within earshot were now looking. His reply was mildly quiet. "Wasn't nothin' special. Just doin' my job."

"Don't be modest now… you laid some big tracks, boy! Got the whole story from our area supervisor, Gator Hawkins, two hours ago. He rode in early from Pasco just to tell it and report on Ollie. Half the town knows by now, the other half by sundown! There's a bonus for your pay, too!"

Jericho nodded his head with a half-smile, just wanting to get to his meal and the cup of coffee. He came right to the point. "So I can go on workin' for you for awhile? Ollie's laid up and your other man's down… the one who was bad sick yesterday. I can work as long as you need me, I can."

Zeb's expression suddenly turned solemn and guarded. His words came quieter. "Well, you see… the thing of it is that Horace… he's the man that was sick… Horace is better today. Had a bad bug yesterday, throwing up with fever, but it's passed now and he's our regular man… a good man. Got a wife and two kids. He needs his job. He'll ride with the deputy back over to Pasco."

"Sure… sure," Jericho said. "But Ollie won't be up and running for a while. You're still one man short for a while, ain't ya?"

Zeb frowned and shook his head. "Well, our station agent over to Pasco has a younger brother that's been tryin' to get on, so he'll take Ollie's spot till he's better. That was the other news Gator brought from Pasco."

"Okay then… I'll draw my pay," Jericho said.

"I sure am sorry about it, Jericho," Zeb said as he pulled out the cashbox. "So you got three dollars in pay… a dollar fifty for each way. Then you're getting a bonus of seven dollars for saving the run, the payroll, and likely Ollie's life. That's an even ten dollars. There you go, son. Oh, and you get one more free night in the hotel and another free go at the dining room. Get all you want to eat on us. I wish I could do more for you."

Jericho took the silver dollars. "I'm much obliged, sir. You been plenty fair. I'll be around for a day or two 'fore I make on out. If ya end up havin' need or hear of any, just let me know."

"I'll do it," Zeb said.

Jericho turned and walked for the dining room. He was suddenly very hungry and there was no hurry on finishing his meal.

4

Jericho spent a few hours of the day walking the town, checking all possible employers with whom he might have any aptitude. The ones that knew about the thwarted stage robbery and realized who he was paid their sincere respects, stating they wished they had work for him. But none did. Worries did not plague Jericho, though a slight uncertainty now crept forth like doubt in the night which knows no taming. He needed work and if he couldn't find it, he needed the simple pursuit of it.

Down the years, his movements from town to town always provided purpose for the possibilities that loomed. He swept like the wind over the plains and mountains, through forests and all manner of valleys and canyons, veined by rivers and lakes. The trail was always onward with a prospect or dream on the horizon. He figured it kept him in purpose to God and true to himself. And he knew it was his youth that fueled his restless energy. He also knew a time would come when he would slow to a more settled life. But for now he burned like gunpowder across the western frontier. With no more current prospects in this town, he would soon be making dust toward another.

When night came, Jericho had supper and left the hotel dining room, happily satiated with a good meal. He walked outside onto the dirt of the street where a full view of the night sky presented its majesty, the stars abundant and twinkling with a crescent moon giving punctuation to eternity beyond. He lit his smoke and dragged on it, listening and looking. Then he walked on, drawn to the wonder of resonance that could only be the saloon. His pace was easy and precise, the simple pleasure of it not lost on him. In his travels, he'd seen many cripples and maimed folks who would have paid for the pleasure of strolling up a town street under a beautiful evening sky.

The sound of night life drifted easy from the Rusty Spur Saloon. It was the next biggest building in town after the hotel. The bar was fifty feet long, inside a sprawling room that had a small stage and dance floor with tables and chairs all about. The far end had several tables dedicated to card games. A collection of men stood at the bar while people at tables talked and laughed, telling stories and socializing, some singing or dancing as a piano, banjo, and fiddle played in background to it all.

As the bar filled with the evening crowd, each new entry through the batwing doors was met with appraisal by some while others took little notice. When Jericho walked in, a few men at the bar looked. One of them waved Jericho over. Jericho glanced around, thinking the man must have been waving to someone else. But when he looked back, the man was pointing directly at him and waving him over.

"Let me buy you a drink," the man said to Jericho as he arrived at the bar. "I'm proud to have a drink with the man that saved Ollie and the stage. What'll you have?"

"I'm most partial to whiskey, sir," Jericho replied to the stately-looking man.

"Well then you'll have it! Cal, set this man up with your best whiskey!" He turned his attention back to Jericho. "I'm Heaton Wrenn," he said, extending his hand to shake Jericho's.

Jericho shook his hand. "Jericho Buck… much obliged for the drink, Mister Wrenn."

"Call me Heaton."

The bartender brought the glass and poured a shot for Jericho.

"Leave the bottle, Cal," Heaton said.

"Yes, sir, Mister Wrenn."

Heaton poured a shot worth into his beer and held his glass up to toast. "Here's to true action when it's most needed!" he said, then clinked Jericho's glass and proceeded to drain his beer as Jericho threw back the shot.

"I can speak on two things I know to be true," Jericho said. "First off, this is the biggest saloon I ever been in."

"There's a lot of folks pass through here going east or west… some north or south, but mostly west," Heaton said. "A lot of trail business keeps this place full. What's the other thing you know to be true?"

Jericho's face took on a more somber expression. "That feller I shot in the head yesterday was the first man I ever killed."

Heaton frowned and refilled Jericho's glass. "It wouldn't do to make a habit of it, but when a man needs killing, it's best to think of the other folks present that don't… including yourself. You did a good thing. You did your job."

Jericho nodded. "Yep, that's all I was doin'… my job. Now I ain't got one. I was kind'a hopin' I could stay on temporary, but she didn't work out. Just got here two days ago. My mind fixed I'd stay a fortnight 'fore I moved on."

"Just where is it you're moving on to?"

Jericho showed a faint smile. "I'm part'a that crowd goin' west. Mosey on over to California and maybe see if I can scare up some gold… or tie into some goin' concern. Never been in that country, so thinkin' I might like to see it. But a man never knows… might fall on opportunity anywhere. I generally take my time and take a good look at the places I pass through."

Heaton nodded. "Well, if it's temporary work you want, I've got it for you. I own the High Eagle Ranch six miles north of town.

You come see me… I'll put you to work for as long or short as suits you."

Jericho looked Heaton in the eye with appreciative steel. "Thank you, sir… that's a mighty nice offer. I can cowboy or anything else you need."

"All right," Heaton said. "There's a trail out the backside of the livery… easy to see… comes right to my place. Mike Tope is my foreman. We've got a good outfit, good bunkhouse, and great grub. Two dollars a day. Come on if you want."

"Can't thank you enough, Mister Wrenn. I sure would give you a good day's work every day."

"I believe you would," Heaton replied.

Jericho and Heaton talked on for another half hour and put a fair dent in the first half of the whiskey. Then Heaton bid goodnight to Jericho and took his leave, expressing his hope he'd see him again soon. Then he was gone in a blink.

Jericho felt properly lit from the numerous shots of whiskey he'd had. He grew ambitious as he looked to the corner of the room. Jericho took the beer he'd ordered and made his way over to one of the card tables where he sat down in an empty chair with three other players and a dealer.

"This Blackjack?" Jericho asked.

"That's right," the dealer said, not looking up as he dealt to the three players. "The other three tables are Faro if that's what you're looking for."

"Nope," Jericho said. He fished his money out and counted it. He had a pair of twenty-dollar gold pieces and another eleven dollars and thirty cents in silver. He palmed five silver dollars and returned the rest to his coin pouch, then watched as two players busted and the third held at eighteen. The dealer had a king and a five. He dealt himself another five.

"Damn!" the man with eighteen said as the dealer raked the bet.

As the dealer shuffled, two of the men placed their nickel bets, and the third slid a quarter forward. He was the well-dressed older gent who'd lost on eighteen. Jericho put his stack of five dollars on the bet spot. The other men cast shocked looks.

"Are you wanting change?" the dealer asked.

Jericho broke to a long, easy grin. "Nope… that's my bet."

"Three-dollar limit," the dealer said as he continued to shuffle.

A pit boss had moved to within a few feet behind the dealer and had already sized Jericho up. "Take the bet," he said.

The dealer nodded. "All right, gentlemen, bets are down."

Jericho sat in second position. The dealer dealt him a jack of spades.

"No double down on a bet exception," the pit boss instantly declared.

"You mean doubling my bet?" Jericho asked.

"That's right, kid," the dealer answered.

"Why would I want to do that?"

The older gent next to Jericho turned his head to him and leaned in as if delivering a secret. "If you get the ace of spades, your bet pays ten to one," he said.

Jericho smiled again. "Got'a be long odds of that happenin'. That's the biggest bet'a my life right there. Wouldn't think of doubling it."

A moment later, the dealer dealt Jericho's second card. It came drifting down, face up, like an autumn leaf on a breeze, light and airy. But it landed like a wheelbarrow of bricks.

"Whoooeeee!" Jericho bleated as the other players gave audible grunts and outburst at the ace of spades now paired with Jericho's jack of spades.

Two of the other players had seventeen, the third had nineteen, and the dealer had a nine showing. All the players stood pat. The dealer flipped his hole card, a seven. The dealer hit himself with a king and busted.

"Winners all around!" the older gent said. Then he turned to Jericho. "And you, young man, certainly know when to place the biggest bet of your life! Five dollars to win fifty in one hand!"

Jericho nodded disbelievingly then began to collect the stacks of silver dollars that the dealer looked to be grudgingly pushing to him.

Jericho glanced to the older gent and said, "I know when to quit, too… and I'm thinkin' this is it."

Jericho pushed two dollars to the dealer then stood up and stuffed the rest of his winnings into his pockets. "Good luck to you men. I got a job to be at in the mornin'. Adios."

The pit boss whispered into the ear of one of his heavies. Jericho was walking for the exit when the bigger man stepped in front of him and grabbed him with brute force on the side of each arm just above the elbow. The big man squeezed Jericho's arms with a crushing vise grip.

"Where you goin'?" the big man asked with deadly intent. "You're gonna go sit back down and keep playin' till I say you can leave. You got it?"

Jericho stared him in the eye with simple resolve. "Mister, I don't take orders from nobody but my boss. I don't have one at the moment, so you best take your hands off me or I'll blast your privates off."

The sound of a pistol cocking immediately followed Jericho's declaration. The big man slowly looked down to see a cocked pistol in Jericho's hand with the tip of the barrel an inch away from his pants.

"I ain't funnin'," Jericho calmly said. "Unless you're partial to bein' known as Mister Steer, you turn me loose in the next two seconds or you'll be nutless in three."

Jericho started counting. The big man immediately let go and backed up a step.

"I won that money fair and square. Don't brace me again or I'll have to kill ya."

Jericho walked out the door and into the cool evening, his stuffed pockets clinking of silver dollars with every step he took.

5

Darkness of the night hung full and still, yet it would be only another half hour before light of the eastern horizon would show its faint promise, growing quickly with every passing minute to a complete affirmation of a new day arrived. Jericho awoke and lit the bedside lamp. He took his pistol from the bed and returned it to his holster, having kept it close in the event of someone from the saloon trying to do him harm or rob him. He walked softly to the table and used the pitcher and washbowl to clean his face and hands. Then he tapped the dental powder onto the bone-handle brush and scrubbed his teeth. Moments later he was dressed and packed. With his saddlebags over his shoulder, he moved to the door and turned the skeleton key to unlock it. In seconds, he descended the stairs, their slight creaks hardly betraying something more than a cat going down. Having passed on his room's chamber pot, he slipped outside for the privy.

The dining room lamps were lit and the coffee was fresh, hot, and strong enough to take paint off a barn. Just right, Jericho thought. He had a slab of ham with three eggs and as many biscuits. Jericho marveled over the homemade peach marmalade, slathering it on thick enough to hide each biscuit. Then he licked his fingers after each to get the excess of peachy confection remaining on his digits. The marmalade was enough to make him contemplate taking up permanent residence at the hotel.

Other hotel guests and a few townsfolk began to drift in as

Jericho enjoyed a final cup of coffee. Then the stage station agent, Zeb, walked in. His eyes got big when he spotted Jericho. Zeb immediately walked in his direction.

"Good morning, Mister Buck!" Zeb said cheerily as he pulled out a chair and took a seat opposite Jericho. He leaned forward, putting his elbows on the table and sporting an expression as though he were going to stay someone's execution. "I have some news that you might be particularly interested in," he said.

Jericho waxed expectant. "You got a job with the stage line for me after all?"

"No… no. But a man like you… it might be right up your alley. You'd have to move quick though."

Jericho cut right in as though it didn't matter what Zeb was going to tell him. "Well, truth be told, I already got a job. Mister Heaton Wrenn of the High Eagle Ranch said he could put me to work. Two dollars a day! Better'n average pay for cowboyin'. I'm headed to the High Eagle right after I finish this coffee. Just the same… what is it you're talkin' about?"

"The Pony Express!"

Jericho's eyebrows hiked up. "Say I heard'a that. Some kind'a mail delivery?"

"The fastest in all the land! Going for almost a year now," Zeb said. "Mail taken from St. Joseph, Missouri, to Sacramento, California, by Pony Express riders in ten days flat. Two thousand miles!"

Jericho looked skeptical. "That don't even sound possible. How could anybody do that?"

"Well, they got eighty or so riders going all the time… forty going each way. Each man rides sixty, seventy miles or more, changing horses every so often so they can just ride like hell."

"That's a lot'a horse changin'. Where do they change horses?"

"They got more than a hundred and fifty stations spread clear across from Missouri to California! Fresh horses at every one of 'em. And they got fresh riders at every fifth station or so, called home stations."

"You tellin' it true?" Jericho asked, his skepticism stuck in his craw.

Zeb continued, "One of their station agents came through here last night. I talked to him on the porch out front here. He might have even put up here for the night. Don't know... but he was telling me that they're short of riders. Lost a fella just a few days back and they need someone right quick for the route between Dry Creek and Cold Springs. Pays one hundred and fifty dollars a month!"

"Is that right?" Jericho asked, shocked.

"Yes sir! Surprised me, too! Said that's what they pay for their most dangerous routes. Lot of Shoshone and Paiute up in the Sedaye Mountains and Lookout Range. Tough country."

Jericho nodded. "Wouldn't 'spect nothin' less for that kind of pay."

"Well, I told this agent I knew a young man with all the sand in the world that was looking for work. Told him about the stage fracas. He asked me how big you were. Told him I figured you about five-foot and seven, and maybe a hundred-forty pounds. He said that was on the top end, but as long as you weren't any bigger you'd be all right. Are you bigger'n that?"

"I don't think so. Five foot and seven's right. Stepped on a freight scale once, couple years back. Man said I was a hundred thirty-six pounds. Don't think I'm any more now... well, maybe a little bit after all the eggs, ham, biscuits, and marmalade." Jericho shook his head. "Man alive! If they had that marmalade at the other end of that route, I'd ride through flamin' arrows and scalp-seekin' savages all day to get to it."

"You'll have to get there fast to try your luck. He said they have a lot of takers for that kind of money."

"I don't know either one'a them places you said. Where would I go?"

"Dry Creek is what that agent said. 'Bout eighty miles northeast of here. The livery owner, Pepper Jack, can give you the skinny on how to get there. Knows the trails… landmarks… distances."

The interest was etched deep on Jericho's face. "Boy… Sure sounds good. But eighty miles… it'd be two hard days gettin' there. Likely run my horse to near death, still end up second or third man in line."

Zeb shook his head. "No, I don't think so. That agent talked like the call was fresh as a hot loaf. And I don't believe there are any sizable towns closer than us. He said whoever got traveling right quick would hold the best chance."

Jericho drained his coffee, then threw four bits of silver on the table for his breakfast. "I like havin' the best chance. So long, Mister Purnell. I'm off to see about it."

6

Jericho collected his horse at the livery and listened carefully as the livery owner, Pepper Jack, described the route in great detail, prompting Jericho to get out his pencil and writing paper and take a few notes.

Pepper Jack hit the end again. "When you come out of that draw, you'll see that butte to the north. Keep pointed right at the eastern tip of it and you'll come across the stage trail after a mile or so. Follow that trail northeast seven or eight miles and she'll take you right into Murphy… nothin' much more than a stage stop and Murphy's saloon… always open save for the middle of the night, and even then sometimes. You're close then. Talk to Murph. He'll get you the rest of the way. Not much farther I don't reckon."

"Thank you, Mister Jack. I'm much obliged," Jericho said.

Pepper Jack was grizzled and sure. He flashed a grim smile. "I heard about you winnin' the money last night and shuttin' down Moss Oak when he tried to keep you from leavin.' Probably best you're movin' on. He's a devil… be layin' for you if you're around."

Jericho nodded, "He's got about half a minute more of me being around. Hey, if you see Heaton Wrenn, tell 'im I sure appreciate his offer of work, but I moved on to somethin' I'm better suited to. Best to ya, Mister Jack."

Jericho led his horse out of the barn. The sun was cracking the horizon of a cloudless morning.

"Need a shine, mister?"

Jericho turned his head to the voice. The old man sat on a wood crate against the outside wall with two other crates in front of him, a taller one for the customer to sit on, and a smaller one for the shoe being shined to rest on. The old man hadn't been there fifteen minutes earlier. His clothes were ragged and his appearance disheveled as he squinted into the sun from under a worn bowler.

"Just a nickel," he added. "I'll put a gloss on yer boots. They'll look real fine. I surely could use the work. Got an old dog to feed."

Jericho led his horse over to the old man and stopped. He reached in his saddlebag and pulled out two felt-wrapped stacks. "I ain't got time right now. Maybe if I get back through this way. I'll pay in advance now."

Jericho handed him the wrapped stacks and then immediately mounted up.

The old man stared at them a moment then pulled back the felt and glimpsed the twenty silver dollars that he held in his hands. He looked up. "What are you doing, Mister? This is your money… not mine."

"It's yours now," Jericho said. "I got a long ride ahead of me and my horse don't need the extra weight. Feed that old dog good."

Jericho put light heels to his horse and broke to a lope out of town heading northeast.

****

The country was arid and wide open with the stark beauty of distant mountains, buttes, and expansive valley that stretched out, heaving in elevation drops and gains, cut by arroyos and speckled with the chartreuse and hunter of intermittent cactus, sage, rabbit brush, and piñon pine. Jericho's horse, Buddy, was well rested after several days of oats and inactivity. He took to the open country with sauce in his trot, keeping a good pace as they swallowed up the miles in the mild, late-winter temperatures. Jericho saw the landmarks, remembering most, and looking at his notes and compass only a few times. By mid-afternoon, Jericho spotted the humpback rock formation that Pepper Jack had told of. He made for it and found the spring, cool and inviting with a cluster of desert willows along the grassy banks, throwing shade like an oasis.

"The man knew what he was talkin' about," Jericho said to Buddy, knowing his horse was in full agreement. "And he said this spring was every bit'a halfway! Good day's work, partner."

Jericho stripped his saddle then made camp as Buddy drank his fill and chomped the grass. The rest of the afternoon fell away quickly, bringing forth the silver sliver of crescent in the night's clear sky, flooded with luminous, shimmering orbs against the grand blackness. He ate the jerked beef and hardtack, all the while reminiscing about his morning's feast, topped with marmalade. Before he fell asleep, he smoked a cigarette as he lay stretched out with a blanket, his head resting on his saddlebags and his eyes fixed on the heavens. Buddy stood tethered to a willow. The evening held calm as the man and his horse drifted off in sleep.

Sometime in the night, Buddy neighed and snorted, instantly waking Jericho who grabbed the rifle by his side and sat up as he cocked it. He quickly turned his head from side to side, looking about. Then his eyes fixed to the bank of the spring pool. It was black but Jericho could make out the shapes that stood cautiously, startled by Buddy's snorting or perhaps the cocking of the rifle. He stared hard to the spot less than a hundred feet away. Several wild mustangs made their way down to the water and began to drink. Then the other smaller shapes began to move closer to the water. Jericho could see the gait and knew they were deer.

He whispered softly to Buddy who had begun to settle more, "It's all right, boy… just some locals, thirsty like us." Minutes later, Jericho's light snoring cut the air with exquisite calming on all that could hear it. Rituals of the night continued.

At first light Jericho was up. After his personals, he filled his canteen and was mounted up and riding within minutes. He would have liked coffee, but not enough to search for fire fuel that wasn't readily apparent. He had no bacon to cook, nor anything else fresh, so he ate more jerky and hardtack as he admired the country in the cool morning from atop his saddle.

Buddy's step was not as lively during the second day of the journey. They made Murphy's Saloon in the late afternoon, an hour later than Jericho had hoped for. And they would still have some miles to go to make the Dry Creek Pony Express Station after that. He'd have to make it before dark or he'd never find it. If he didn't make it there this day, he was damn sure somebody else would, and he'd have come a long way for nothing.

"How far to Dry Creek?" Jericho asked the bartender as soon as he was inside the door and within earshot.

Murphy looked up and considered the young man striding his way with urgency. He knew what the urgency was about and couldn't resist. "Seems you're in a hell of a hurry for these parts, son. 'Course, you'd be the fifth young man today askin' how far to Dry Creek."

Jericho stopped cold in his tracks like all the wind had just sucked out of his sails. His mouth hung open and his head dropped to one side. "Is that right? Four been through already?"

"Nope, it ain't right," Murphy said, his eyes sparkling with mischief, and a grin breaking from under his walrus mustache. "But it sure did take the hurry out of you. Only stagecoach folks been through… and they all kept goin'. I'd say you're the man if you make it today. It ain't but six more miles, so slow down and have some of my famous bullhead stew."

Jericho's eyes relaxed. "You got'a peculiar sense of humor, mister. What's in the stew?"

"Fresh whitetail, onions, peppers, carrots, garlic, and some other secrets… all in a fine gravy sauce over mashed potatoes. My sense of humor heeds to a serious sense of delecti where my cookin's concerned."

"How'd you get all those vegetables and fixins?" Jericho asked. "Didn't see anything growin' about in these parts."

"Stage hauls all the vegetables I need once a week from Soda Springs. Got a standing order. I hunt the whitetail myself. Sometimes elk… but the whitetail are fine eatin'!"

Jericho nodded. "All right, Mister Murphy. You give me good bearings to Dry Creek Pony Express Station and I'll have a plate or two of that stew. Say, why do ya call it bullhead? Why not just deer stew… or whitetail stew?"

"Well, a bullhead sticks… and so does my stew. Stick with you all the way to Dry Creek and the rest of the night, too!"

As Murphy told the details of the way to Dry Creek, Jericho ate two plates full followed by a beer just to put out the fire.

"Mighty tasty it was," Jericho opined as he put silver on the bar and began walking for the door. "But I'm of a mind it's more suitable to bein' called hot-hole… as it surely will cause such on the way out."

"Hope you get the job," Murphy chuckled as Jericho disappeared out the door and mounted up, all within twenty minutes of having arrived.

An hour later, with the sun hanging low behind a western horizon of clouds, Jericho came over the climb and saw the valley below, thick with scrub oak. He pulled his spyglass from the saddlebag and spotted on the structures a mile away. The log cabin slung low, yet was good size in width and depth and sat close to the river that meandered along the valley floor. There was a big corral with a dozen horses and a horse barn. Another smaller corral sat nearby with a few more horses. There was a small stone building and a few other small outbuildings. He knew it was the pony express station of Dry Creek. It was just as Murphy had described.

Jericho put his glass away then saw the faint dust of a rider directly across the valley coming from the opposite direction. He looked to be about the same distance from the station as Jericho, who immediately imagined he was about to be bested for the job if the other rider got there first. He kicked Buddy a stiff one.

"Heyahh, Buddy! Git!"

Buddy bolted down the long, steep grade as Jericho leaned back, reining his horse with nerve and precision on the best ground to avoid a fall. Jericho thought the other rider might be closer to the station, but was unsure because of the two differing paths of approach. It was going to be close either way. He kicked Buddy again and yelled wildly, knowing Buddy was played out but still giving all he had. The grade began to flatten out with the scrub oak now presenting a visual barrier to the station. Jericho sat tall in the saddle, trying to keep eyes-on as he weaved in and out of the scrub oak, no longer concerned with the other rider but only reining Buddy on the best line possible. He kept at it, urging Buddy on and reining him at a full gallop around the bushes like some kind of rodeo contest, sometimes picking the right opening and sometimes not, getting squeezed and scraped as they busted through the bush.

Then the scrub oak suddenly gave way to an open stretch for the last hundred yards to the station. He didn't see the other rider, but a man stood to the side of the building with a saddled horse. Jericho galloped to the hitching post directly in front, reining up abruptly in the last few feet as he jumped from the saddle before Buddy had stopped. In an instant he had Buddy tied. The other rider reined up to a far hitching post where the man with his horse waited. Jericho watched a moment as the rider handed off the mochila filled with mail to the other man who quickly hooked it over his saddle horn. A moment later the other man was mounted up and galloping off to the east. Jericho quickly made for the door.

7

One side of the large room had a settee and two big armchairs with ottomans, all of it handmade, crude log furniture with cowhide cushions. A nearby bookcase held a few offerings of fiction hardcovers and stacks of old newspapers and bulletins. The other side of the room had a counter against the far wall above which were shelves that held plates, bowls, cups, pans, and various utensils. A cook stove occupied a section of wall adjacent to the counter. The stove sat on a hearth with a full woodbox and some stove utensils and cast iron pans hanging up. A heavy plank table with benches on each side sat in the middle of the room, easily capable of seating six or more men. The far wall opposite the front door had its own door, which Jericho guessed led to the bunks room. And there at a desk on the back wall sat a man in buckskins studying some sort of logbook. His hair was long and he wore eyeglasses perched on the bridge of his nose. Jericho guessed him to be in his mid-forties. He hadn't looked up yet, but finally did after Jericho stood looking for ten seconds or so.

"Who are you?" the man asked with a bellow.

"Your new rider, I hope. Name's Jericho Buck. I heard you needed another man so I came quick."

"Quick enough, it seems. Pull up a chair and sit down. I do need another rider. We'll see if you fit the bill."

Jericho strode across the room like a peacock on the prowl, offering his hand to shake as he sat down.

The man shook his hand and gave him a hard stare, sizing him up. "I'm Willie Brock, the Station Keeper. Where you from?"

"Right here in the territory… far east… by the Colorado River."

"How much you weigh?" Willie asked.

"Bout a hundred thirty-five, I reckon. Don't get on a scale regular like. Ate a lot'a stew over to Murphy's saloon an hour ago. Might be a hundred thirty-six right now."

Willie's eyes sharpened a bit. "Yep, that's about what I'd guess you at. The cutoff's a hundred and forty. If you ain't there yet, you won't get there working here. You'll be riding hell bent at least eight hours a day… sometimes more depending on need and circumstances. No time for eating in the saddle. And you'd find out quick it's a miserable deal hitting the saddle with your belly overstuffed. It ain't leisure riding. What's your age?"

"Twenty-one."

"Can you read and write?"

"I sure can," Jericho said with pride. "My mama learned me up good. Even went to school for three years."

"Well it ain't a requirement," Willie said. "But it's another point to your side. You ever been in jail for more than a night or two?"

"No, sir… not for more'n a night or two."

Willie's eyebrows hiked up. "What was the charge?"

"Drunk and disorderly."

"You got thrown in jail?" Willie asked.

"Yep… for one night… me and the other feller."

"Do tell," Willie said.

"Well, it happened a couple years back. Wasn't my doin'. This dude braced me over a gal he liked. She seemed to like me better. It was a backwards dance over to Kansas Territory. Girls ask the man to dance. She asked me more'n twice and he didn't much care for it. He tried to kick the hell out'a me. Had to defend myself. Shame, too. I was bein' real polite till he started in."

"What about the drunk part?" Willie asked

Jericho seemed innocently confused. "What about it?"

"You were drunk?"

"Sure was. Couple'a them boys had some real good shine. Just tryin' to be sociable."

Jericho saw the scowl on Willie's face. "Well I ain't no kind'a regular drunk or nothin'," Jericho said. "But I'm a hard workin' man who's alive in the West. I'll take a drink once in a while in a sociable setting."

"You can't drink here or any station," Willie said flatly. "You'll have to take the rider's oath. You break it, you're fired. You get four days off a month. You go to town and have a drink then… nobody will care unless you get arrested for drunk and disorderly. Understand?"

"Yes, sir. I work hard and follow whatever rules my boss gives me."

The front door opened behind Jericho. In walked the tough, young rider that Jericho had raced to the station. He was wiry, bow-legged, and jovial of expression. He collected a plate and headed for the pot on the woodstove.

"Can you ride like a demon and shoot while doin' it?" Willie asked Jericho.

"He rode down Thompson grade like he was the devil himself!" the rider at the stove chimed as he dished himself up a plate of the evening's fare.

"And I can shoot, too," Jericho added with teamwork timing, then looked over to the rider, who flashed a quick smile.

"You'll likely get your chance," Willie said flatly. "A year ago, the Simpson Park Station was attacked and burnt down by Shoshones. They killed Charlie Loney, the Station Keeper… took all the stock. Shot another rider on his way here. He made it back but died from his injuries the next day. There's Paiutes in these parts, too, along with marauders, horse thieves, and every lowdown, two-legged varmint that ever took robbery to mind. When they ain't about, you better be lookin' for snakes and bears… lost riders to them, too. This is dangerous work."

"That don't bother me none," Jericho said, suddenly sitting up a little straighter. "I like ridin'… the adventure of it, and I heard this pays a hundred 'n fifty dollars a month. Is that right?"

"Yep, the route you'd be riding does. Ain't a longer one anywhere from St. Joesph to Sacramento. It's a hundred miles from here on over to Cold Springs, changing horses at Simpson Park, Jacob's Spring, Smith's Creek and Edward's Creek. Bed down at Cold Springs and bring eastbound mail back here the next day. The Sedaye and Desatoya Mountains hold Indians and Lord knows what else. Sometimes you might have to ride extra, and you have to defend whatever station you happen to be at from attack if you're there. You believe you're up to it… Mister Jericho Buck?"

"I am… on my word, I am."

Willie nodded his approval then opened his desk drawer and pulled out the sheet. He handed it to Jericho.

Willie looked over to the rider who was at the table with his plate. "Hags, come and sign as witness to his oath," Willie said.

"I'm listenin'," Hags answered. "I'll sign when I'm done eatin'."

Willie looked at Jericho. "Stand up, raise your right hand and read the oath. Say your name where the blank is in the beginning."

Jericho stood up and raised his right hand, holding the pledge close to his face with his left to see the words in the fading light. He read with a clear, strong voice, filled with a tone of resolve.

"I, Jericho Buck, do hereby swear, before the Great and Living God, that during my engagement, and while I am an employee of Russell, Majors and Waddell, I will, under no circumstances, use profane language, that I will drink no intoxicating liquors, that I will not quarrel or fight with any other employee of the firm, and that in every respect I will conduct myself honestly, be faithful to my duties, and so direct all my acts as to win the confidence of my employers, so help me God."

"Good!" Willie said. "Glad to have you take up the run!"

Willie and Jericho shook hands. "Sign and date the book right here," Willie instructed. "Today is February twenty-fifth, eighteen and sixty-one. Provision wagon comes through once a week with food and feed. If you're in need of something you can put in an order that will generally get filled within two weeks."

"I'm Steve Haggerty… most call me Hags… happy to make your acquaintance," the rider said as he shoveled the last bite in and sprang from the table. He walked a brisk few steps over to where Jericho finished signing.

Jericho extended his hand to shake. "Good to know ya. I'm Jericho Buck."

Jericho guessed him to be about the same age. They shook hands like they were trying to see who was stronger, squeezing the blood from each other.

"Hags is on loan from Cold Springs… usually riding west." Willie said. "He'll be showing you the route from here to there. Hope you're a fast learner. They'll need 'im back soon… then you'll be on your own."

"Got a compass?" Hags asked.

"Sure do."

Hags nodded. "That'll make it fast. I got it all wrote down on cards… each station's heading from landmarks. You'll know 'em in no time."

"Pick an empty stall in the barn and put your horse up," Willie said. "We got two stock tenders that'll see to oats and water. Got a tack rack for your saddle and such. Won't be using yours here."

Jericho sparked curious. "No?"

"Too heavy," Willie answered. "And every fresh horse you get will already be saddled… time savin'. You'll use our rigs. Light! Saddle and bridle about thirteen pounds. Our horses are mostly mustangs, no more than fourteen hands and eight to nine hundred pounds. Short, sturdy and fast. We'll give you a Bowie knife and a .36 caliber Navy Colt." Willie suddenly took notice of the pistol Jericho was wearing. "Just like the one you're wearing!… extra holster too if you want to strap it on opposite yours. The mail rides in a mochila, about fifteen to twenty pounds full. Goes right over your saddle. Get some grub then pick a bunk… through that door. Tomorrow you take up the run at 6:00 a.m."

8

The smell of bacon, biscuits, and coffee permeated the front room at dawn as Willie tended the cooking by lamplight. He moved the bacon briskly about in the iron skillet, popping hot grease. A big pop sent a spatter that hit Willie on the high cheek just below his right eye. He flinched at the searing burn.

"Damn swine!" he half yelled then hooked the top and lidded the skillet. He moved it off the burner plate and poured himself a cup of coffee.

The two stock tenders, Clyde and Billy, walked in the front door like they were on their way to a fire. "Mounts are ready," Clyde said as he and Billy grabbed their cups and plates.

"We ready here?" Billy asked, crowding in toward the coffee pot.

"Course we're ready!" Willie said, squinting from one eye with the grease burn below it. "You hornswogglin' hogs always gets your feedbag on time. Let me through!"

Willie hustled toward the table with his coffee, getting out of the way of the two wranglers who'd horned in like they'd run roughshod over a church gathering if they needed to. They quickly loaded up and hustled to the table.

Jericho and Hags came in from the bunk room.

"You boys better get to it," Willie said. "The westbound'll be in soon. If he's early you won't get to eat."

Jericho followed right behind Hags, who grabbed a plate, cup and fork then made for the stove where he poured coffee, collected two biscuits, and pulled the lid from the skillet. Hags gave each biscuit a quick dunk in the hot grease and forked out several pieces of bacon. Jericho followed his lead, staying measured in how much food he took. It required restraint. He was hungry, having not eaten anything since the late-afternoon stew feast at Murphy's saloon the day before. Jericho stared at the skillet, guessing it held four pounds of bacon heaped high in a sea of grease. He took a modest amount, remembering Willie's admonition that he'd be miserable if he ate too much. Being miserable riding after a meal was not something Jericho could remember from his own experience, but he would heed Willie's advice the first time; he had never ridden so far and so fast. A hundred miles in one stretch of daylight excited his thoughts.

After a gruff round of "Morning," and "Good morning," said from each man to the others, the table fell silent of conversation as the only sounds came of fast eating and cautious slurping of the scalding hot coffee. Jericho wolfed down his first biscuit and some of his bacon then took a few hot sips as he thought. What Willie had said just minutes earlier stoked his curiosity.

"The westbound will be here soon?" Jericho asked of no one in particular. "The mail that Hags and me is takin' to Cold Springs… will be here soon?"

Clyde and Billy glanced at Hags and Willie, and then each other.

"That's right," Willie answered, looking to the cuckoo clock on the wall which showed about 5:42. "Usually here by six… sometimes a little earlier, sometimes a little later… mostly a few minutes later."

Jericho frowned and took a bite of his second biscuit. He swallowed quickly and shook his head slowly. "I reckon I'm the fool… thinkin' the mail we's haulin' was already here. But there ain't no way in creation mail's gettin' two thousand miles in ten days unless it's movin' all the time! You got riders goin' all night, too!"

The men chuckled.

"All day, all night, all the time," Willie said. "Westbound riders leave here at 6 a.m., 2 p.m. and 10 p.m. Eastbound at 11 a.m., 7 p.m. and 3 a.m. The two boys sleepin' in back… Purdy and Hambone… Purdy'll take up the run eastbound at 11 this morning, and Hambone'll be heading west at 2:00 this afternoon."

Jericho swallowed another bite. His eyes widened a bit. "So each man is about eight hours on and eight hours off?"

"No… don't work like that." Willie answered. "The run to and from Cold Springs is the longest run on the route… hundred miles… every bit of eight hours. You'll get about thirteen hours off up there before you leave with the eastbound at 3 a.m. and get back here about 11 a.m. Then you'll get about eleven hours off until you take up the westbound again at 10 p.m. Your departure times from each end of the route keep shifting."

Jericho shot a confused look. "So I get thirteen hours rest at Cold Springs and eleven hours rest here? That always stays the same because my departure times shift?"

"Yes sir! That's it. The boys that ride east from here or west from Cold Springs don't get as much time off because their saddle time ain't as long to the next home station… sixty miles going east from here… only fifty-two miles going west from Cold Springs."

Jericho shook his head. "I ain't gonna try to cipher that. Just happy I get to ride the first time while the sun's out. Tall order ridin' the whole thing in the dark, ain't it?" Jericho asked.

Willie's eyebrows hiked a little. "Most riders reckon it's less danger from Indians and such at night… and it's a lot cooler in summer, but colder than hell right now. Biggest worry is your horse steppin' in a hole… taking a fall. Rare thing though. Mustangs are sure-footed as any animal."

Billy jumped in, "Them horses can smell their way from station to station! They know their routes. All you got to do is hang on."

"That's a fact!" Clyde added. "You get your eyes poked out somewhere and your horse'll get you home."

Jericho gave a toothy grin. "Not lookin' to find out if that's true… but nice to know you boys got that confidence."

Willie slapped the tabletop with an open palm. "I got confidence that you and Hags better get out front and look for a rider comin'."

Jericho stuffed the rest of the bacon and biscuit in his mouth as he stood up and headed for the door like a man who didn't want anyone waiting on him. The rest of the men kept at their food or coffee, paying no mind to Jericho's silent departure.

Hags nodded. "I think he'll be all right."

****

Jericho stood outside gazing east in the cool air. He pulled out one of his rolled smokes and lit it, then dragged on it, looking toward the prominent semicircle of light where the morning sun would soon rise. Against the crystalline blue of the cloudless sky's horizon, he caught the faintest glimpse of rising dust. He stared and dragged on his smoke, unable to yet see the rider but knowing it had to be him. The front door opened behind him.

"He's comin'," Jericho said.

Hags squinted. "You got good eyes."

The door opened again and Billy came out. "Ah, well there he is…'bout two miles out. Time to shake it."

Billy walked toward the end of the building where two horses stood tethered to the hitching rail just around the corner. Hags and Jericho followed.

Hags glanced at Jericho. "Hey, if you got'a piss or shit, best get it done right now. We'll be at a gallop about one minute after he gets here."

"Nope," Jericho said. "I'm all set."

They arrived around the side of the building. Billy stood to the side of the horses taking a bite of plug tobacco.

"You take the gray," Hags said. "He's all business."

Jericho nodded and moved to the pony. He gave a quick tug on the cinch and eyed the stirrups. "Looks set just right," he said.

Billy spit in the dirt. "That's 'cause they are."

Jericho took another drag as he examined the rig and the small canteen lashed tight. "You weren't funnin' about the saddle. Ain't much to it."

"Tooled for weight and speed," Hags said. "You'll get used to it… but you'll be sore the first week."

Jericho moved forward and rubbed his horse's neck, and then along the jaw line and on the forehead between the eyes. He leaned in as the horse nuzzled him. "All business, eh boy? Suits me right." He patted the horse once more then walked to where Billy and Hags stood watching as the rider neared at a full gallop, getting the last out of the horse that would soon be resting, like the rider himself.

A moment later he came in hot with a cloud of dust, reining up and coming out of the saddle as if he could fly like a feather on a breeze. He hit the ground effortlessly and smiled.

"What's Willie got ready?" he asked.

"Bacon and biscuits," Hags said. "Say hello to our new rider, Jericho."

"Pleased to make your acquaintance… I'm Huck Hurry… and I'm in a hurry to eat!"

"Well, get to it," Jericho said, shaking Huck's hand.

Huck strode toward the door as Billy held the reins of his horse.

"Swap 'er out… the mochila's ridin' with you," Hags said to Jericho.

Jericho looked at it for an instant then pulled it from Huck's saddle. The leather mochila had a hole at the front that slipped over the saddle horn. The rest of it covered the saddle seat and draped down each side, ending well above the stirrups. It had four mail pouches, two on each side, one each in front of and behind the rider's legs that held a combined weight of up to twenty pounds of letters and such. Each pouch had a flap cover, but one also accommodated a small padlock used to secure government communications.

"Those pouches are called the cantinas," Hags said to Jericho who had the mochila transferred and positioned on his saddle inside of half a minute. "Don't worry about the one with the lock. Only the Station Keepers have the key."

Jericho and Hags mounted up.

"So long, Billy!" Hags exclaimed. "We're takin' up the run!"

The mustangs jumped to a hot dash and left the yard headed west with rising dust in their wake.

9

Jericho and Hags made the first twenty miles over to the Simpson Park Relay Station in an hour and a half, alternating between a gallop, a lope, a fast trot, and even a brisk walk at the most challenging ascents and descents, down through arroyos and up steep trails to ridge lines above. Along the way, Jericho had studied the card that Hags had given him, noting landmarks and compass headings for Simpson Park and finding the information to be spot-on. And he mostly gave his pony its head as it seemed to know right where it was going, just like the stock tenders Clyde and Billy had said.

The country swept wide and bold with arid landscapes that transitioned to pine forest as they had climbed the last few miles toward Simpson Park. Then they came out of the trees and saw the station amidst more scrub oak in an open valley below, much as Jericho had come upon Dry Creek Station just the day before.

They rode hard the last mile to the station then threw down with fast dismounts and quick movements. Jericho moved the mochila to his new mount and shook hands with Gabe the stock tender.

"Glad to know ya," Jericho said when Hags introduced them.

Gabe nodded with a half grunt, "Yep."

Then they were up and bolting away again on fresh ponies ready to run. Gabe yelled something he'd forgotten just as they were galloping away.

"Hey!… eastbound saw a half-dozen Shoshones up near Bear Point late yesterday! Keep your eyes open!"

Hags held up his right hand a moment to acknowledge he'd heard it. Jericho was galloping abreast of Hags and looked over at him. Hags looked unfazed and offered no words.

After a moment more, Jericho yelled loud enough to be heard above the wind and pounding hooves. "Where's Bear Point?"

"'Bout five miles out! More forest. Couple ways through. We'll take the slower route… more wide open… less chance for an ambush or meetin' we can't see comin'!"

"I'm for that!" Jericho answered.

"Maybe nothin' more'n a huntin' party anyways… with only six of 'em," Hags opined. "Likely long gone by now."

Twenty minutes later they began riding through sparse pine that began to grow rapidly denser. Hags pointed ahead. "Usually ride through that draw over there… she's faster. But we'll swing south here… stay to the open country."

They rode south for two miles, then turned west along the rolling plain patched with stands of pine standing thick like small islands, each an acre or so in size and separated by the swelling, vast, open ground, green of spring grass fed by shallow aquifers and spidered stream beds of the season.

They'd ridden another mile west when three cracks of sound out of the south broke almost as one, cutting the morning air with reverberation that echoed to them over the mild rise from their left flank. Then a low rumbling thunder washed over all the plain as a wave that seemed to be moving.

Hags reined his horse from a lope down to a trot as he looked to his left, confused by what he had heard. Jericho slowed with him.

"Was that lightning? Did you see a flash?" Hags asked.

Jericho shot Hags a look of disbelief. "Hell no! Those were rifle shots, and we best get runnin' 'cause I got a bad feelin' regardin' what'll be comin' over that rise!"

Their horses were agitated at having slowed as the ground began to tremble. The rumbling grew louder and then consumed the morning as several thousand buffalo nearly a mile wide crested the horizon on a dead run right at them from half a mile away.

"Hyah!" yelled Jericho as he and Hags kicked their horses to a full gallop heading west, trying to clear the north-running wall of thundering bison coming from their left flank, threatening to T-bone them if they didn't turn north to run directly away. But riding any direction other than west meant losing more time, and they were Pony Express riders. In moments more it became clear to Hags that they wouldn't clear the west end of the stampeding herd in time. He started to rein his horse to a right turn.

"We won't make it! Turn up!" Hags yelled.

But Jericho was fifty feet ahead and riding into a stiff wind that blunted Hags's voice as the ominous roar of pounding tonnage grew more deafening by the second. By the time Hags realized that Jericho wasn't turning, he'd already committed to his new course. If he turned back to follow Jericho now he'd be done for sure, he thought. So he galloped north as Jericho continued west, each man giving it all he had.

"Hyah! Hyah!" Jericho yelled over and over as he leaned low and kicked away, watching the ground in front of him. The long line of charging beasts still showed a quarter mile ahead to the west, closing on his flank with murderous speed. He fought to understand if he'd make it or not, knowing it would be so close that it would only be the last seconds that would tell the tale.

"Run, you devil buckin' horse! Run! Hyah!" he yelled.

Then the noise came as if he were in a tunnel. He was unable to hear himself or the sounds of his horse's hooves and ragged breathing, only the ground that shook violently beneath the approaching brown swarm. They were close, and running every bit as fast as his horse. He wasn't going to make it. His horse instinctively veered right in the final seconds. Jericho gave him his lead and yelled his fury into the sky, hoping his voice could stave off doom. Then he saw the very end of the buffalo line just about to trample him. And then they were gone, having folded inside just behind the rear of his horse, missing by only feet.

For an instant, a wind pushed at his back from the force of the passing stampede like the reaper denied. Jericho galloped on for another hundred yards before he slowed to a trot and turned back to look.

The many thousands of buffalo ran north, quickly fading away in the dust of their wake. Jericho watched a moment in astonished wonder at the sight, grasping his luck at having not been stomped to his end in the midst of it. Then, just as quickly, his thoughts were stolen to the realization that Hags was nowhere to be seen. He scanned the flattened plain behind him, hoping he would not see the lump of a trampled man and horse somewhere in the distance. But there was nothing. And little more of the herd could be seen to the north in the veil of dust. After another minute, the recessed thundering of hooves began to wane as the fatigue of the buffaloes took hold and their gait slowed.

Jericho guessed that Hags had turned north long before, perhaps heading for one of the island stands of trees that dotted the ascending plains. They were behind schedule. Time had already been lost, but Jericho would go and look, hopefully reuniting quickly and carrying on the run. He took one last glance to the southern rise, where the buffalo had crested minutes earlier. Four Indians on a dead run were galloping directly at him from at least a half mile away. He stared a long moment in an unhurried taunt, mad that he had to abandon searching for Hags. Jericho turned back west and put the pony to a gallop once again, hoping he could find his way to the next relay station at Jacob's Spring.

10

From a mile out, Jericho caught sight of the small buildings and horse corral. He became immediately hopeful and put his pony to a full gallop once more. Half again closer, Jericho saw the man and horse standing in the yard and knew he'd found Jacob's Spring Station. Jericho galloped to a hard finish then reined up and swung down, quickly tying to the hitching rail and removing the mochila from his lathered, tired horse.

The tender stood holding the reins of a fresh mount. His words had an inquisitive tone. "Heard a new man was making the run… but I thought Hags'd be with you."

Jericho talked fast as he walked the mochila over to his new pony. "Well, if he ain't here, I hope he's close behind! We was together till near Bear Point… got split up in a buffalo stampede that damn near took us both. Must'a been ten thousand of 'em came over a rise at us… started by a huntin' party of Indians… Paiutes I reckon. Some of them boys chased me out'a there 'fore I had a chance to look for him. I'm Jericho Buck." Jericho held his hand out to shake.

"I'm Yerkey," the man replied as they shook hands. "Good you found your way after all that."

"Yeah, well now we'll see if I can find my way to Smith's Creek, Edward's Creek, and Cold Springs," Jericho said.

"You ain't gonna wait to see about Hags?" Yerkey asked.

Jericho shrugged. "Already behind schedule, ain't I? It don't do to run late your first day… or any day for that matter. I got cards with the landmarks, and Billy and Clyde over to Dry Creek told it right about these horses knowin' their way. I'm pressin' on!"

Jericho swung up onto the saddle and felt his new horse's muscles quivering beneath. The animal stood ready to run.

"If Hags shows, tell 'im I'm fulfillin' the obligation of my oath to the company. Hope to see 'im up the line! Say, what's my first sightline out'a here?" Jericho asked.

Yerkey pointed southwest toward a patch of mesquite and a boulder formation a mile on beyond. "Head right for those rocks," he said. "When you get close, you'll see the chase trail bend to the right down through a gulley. It'll lead you around the north side of 'em and straight down a wide corridor of saguaros, look like they's a road for the occasion. Stay to the middle of 'em for a couple miles more. Billy and Clyde's right. Give your horse his head and he'll get you to Smith's Creek."

Jericho nodded. "Obliged! See you next time." He flicked the reins and tapped his heels, prompting his mount to a gallop out of the yard.

"Fare-you-well," Yerkey said under his breath to the vanishing rider.

****

Jericho found Smith's Creek Station and Edwards Creek Station with little trouble. He rode the last leg toward Cold Springs, each mile bringing awareness of how sore his back and groin had become.

"Ohhh," he groaned as if informing the open country of its complicity. "A hundred miles of ridin' hard on fresh horses'll leave a man feelin' like he'd been dragged the whole way!"

Jericho chuckled at his declaration to the blue sky and realized the pile of easy money he thought he'd be making would be hard earned after all. He lit a smoke and let his horse slow as they began up a hill. With loose reins hooked behind the saddle horn, Jericho smoked and stretched as his mount trotted in a meandering course among the ground cactus and more prominent rocks. At the top of the grade the view opened to a wide horizon. Jericho's horse stopped, then started, then stopped again.

"Whoa boy," Jericho commanded, reining to a stop. He sat looking at the possible paths, knowing his horse had strayed and needed his rider's lead.

"Well, let's see what we got," Jericho said as he fished out the cards and found the one for Cold Springs. He read the list of landmarks, remembering a few but not the ones farther down the list. His eyes came up and looked northwest, sure that he was south of where he should be. There was nothing that directly coincided with the landmarks on the list, but the terrain northwest showed the most promise. Jericho pulled his compass then reined his horse around and sighted on the path he'd just come, being able to see a mile of it.

"Yep, we been drifting south. You tryin' to give me the grand tour?"

The horse snorted as if disgusted by the question.

"No offense intended. I know you come by your missteps honest as the day is long." Jericho reined around again and took a sighting to the northwest then quickly stowed his cards and compass. "The oats are waitin' for ya and I'm leadin'. Make some dust!" Jericho said, giving a light kick that brought the horse to an instant gallop.

After a mile of riding northwest, Jericho caught sight of the sharp triple-tooth part of the distant mountain range that hadn't revealed itself until now. He pulled the Cold Springs Station card once more for a glance then stuffed it away. It was the last landmark to the station. Jericho reined toward a sightline line just north of the teeth then rode over hill and dale for two more miles before spotting the lone structure on a barren valley floor. A waiting rider and horse stood just clear of the buildings.

"Hyah!" Jericho sharply clipped, putting his mount from a lope to a full gallop once more.

11

Jericho made a hot stop, coming out of the saddle and hitting the ground before the horse had come to a halt. It was the only kind of dismount he'd witnessed, so he decided that anything less wouldn't properly display an urgency of mission. A dust cloud from his arrival rolled over him and the man who walked briskly toward him to remove the mochila from Jericho's played-out horse.

"Just tie 'im to the rail," the lean, young rider said as he pulled the mochila and strode to his own mount. "Danny's inside… he's the tender. Be out in just a minute for your horse. You don't need to do nothin' more 'cept collect some beef stew and biscuits that's fresh this minute. Then some sleep. Bet you're ready for it after that run."

The new rider set the mochila over his saddle and then walked over to where Jericho stood stiff, like he couldn't move.

"Pooch Stavely," the young man said, extending his arm for a handshake. "Good to have you on the run, Jericho!"

Jericho nodded as he shook Pooch's hand, realizing his wild-west dismount had set every joint in his body ablaze with fatigued pain.

"How'd you know my name?" Jericho asked.

Pooch smiled. "Got'a go. Little behind schedule."

In two seconds more, Pooch had turned and leapt onto his horse, putting it to a run and creating his own dust that drifted to the west, obscuring the vanishing rider.

Jericho tied his horse to the hitching rail then began hobbling toward the station door. It seemed a cruel distance at present. Each step rubbed his chafed groin and radiated stiffness from his neck down through his shoulders and on down his back to his buttocks, which felt like they'd been beaten with a branding iron. A muscle in his abdomen suddenly began to cramp in a knot. Jericho stood up straight and arched his back, pushing his belly out, trying to get the knotted muscle to unwind.

"Ahhhhh!" he cried out, bending farther back for all the stretch he could get. He held his stretch for a good half minute then cautiously resumed normal posture and hobbled on, his legs widening as he walked to avoid the stinging chafe.

Hags was standing up, waving his hands telling it to three seated men who were listening to him with rapt attention. "Yeah, it was the biggest damn herd I ever saw! Between that and them injuns, I'm feeling lucky to… well, looky there! Here comes the other lucky one!"

The men all turned and stared as Jericho came in, doing his best to walk normally rather than appear the bedraggled heap of hurt he was. Jericho's eyes widened at the sight of Hags.

"That last horse got a bit sideways on the way here," Jericho said. "But I didn't reckon it was enough time for you to beat me."

"I done this a few times now, kid," Hags said with a breath of chuckle. "Damn impressive you makin' it here as fast as you did… but you ain't as fast as me yet!"

The men laughed and stood up as Jericho made his way over to Hags and shook hands.

"Leastways, I'm glad to see you didn't get run down by them buffalo or scalped by them Indians!" Jericho said, shaking Hags's hand with the force of their both having survived.

Hags looked him in the eye with knowing appraisal. "We done cut it close!" he said. Hags nodded to the three standing men.

"Jericho, say hello to Stan Brock, the Station Keeper here at Cold Springs… Danny, a tender here… and Skinner, one of the westbound riders."

"Glad to know ya," Jericho said as he shook hands with the three men who all looked older to Jericho, particularly Stan, who was a big man with a long graying beard. Jericho waxed curious at the resemblance.

"You a relation of Mister Brock over to Dry Creek?" Jericho asked.

Stan nodded. "Willie's my brother."

"Well, I sure am obliged to him for givin' me this chance," Jericho chimed.

"He picked the right man for the job," Stan said. "I don't know if he could have gotten a better one from a line of a hundred. You proved that much already."

Jericho looked grateful. "Thank you, sir."

"Call me Stan," the rough-looking station keeper replied as he walked over to a cabinet and grabbed a jug and five cups, hooking three on the fingers of one hand and two on the other. He strode to the table and put the cups down, then pulled the cork and talked as he poured. "You got about twelve and a half hours 'fore you take up the run back to Dry Creek. From the look of you, you're hungry, tired, sore all over, and likely need some axle grease for your crotch. Good thing we got some liniment that'll work even better. But first!… First! We'll toast to a job well done on your first run! Gather round and throw 'em down!"

Jericho, Hags, Danny, and Skinner walked to the table. Jericho looked unsure as they all grabbed a cup and held it up for a toast.

"What's the matter, boy? You don't drink?" Stan asked Jericho.

Jericho looked solemn. "No, that ain't it. Just that… well, wasn't but yesterday that I took the company oath in front'a your brother Willie, sayin' I wouldn't drink no intoxicatin' liquor at any station."

Stan smiled. "If Willie were here, he'd drink it for you. That oath is a statement of intention… meaning you intend to do your job no matter what. This toast ain't a regular thing… and it ain't no small thing. It's ceremonial, in honor of surviving this far. It's a hard life… and harder yet around the next bend. Bitter and sweet in magnificence… and always demanding of a man who meets his obligations and responsibilities. That's what you took an oath to. Now we toast those obligations and responsibilities and thank God for the wherewithal to have them and thrive."

Jericho's eyes widened. He picked up his glass. "I'll drink to those words anytime!"

"This ain't anytime," Stan said, "it's this time… here and now. In twelve hours you'll be hard at it again… sober. To sunny days and prosperous ways!"

"And women that smile come the end of the day!" Skinner added.

The men clinked cups then threw back their shots in unison.

"Whoooeee!" Hags squealed as the men returned their cups to the table.

Stan pulled the cork again and poured. "One more just like before… and that's it."

The men collected their cups and held them up.

Jericho called it out. "Here's to horses that carry us through, and one more drink before the beef stew!"

"Hear, hear," Hags seconded.

Again the men drank. The shine was firebrand and strong as lye soap. Jericho put his cup down and coughed. A glow rolled over him like a wave of warm honey. He steadied himself, feeling his muscles relax as his full-body ache began to subside.

"I sure do thank you for the fine moment of a toast, sir," Jericho said, his words just a bit warbled.

Stan eyeballed him. "Well, Mister Buck. There's one other thing about a ceremonial toast that all that partakes abides by. We don't mention it to nobody else… ever."

"Mention what?" Jericho said with a look of mischief. Skinner cackled as the others gave wry grins.

"Course, maybe you should tell me if ya got any other brothers at any stations," Jericho said, now clearly lit as if he might break out in song.

"Well, there is another of us," Stan said. "My brother Pete! But he's a few thousand miles away… back in Boston."

"Say, I heard'a that," Danny said.

"Me too," Skinner said. "Where is it?"

"East," Stan answered. "Clear across the whole country… right up against the Atlantic Ocean. Pete's the captain of a whaling ship."

"Whaling ship? You mean they can catch 'em?" Danny asked.

"What's a whale?" Skinner instantly queried.

Danny looked at Skinner. "It's a giant fish! You ain't never heard of a whale?"

"I heard the word one time somewhere," Skinner said. "But I don't recollect where or knowin' what it was. I only ever caught rainbows, browns, and such. Never seen an ocean. They got any of these whales 'round these parts… in the rivers or lakes?"

Hags jumped in, blurting it out, "No, Skinner! They's fifty feet long!… and longer!… maybe a hundred feet! Ain't gonna fit in some river!"

"Could fit in a lake, I reckon," Skinner said defensively.

"They sure could," Stan said quickly, "but they're saltwater creatures… only live in oceans. Oceans are all saltwater. If there were saltwater lakes, whales could sure enough live in 'em. There's likely some inlet water… saltwater bays and what not, along the coasts where whales hole up now and again."

Skinner smiled, showing what was left of his broken, brown teeth, feeling better that Stan had taken up with an explanation that muted Hags's incredulity. "Nothin' but saltwater in them oceans, eh?" Skinner said.

"Nothin' but," Stan said.

"I'd like to see one of them oceans someday… just as far as the eye could see, I reckon. Like to see one of them whales, too," Skinner said with mystery in his eyes.

Jericho spoke up. "My ma told me Bible stories when I was a boy. I most liked that one about Jonah and the whale."

"Yep, that was a real good one!" Danny seconded.

Skinner's face turned to puzzlement. "Didn't get any Bible learnin'. What happened?"

"Well," Jericho said, "God told this fella Jonah to go preach to some wicked people over to a place called Nineveh. But Jonah didn't cotton to that idea so he quick got on a boat goin' a different way. Well, God didn't like him runnin' away so he set a storm upon the boat… and the boat people figured it was Jonah's fault so they threw him in the ocean. God didn't want Jonah to drown, so he had a whale swallow him up… and Jonah was safe inside for three days until the whale spit 'im out. And where do you suppose ole Jonah landed?"

Skinner looked deep in thought and taken with the question. He glared at Jericho with a confused gaze. "I ain't got the first goddamn idea! Where'd he turn up?"

"Right there in Nineveh, where God had told him to go!" Jericho said, smiling.

"Don't that steal the bacon!" Skinner declared.

The men laughed.

Skinner turned to Stan and asked, "Did your brother Pete tell you how in hell they get a fifty- or hundred-foot fish on the boat after they get it caught?"

Hags and Danny looked at each other, taken with Skinner's question and that they hadn't considered it themselves.

"Yeah!" Hags exclaimed. "How would they get one'a those monsters up onto the ship?"

Stan looked at the men, all their attention squarely focused on him for what had just become the most perplexing question of the day.

"I wondered the same thing," Stan began. "Pete told it like this. He said they catch the whales with longboats… much smaller than the ship… maybe thirty feet or so, and six or eight men in each, throwing spears with ropes tied to them. They tire the whale out from bleeding it… and in time they drown it. Then they have to tow the whale back to the ship where they chain and tie it up along the side of the ship. Then they spend the next four or five days, a week maybe, butchering it while it's in the water… cutting big pieces off it and boiling them on the deck of the ship in big pots. Then they barrel up all the oil that comes from boiling all the pieces. After they get all the oil they can, they turn the carcass and other waste loose back into the ocean. So they never do bring the whale up on the ship… save for in pieces. Dangerous work! If the whale don't smash them to bits while they're in those longboats, they have to keep from getting eaten by sharks while they're butchering him in the water!"

"They hunt 'em just for the oil… not the meat?" Skinner asked.

Stan appeared quizzical. "I don't believe there's much meat on them, mostly just blubber… fat. Pete said they keep some of the whale bones and cartilage too… but it's mostly about the oil. They use it for lamp oil… oilin' machinery… all kinds of things. There's big money in it."

"Ain't that somethin'!" Hags proclaimed.

"I need to eat," Jericho suddenly said, weaving just a bit and feeling unsteady on his feet. "I feel like I been butchered."

"I'm ready myself," Hags agreed.

****

A nagging poking commenced as Jericho was deep in a dream, standing in a meadow with two dozen elk and a pack of wolves that were stalking them. He imagined it was the rack of one of the elk poking him in the shoulder.

"Get up… time's drawin' near," the elk said.

Jericho couldn't believe what he was hearing. Then the poking came again. "Jericho!"

He opened his eyes and saw Hags standing over him in the dim, candle-lit bunkroom.

"We ain't got long… half hour at best," Hags said then headed out to the main room.

Jericho rose quickly and silently. He'd slept like the dead but now felt fully alive and rested. He slathered himself once again about the crotch, inner thighs, and buttocks with the magical salve that Stan had provided. It numbed the area with soothing relief like nothing he'd ever used before. Stan had given him the jar, saying they had plenty more, but Jericho would have to buy the next jar for two bits. Jericho thought that was the best deal he'd heard of in years and had immediately put a dollar on account for another four jars.

"Well, don't use too much at a time," Stan had told him. "Helps the pain but it'll stone you good if you take too much."

Jericho speedily dressed. Minutes later he stood outside with a cup of coffee, eating a second biscuit as distant coyotes yipped in concert under the half moon. Hags smoked a cigarette as Danny stood by the saddled horses peering into the western darkness.

"He's comin'," Danny said with certainty.

A moment later, Jericho heard the faint sound of pounding hooves. He stuffed the last piece of biscuit in his mouth and slurped the coffee to aid in getting it down.

Hags spoke easy to Jericho. "I got a notion you'll only need this one night-run together before you can ride it on your own."

"I'd bet on it," Jericho agreed. "I could do it alone right now if you're feelin' ready for some more biscuits and bunk time."

Hags shook his head. "No… no! Willie would roast me alive if I didn't stick with you for the first night-run."

"It'll be light in three more hours," Jericho countered.

"A man can get good and lost in three hours," Hags said, throwing his cigarette to the ground, "not to mention freeze to death!"

The dark figure could be seen the last quarter mile, moving like a force of the night in full gallop under the faint light of the half moon. Dust rose as he entered the yard and hard-reined to a stop, throwing down in pure Pony-Express-rider fashion like he'd been doing it all his life. He had his mochila off his horse in seconds more, looking instantly at Jericho and Hags to see who was taking it. Jericho took it with a silent nod and had it on his own saddle nearly as fast.

There were no words exchanged, no introductions, as if it were a custom of a night transition that Jericho instantly understood. He felt a pulse of pride at being one of the riders, a rider for the famed Pony Express. These men could ride, all of them. And if they couldn't, or weren't up to the demands of the job, they'd be weeded out in short order. But that would never happen to Jericho Buck. He knew that much already.

Jericho and Hags bolted east out of the yard, the cool air rushing over them and enlivening their senses with the secrecy of the night.

****

Jericho and Hags dismounted back at Dry Creek Station at 11 a.m. sharp. The mochila continued east within a minute of their arrival by way of a boy not much more than fifteen or sixteen, Jericho guessed. Clyde took their mounts and began leading them toward the barn as Jericho watched the rider's dust trail ascending up the outlying grade.

"That one's a youngin', Jericho said to Hags.

"Youngest we got. Seventeen," Hags replied. "I heard there's some fifteen-year-olds back east… over to Nebraska Territory and such."

Hags was walking toward the station door when he glanced back and saw Jericho still standing in place, smoking a cigarette and looking after the rider who would soon disappear over the ridge.

"You comin'?" Hags asked, taken by Jericho's statuesque trance to the east.

Jericho turned and looked at Hags as he took a drag and slowly exhaled it, watching the smoke vanish in the breeze beyond his lips.

Hags frowned. "You contemplatin' the nature of smoke in the wind?"

"Among other things," Jericho drawled. "Say, you know what's in the salve?"

"The what?" Hags asked.

"The salve… the liniment Stan gave me."

Hags stared at Jericho for a long moment. "Lordy… you're pickled as shit! I knew it. Couldn't put my finger on it. Didn't see you drinkin' or nothin' but you been uncanny as a squirrel in a briar patch."

"Not so much now," Jericho said. "Mostly just wore down to nothin' but mush at this point. But I sure enough saw the night moon and rising sun in ways I never did before. What's in that salve?"

Hags chuckled. "Well, I don't know all of it… but it's got those poppies in it that'll head-thump like no kind of shine. I recollect Stan telling you to go easy on it just before you went to bed last night."

"I did go easy on it last night," Jericho said. "Slept like a log twelve hours… never felt the chafe. Worked so good, I figured I'd lay it on good just before we rode. It sure got rid'a the saddle sore… but my head feels like it soaked in a wash bucket," Jericho abruptly started striding toward the station door. "I don't know what poppies are but I need some sleep."

"Damn good thing I rode back here with you," Hags said. "No tellin' where you'd be now if I hadn't."

"Nowhere near here, I reckon," Jericho replied with a small skip in his step.

"Well, likely best you don't tell Willie about your grand salve adventures right now."

Jericho nodded. "I'm headed straight for a bunk."

12

A warm wind blew over the upper plains, bending the tall, green grass of spring against the backdrop of the Sedaye Mountains with their patches of birch and aspen newly in bloom. The unusually heavy rains of April had yielded mountain wildflowers of lupines, false baby stars, blue dicks, yellow monkey-flowers and Indian paintbrush with minarets, all gracing the contours of the high country under the ever-warming skies of late May. Jericho took in the beauty of it like the lucky audience of one to a grand show, all the while working his horse for speed when the terrain was best, then restful moderation when it wasn't. And nobody could do it better.

It had taken him a full, brutal week to get past the worst of his initial saddle chafe as he opted to forego any more of the magic salve while riding. The pain had finally relented, replaced by a sense of dues paid and hardened will. Now he'd been on the job nearly three months and had proved his mettle, being one of just a few that rode the longest run of the entire Pony Express route. The one-hundred-mile stretch was replicated in only two other runs along the two-thousand-mile route from St. Joseph, Missouri, to Sacramento, California, though the other two routes were much farther east in the flatter lands of the Kansas and Nebraska territories.

The land was changing, too. Just a month and a half earlier, in March, the Utah Territory had been whittled down when the Nevada Territory was officially created, taking the westernmost lands of Utah, and placing Jericho's entire route from Dry Creek to Cold Springs under the jurisdiction of Nevada Territory, with its capital, Genoa, on its western border.

Jericho was quickly becoming renowned beyond just his own route. His meteoric rise grew with his willingness to take on any job and see it through. He had volunteered several different times to pick up additional routes when sickness, injury, or emergency business had left Cold Springs westbound, or Dry Creek eastbound, temporarily shorthanded. He never got lost and was seldom more than half an hour late along the new routes unknown to him, completing stretches of nearly twenty-four hours before getting to rest.

Jericho was making more money than he'd ever made, but he saw the pay only as one of the benefits. He relished the country he rode and the endurance challenges he took on. Youth and stamina were fleeting things, so he burned hot, propelled by forces within for as long as his being could muster. He understood his prime and extracted every drop of life as his purpose.

Over the months, Jericho had come to learn shortcuts between certain stations that cut bits of time off or merely changed the scenery. Such was the mountain pass he approached now. It cut off distance but not time. No matter to him. He was ahead of schedule. The wildflowers that graced his path were rare and delighted his wonder of creation. And a mile farther ahead was a valley in which a lake of crystalline blue water mirrored the sky above and the tall pines that ringed its shores.

The gray that Jericho rode sprang heartily in the surroundings, knowing them from the previous re-routings of its rider. Soon the valley ahead would slow the pace to a lope as the abundance of trees would come to bear. But for the moment, the gray galloped over the open meadow toward the pass entrance that was narrow and elusive to the eye. A quarter mile fell away. Then he rounded the granite rock face that rose for a hundred feet, obscuring the entrance to the pass, which majestically widened after another quarter mile, giving view to the mile-wide valley, rich with pine, aspen, birch, cottonwoods, and a variety of high-valley bush.

Jericho slowed to a lope and lit a cigarette. He smoked and rode, alternating between a lope and fast trot as he weaved amongst the bush and trees that came densely and then gave way to short expanses of open ground. The lake flashed through the trees to his right, with an occasional full view. And the sound of a stream running briskly to the lake lay ahead. The notion took him. He would make a few minutes to swim in that lake on a day when he was ahead of schedule during the coming summer. It would sure be nice, he thought. His musings were suddenly stolen.

The shots came loudly, eight rapid-fire blasts reverberating from close by, followed by a piercing scream, a woman's scream, coming from the thicket of trees only a few hundred feet ahead. Jericho kicked his horse to a gallop and drew his pistol, riding low and hard as he reined his way through the trees and caught first glimpse of the scene ahead. His horse took the fast- running stream in one bound, and then he was within a hundred feet and could see it all.

In an open spot, four men on horseback with pistols drawn were facing a young Paiute woman atop a horse. Two Paiute warriors, one on each side of her, lay dead, their bullet-riddled bodies full in the afternoon sun upon the small clearing. Their horses stood a ways off, having bolted when their riders were shot off them.

The sound of the stream had masked Jericho's approach until he'd cleared the water. But now they turned and looked at his approach. Two of the men pivoted their horses and their pistols toward him. Jericho slowed to a trot and then reined to a stop thirty feet away. The men were on his right, the woman to his left. He holstered his gun as he glanced at the two dead Paiutes, noting that neither had been armed besides their sheath knives. Their rifles still rested in the scabbard skins on their horses standing fifty feet away.

Jericho saw the silver badges that each man wore. They were hard-looking men, but something else, too. He eyed the horse of one of the men that had turned toward him. Then he looked for an instant at the man who rode him.

"I heard the shootin' and a woman scream," Jericho said calmly.

"Who the hell are you, mister?" one of them asked as the other two men also turned their horses toward Jericho.

"Pony Express rider!" Jericho said.

"You're off the beaten path," the man shot back.

Jericho shrugged, "I know a lot of paths. Change 'em up from time to time. You lawmen?"

"That's right!" a man with long, stringy hair replied.

"Where from?" Jericho followed.

The meanest-looking one reined his horse forward a step as if to make it clear he was the leader. He spoke with contempt in a mocking tone: "Where from? Hereabouts, thereabouts, wherever we's abouts."

The other men chuckled as Jericho looked to the young Paiute woman. She was beautiful. Their eyes met and held for a brief moment, her fear clawing at him. He hoped she had read his gaze on her and somehow understood he was on her side. He knew what these men planned for her.

"Well… I got mail to haul… best be gettin'," Jericho said nonchalantly.

"Don't you move, mail boy!" the leader said. "Truth be told, we're robbers posing as lawmen so we can get the drop. Didn't need it with them… or you. This valley's our hideout when we're not workin'. Your misfortune was to come through here today… her misfortune, too. Before we kill her, we'll find out how many ways we can pleasure ourselves. But you? Well, the mail ain't gettin' through today."

All four men were staring hard at Jericho, two of them with their guns already drawn and trained on him.

Jericho cocked his head just a bit and said matter-of-factly, "I reckoned it might be such. That soft pud on the brown there turned tail and ran when I killed two of his partners tryin' to rob a stage I was on a couple months back."

The man Jericho referred to suddenly straightened up a little, his eyes widening as he remembered.

Jericho continued, "Yes sir, a man never knows when his time is up, but I'll swear to God I know when it's time to stop talkin' and start shootin'. Run!" he yelled at the woman.

His gun was already coming out of his holster with lightning speed as he finished the last word and kicked his horse straight at them. Shots ripped the air as Jericho fanned his pistol and felt the burn of two bullets taking him in the arm and side. But his shots were true on the two men who'd had their guns drawn and had fired just an instant before he had. Jericho took the man on the brown through the throat and shot the other man center-chest, sending both tumbling from the saddle. The leader's gun had come level and he was firing as Jericho ducked down to his horse's neck, about to ram the leader's horse. They fired simultaneously. Jericho felt his horse going down as a bullet took his mustang in the head. Yet Jericho's shot had found the mark, boring straight through the leader's heart, killing him instantly.

Jericho slammed the ground, rolling over his right shoulder to absorb the worst of it. He heard the shooting continue and knew it was the outlaw at the end of the line, the one closest to where the Paiute woman had been. She had made it to the tree line before a shot took her horse in the rear flank, causing the animal to stumble badly. She pitched from her mount, slamming her head on a tree on the way down. She lay motionless.

Jericho fumbled a moment on the ground, searching his body for his other Navy Colt pistol. He got to his feet with the fully loaded piece in his hand as the last outlaw turned toward him, still atop his mount. Jericho ran at him, fanning his Colt as he charged, his shots mostly finding the outlaw's torso. The outlaw jerked from the impact of the bullets as he tried to fire his pistol. He was empty. But he had enough gumption left to throw the heavy piece with every ounce of remaining strength. Jericho took the pistol square in the forehead and collapsed unconscious just a step away from the outlaw's horse. Shot to ribbons and bleeding badly, the outlaw gazed about to see his three partners, all dead. Then, in shock and delirium, he put his horse to a trot and made it to the shade of the trees before he fell from his mount and thumped the ground. He managed to roll to his back and look up at the blue sky, wondering how he had come to be there. A minute later he was dead.

13

Shimmering moonlight stretched long on the lake's quaking water, pushed by a cool breeze. Jericho opened his eyes and stared at the stars, thinking that he should have been able to see more of them. He turned his head and saw the moon, robust in the clear sky and perhaps only days away from being full. The events of a few hours earlier flooded his mind. Lying still on his back, he began craning his head around to see the shapes of the dead upon the ground.

Pain radiated throughout his body. He knew he'd been shot and began feeling his arm. His fingers quickly found the entry and exit wounds for his arm and his side. The bullets had gone all the way through, missing major arteries and organs, but he felt like one of his ribs was broken from the shot through his side. His shirt was soaked. He had bled a lot and was very weak and thirsty. Grunting with the strain of a simple task, he rolled over and began crawling toward his dead horse thirty feet away. He was shocked at his weakness, knowing he likely couldn't have stood up. When he finally got to the mustang, he had to rest for a minute before unlashing his canteen and drinking. He drank half of what was left and lay back, exhausted. There were several horses still nearby, cropping grass in the ease of the night.

I can catch one, tomorrow… after I've rested, Jericho thought. He looked and saw part of the mochila caught under his dead horse.

I'll get it loose and take up the run again tomorrow, when I'm rested. I just need to rest, he thought, and then passed out again.

Deep and dreamless were the hours unknown. Then in the gray of dawn his eyes came open again, prompted by a voice in his face, angry and loud, the words unrecognizable. A Paiute stood over him yelling down as a score of other Paiute warriors moved about. Jericho was tied to a travois and hitched behind one of the horses of the outlaws. The two dead Paiutes were draped over their horses. The Paiute standing over him yelled again then stood glaring at him as if he was expecting an answer. "I don't know what you're sayin'," Jericho said raspily. The Paiute swung a club he was holding, hitting Jericho alongside the head. All went black.

Midday sun from high above blinded him as he tried to open his eyes. He managed only slits. His head throbbed and his body ached with pain and stiffness as the travois bumped along. He was bound tightly to the travois by leather straps, preventing him from any movement of his limbs, adding to his agony. Jericho turned his head from side to side, trying to determine where he was, but none of it was familiar. He only knew he was no longer in the valley pass of the Desatoya Mountains. Yet it was still high country; another area in the Desatoyas? Or maybe it was the range just to the north. He'd seen it, but had never ventured there as it did not fall anywhere within his route. Jericho knew the Paiutes and Shoshones roamed far and wide in the Utah Territory, yet nobody seemed certain of where their encampments might be at any given time. They moved seasonally and frequently, following the best hunting, water, shelter and anonymity. They were the explorers and undoubtedly best knew the land and its bounties for their way of life.

He was near the end of the procession that moved along at a lope. Only a few Paiutes were visible to him, bringing up the rear. After being awake for indeterminate minutes, Jericho wanted to yell from the pain of being banged about. He wanted to yell at being in this predicament. He wanted to yell with anger and his failure to get his run delivered. The pain was excruciating. His rib sent stabbing shocks through him with every bump and jolt. His arms and legs were numb with an unbearable need to move them. A thirst curled his tongue and ravaged his senses with the need of moisture. And his head pounded while his eyes suffered an itching burn from blood that had run into them and matted his lashes. He wanted to scream to the sky, but mostly he wanted to be unconscious again, to be free of his suffering. Even those riding at the front turned and looked back when Jericho let loose with a guttural yell that cracked above the sounds of horses' hooves and other noises, lasting for a long, startling moment as it caught all off guard. But the glances and momentary interest of the Paiutes quickly faded upon realization of who had yelled. Then Jericho embraced the reprieve he had prayed for as he passed out once again.

14

The smell was familiar and worked on him in waves, bringing him slowly from the depths back to the living. Jericho's eyes opened to the late-afternoon sky, clear and crisp with brilliantly white bulbous clouds floating in serenity. Sounds of the encampment drew his eyes to the right. Beginning a hundred feet away, scores of wickiups were spread over several acres of flat, grassy ground, graced with cottonwood trees that shaded part of the camp. Paiutes were visible. Some women toiled on making clothing and blankets, and some worked game hides in a tanning process. Others were weaving or cooking over their own small fires. A few men were in their own area fashioning arrows and bows and spear shanks. A fire pit to the center of camp had large flanks of deer roasting, tended by an old woman. Despite his pain, Jericho involuntarily began salivating at the aroma. There was a sweetness of herbs present that gave the roasting meat a most delicious scent, such that it took his mind to hunger instead of his incessant ache and throbbing, if only for a moment.

A Paiute boy who had been sitting just out of his sight, watching him, suddenly noticed that the white man staked to the ground was awake. The boy rose and ran off toward the camp, waving his arms and calling loudly enough to be heard by the multitude who were visible. With the boy's ruckus, several Paiutes looked to where Jericho lay captive, spying him for a moment before returning to their work. The boy disappeared into a tent.

Jericho realized he was naked. He craned his head up to see his feet. They were spread and bound to ground stakes that held each leg firmly. His arms were straight out from each side, also bound to ground stakes that were deep and immovable. Then he saw the Paiute man exit the tent with the boy at his side. The boy ran off as the Paiute walked toward Jericho. His long, black hair hung down on broad shoulders. Unlike most of the other Paiute men who were presently bare-chested, the approaching man wore a buckskin top and pants, and a leather headband that held a turquoise stone in it, about the size of a third eye, Jericho thought.

He squatted down by Jericho's side, his black eyes intense and piercing, yet devoid of anger or contempt.

"I am Crow Talks," he said in perfect English. "Are you able to speak?"

Jericho smiled grimly then mumbled through his parched and swollen lips, "I'll give 'er hell tryin' but I reckon you could make me out better if I could have a little water first."

Crow Talks turned his head to the camp and gave a short whistle, then called out something in Paiute. A woman hotfooted down with a skin sewn canteen and gave it to Crow Talks who promptly began pouring water mostly into Jericho's mouth. After a moment, Jericho could no longer keep up with the pour rate and began grunting as the water overflowed everywhere. Crow Talks stopped pouring and waited as Jericho coughed and gasped for breath.

"Much obliged," Jericho finally said, sounding as if he'd half drowned.

"What happened to our woman and the braves with her?" Crow Talks asked.

Jericho took a few deep breaths in preparation then grimly recounted:"Them four men wearing the badges threw down on your braves. Didn't see it but heard it… got there directly after. They weren't lawmen… they were bad men… just up'n shot 'em looked like. Your boys never got their rifles unskinned. Anyways… came upon it, I did. Your woman was still on her horse not more'n ten feet from 'em. They were gonna do bad for her… and me too… told me so. That's when I told your woman to run, and I shot 'em."

Crow Talks frowned and looked up to the sky a moment then looked back at Jericho. "Where is our woman… our precious Wyanet?"

"I don't rightly know," Jericho replied, his face showing genuine concern. "She broke to a gallop when the shootin' started. Didn't see her after that… what with bein' shot and fully taken tryin' to kill them murderin' varmints. I got knocked out somewhere in it. She wasn't in that clearing when I came awake again last night. Seen the bodies of the others but she wasn't there… her horse neither."

Stern incredulity hung on Crow Talks's face. His lips tightened as he spoke: "You say you are not with the men who died. You say you killed them all… yourself… after they killed our braves without losing a man. I say you tell lies! Wyanet is the daughter of our chief. You will tell me where she is… or you will die slowly… badly. You are dying now, yet you could live if she is well and you tell us where she is." Crow Talks drew his knife and leaned in closer, his face turning to quiet rage as he continued, "If not, I will cut out your eyes… blinding you of the path to the afterworld. I will cut out your tongue so you cannot ask the way. I will cut off your ears so you will not hear your own screams when I let our women cut off your seeds and stuff them in your mouth for you to choke on. What do you say now?"

Jericho's eyes narrowed to a hard stare. "Mister, I killed them men to save the woman and me. That's the truth of it and anything said different is the lie. I never seen those men before. I ride for the Pony Express haulin' mail 'cross the country… from Dry Creek to Cold Springs." Jericho nodded his head slowly, "If you didn't find her there, I reckon she's alive. Maybe 'fore you start cuttin' me into little pieces you ought'a get to lookin'. Maybe her horse is gone because she's on 'im."

"The horse is dead!" Crow Talks snapped, "Shot… and a broken leg."

"She must'a kept runnin'… on foot," Jericho said, "otherwise you'd'a found her."

Crow Talks stood up. "Or there were other men there," he said. "Men you know… men who took her!"

"I didn't see nobody else!" Jericho declared, "And I ain't acquainted with none'a them men I killed!"

Crow Talks flipped his knife, catching it by the blade. Then with a short burst of his arm he threw it down where it stuck nearly a half-blade deep in Jericho's thigh.

"Ahhh!" Jericho grunted.

Crow Talks leaned over and pulled his knife from Jericho's leg then wiped the blade clean on Jericho's bare leg. "Do not take a loud voice with me again," Crow Talks said, "or the next throw will be through your heart."

15

Chief Leaping Elk sat on bearskin at the back of his wickiup, his head bowed in prayer. He was alone, grief-stricken but ever stoic. He wondered how he might go on if his daughter Wyanet was lost to him. It was as if his life was draining from him with each passing hour, his strength, his indomitable will, all fading with the sunset of this day. He had known crushing grief in his life, losing his wife and two young sons to typhus, so long ago it seemed. Yet, he and his tiny daughter had survived, along with two-thirds of the tribe. The illness had struck like the grim reaper, moving from wickiup to wickiup, casting the spell of death with random savagery. It had taken Chief Burning Sky, too, and Leaping Elk had ascended to Chief, taking his new responsibilities as clear purpose in transcending his sorrows and anything that did not kill him. But that had been nearly two decades earlier when he was young and strong. The ensuing years had brought more death and hardship, yet he could always summon the soaring spirit to see him through. But now, having entered his fifth decade of life, he merely felt old and defeated at the absence of his daughter Wyanet.

The flap on the wickiup parted and Crow Talks entered. Leaping Elk looked up and immediately asked in Paiute, "What does the white man know?"

Crow Talks looked contemplative as he answered in native tongue, "He says the four men wearing badges were false... and they shot Coyote Man and Snake Moon without warning. He says he came there just after it happened and Wyanet was still on her horse in front of them. He tells that these men told him of bad intentions for Wyanet and him… and that is when he told her to run and she fled at a gallop. He says he killed the four men and lost sight of Wyanet during the battle.

Leaping Elk's eyes turned to Crow Talks. "What of it is true… and what is a lie? Who is this man… why was he there?"

Crow Talks answered, "He says he carries mail across the land for Pony Express. I do not know this thing, Pony Express… or the word mail. Perhaps the many letters from his saddle bag is this thing called mail." Crow Talks slowly shook his head as he went on, "He is shot in his arm and side, and also has head wounds, yet I believe it is a lie that he killed the four men himself. Still, perhaps he speaks straight about Wyanet galloping away. If there were no other men, perhaps she fled on foot after her horse went down. Perhaps she is hiding now, fearing that other white men would come."

"May the Great Spirit make it so," Leaping Elk said as he abruptly stood up. "I will go and seek her now."

"Is that wise?" Crow Talks asked flatly. "Our Clan Boar search for her now… our best trackers… six who know the land…"

"Silence!" Leaping Elk snapped, cutting him off. "I know all that you say! It was not wise that I let her go a half-sun's ride away with only Coyote Man and Snake Moon. I should have ordered more to go with her."

"She did not want more," Crow Talks countered. "She has not had more for several years. Visits to her mother's grave are a matter of privacy to her. Such it is for her now a grown woman. The Valley of High Bloom is lonely. We have never known of white men there. You had no way to see danger. You could not know."

"I can do what I will," Leaping Elk declared as he put on a buckskin top. He grabbed his rifle and bow and quiver. "Now I will go and seek Wyanet… alone."

Crow Talks knew better than to suggest that any braves go with him. "What of the death dance tonight for Coyote Man and Snake Moon?" Crow Talks queried.

"Have it," Leaping Elk replied. "Our people know of my need to find my daughter, yet the ceremony must go on tonight. Silver Fox will lead it."

"This man with letters… of Pony Express, will die soon if he is not cared for. What is your wish?" Crow Talks asked.

Leaping Elk's gaze fell stern on Crow Talks. "Let him die."

Chief Leaping Elk exited his wickiup and looked to the western sky. The sun was still an hour above the peaks of the nearby range. He knew he had two hours of daylight left. Moments later he was mounted and had a lead rope on a second horse in tow, cantering out of camp as warriors and women alike watched their chief leaving. Leaping Elk would trail toward the Valley of High Bloom by way of a considerably more difficult and unused trail. There were other such trails in addition to the easiest way, and Leaping Elk now guessed that his daughter would take such a route if she were on foot, wanting to remain hidden from any other white men who might still be in the area. She was well familiar with the land, he knew. If she was alive and walking, she would be close now, within a few hours of the encampment. He would traverse the more obscure routes, using his own cluck-whistle that his daughter would recognize and immediately respond to. He broke to a full gallop, praying she was still alive.

****

Blood-red rose the moon, nearly full and peeking in and out of drifting clouds like a serpent of the night. Jericho watched it from a trance, his conscious state absent of all but delusion from a fever that gripped him even as his body trembled with the cold of lost blood. The tribal drums and chanting of the nearby death dance came to him only as the announcement of his own impending death. He welcomed it, eventually closing his eyes in hopes of a speedier end. Then he fell unconscious again to the colorless end of time and existence, vanished like the sun gone deep below the horizon.

His respite ended brutally with searing pain that brought forth his own voice screaming into the night. His eyes flashed open to glimpse the dark figures hovering over him, dropping glowing embers onto him. The red-hot coals sizzled on his bare chest and stomach, filling his nostrils with the smell of his own burning flesh. Jericho screamed for moments more, exhausting what strength he had left as he shimmied violently trying to shake the coals off him. And then he mercifully passed out.

16

The night dragged long and arduous with moaning, whimpering, grunts, cries, and other intemperate utterances from the dying man, staked naked to the ground. He participated in none of it. The escape of his life dwindling away in sounds, unsanctioned of his will, continued intermittently for hours as he floated somewhere close to death, out of body and out of his mind, involuntarily holding claim to existence by expelling noises to prove it. Then, finally, all fell silent in the last hours before dawn.

The steady hoot of an owl marked time as the first gray of light crawled on. Jericho had delusional awareness of the men suddenly around him, cutting him free of his bounds and folding his arms across his chest as one of them shouted instructions in the Paiute language he did not understand. He wondered if he was dead and being prepared for burial, or if he was to be buried alive, or readied for sacrifice. Blankets were put on him and then he was being picked up by several warriors. They carried him hurriedly, arriving at a wickiup where the flap was held back as he was hauled inside and placed carefully on a bed of furs. A fire burned nearby, the smoke drifting straight up and exiting the hole in the wickiup's high point. Warmth of the fire and blankets did little to quell his uncontrolled shaking, but he felt it as a measure of relief and comfort.

Moments later, two women came in and kneeled close in around him. One cradled his head and poured water slowly, carefully into his mouth, waiting for him to swallow before pouring more. The other pulled the blankets from his body and began examining him, tenderly probing his bullet wounds and wood-coal burns. She softly slid her hand under him, searching for an exit wound from the bullet that had taken him in the side. A moment later she removed her hand and reached for a bowl, bringing forth a gooey poultice on her fingers which she began packing in the discolored bullet holes. She expertly worked the medicinal mixture into each of his wounds, first the entry and exit on his upper arm, and then the bullet hole in his side and the knife wound on his thigh.

The woman giving him water said something to him then poured water on his face. She followed with a cloth, cleaning the dried blood from his eyelashes, face and forehead. When she finished, Jericho opened his eyes fully and stared at her, his face expressionless as he gazed on her round face, framed by long, black hair and brown eyes. She returned his gaze, her look softening as she offered a hint of a smile. Then she placed her hands on his shoulder and pulled as the other woman pushed on his hip, rolling Jericho up onto his side. He felt the poultice being kneaded into his back wound, which was noticeably larger. Then they rolled him to his back again and the water woman began feeding him small bites of frybread and deer meat. Jericho was not hungry but knew he had to eat to gain strength. He chewed very slowly, the effort of it causing him to breathe hard but he kept at it.

The poultice woman began applying peculiar-smelling oil, first coating and massaging his legs and feet, and then his upper body, taking great care around the numerous burns on his chest and stomach. Jericho's trembling began to subside as he watched her and slowly chewed deer meat. Firelight cast her silhouette onto the hide wall behind her, its shape bringing his mother to mind and the times she had tended his injuries as a boy. He swallowed the bite and closed his eyes, falling instantly asleep.

Hours later, the two Paiute women were back. He did not know how much time had passed but the fire was out and the day was full with bright blue sky that shone through a hole at the top of the wickiup. Again the woman cradled his head and slowly gave him water and food while the other woman tended the poultice and massaged him with the oily liniment. The women talked to one another as they performed their care. Jericho listened blankly to the foreign words as he lay motionless, so exhausted and sick that it took all his strength just to drink and eat and silently watch them.

Every few hours the ritual resumed and he would awaken for the time that they were there. During the late-day visit when they rolled him up on his side, the poultice woman took his penis and held it to a wide bowl set beneath it. She nodded at him and gave it a tug. A moment later the yellow urine came forth at a trickle but eventually flowed fuller as Jericho groaned with relief. After she dumped the bowl outside, she returned and put her hands over her lower stomach then pointed to her buttocks. He understood what she was asking and managed a weak answer of "no" as he shook his head.

Sometime late in the night, Jericho opened his eyes to the soft glow of firelight, awakened by singing. He rolled his head slowly to the side to see the source of the sound. The older Paiute man sat cross-legged a few feet away, wearing buckskin pants, moccasins, and an ornamental headdress of fine elk hide, inlaid with turquoise, opal, amethyst, jasper, and agate, and plumed with feathers of eagles, turkeys, bluebirds, green and blue teals, and mallards. His necklace hung down his bare chest, fashioned of diamondback snakeskin on which hung the claws and teeth of bears and mountain lions, highlighted by gold nuggets in between.

Leaping Elk sang a spirit song with a burning smoke-pot before him, praying that this white man who had saved his daughter would live. And he prayed he might be forgiven if the man died. The song moved like the changing weather, his chanting melodically meandering over lower and higher notes with ranging intensity of breath, from long extension of glissando and legato, to short, crisp staccato, all in a universe of possibility to please and enjoin the help of the Great Spirit. Jericho watched as Leaping Elk sang with his eyes closed and his head moving in time to his melodic oration. The effect of it became serenely hypnotic on Jericho. His eyelids soon fell heavy with the warmth of his surroundings, and he drifted off.

The next morning while the women were tending him, Crow Talks entered and stood close to Jericho, looking down at him. Jericho met his eyes and spoke weakly but resolutely. "I reckon you found the woman… seein' as how I still got my eyes, my ears, my tongue and my nuts."

"Yes, we have her," Crow Talks said, showing a genial expression.

"I am happy to hear such," Jericho replied.

Crow Talks frowned with sudden repentance. "I did not believe you… but she told us of your bravery… that you saved her life. We owe you a great debt. I am sorry for throwing my knife. Others are sorry for putting fire to you. You are safe now. You must live… get strong again and live."

"Lord willin', I intend to do such," Jericho said, "if I ain't too far gone already. I don't reckon I can stand up yet. Just the same, I ain't hurtin' too bad."

Crow Talks nodded at the two women tending Jericho. "Imala and Chenoa will see you to strength. Imala's frybread will keep you from pain."

Jericho took a deep breath. "Just feel so weak… can't…"

Jericho's eyes closed as Crow Talks asked, "Do you write the letters you carry?"

There was no answer.

17

Late the following night, Jericho came awake with the sense of something near. His eyes opened with his head turned toward the fire pit which had only glowing coals remaining. They emitted a faint circle of light. Then he realized the sensual warmth on his right hand and turned his head to the other side. She was there, sitting next to him, her face faintly visible as she held his hand in hers. His recognition was instant. It was her, the girl he had yelled at to run when he drew his pistol to defend them both. He could never forget her face. Even in her fear of the terrible moment, she had been beautiful. And now, up close with her soft eyes searching his, she was astonishing, filling his senses as if divine, like an angel.

"Hello, ma'am," Jericho said, quietly with a raspy voice.

She began speaking in Paiute, her voice mesmerizing to him, her facial expression showing concern and then waxing to gratitude and love, he imagined. But he immediately thought himself foolish for having imagined it, and then wished for it anyway. She continued on, as if telling a long story in an easy, gentle tone. Jericho watched her every movement, her eyes holding him with expressive emotion as her lips and mouth spoke words he did not understand. It did not matter to him. Nothing else mattered. Her voice was like healing water flowing over him, warm and soothing as she held his hand. She lingered on, speaking until his eyelids became heavy once again. And then she stopped, looking as if she were trying to remember something. The two words sounded strange in her accented pronunciation, but she spoke them in English.

"Thank you," she said.

Jericho's eyes opened a bit wider, surprised. "Thank you, too, ma'am," he replied.

She released his hand then gracefully rose and disappeared into the night.

He slept for hours more before waking to Imala and Chenoa tending him. Imala poured the cool and quenching water to his mouth as he gazed to the hole above. A patch of blue sky shone through like an announcement that he was alive and the world was well. Then she began feeding him while Chenoa redressed his poultice and began her massage with the liniment. Jericho ate quickly of all that came to his mouth, his hunger having awakened with vengeance. Imala said something to Chenoa that Jericho imagined related to how much he was eating. He looked up at her and smiled as he chewed.

"Hungry as can be today. Must be gettin' better," Jericho said.

Imala felt his forehead and said something else to Chenoa who looked up and gave an approving nod.

"My fever comin' down?" Jericho asked.

Imala and Chenoa looked at him with intrigue, guessing from his tonal upturn that he had asked a question. Jericho knew they did not understand him, but he kept talking just the same. "I'm much obliged to you ladies," he said. Then he thought he remembered the names Crow Talks had mentioned, so he risked it and said, "Thank you, Imala… thank you, Chenoa."

The women laughed with surprise and said a few words to each other.

"Wish I knew what you were sayin'," Jericho said then lifted his hand weakly and pointed to his chest. "Me… I'm Jericho. My name is Jericho… Jericho." Then he put his fingers to his mouth and pulled them slowly away as he said several times more, "Jericho… Jericho. Imala… Chenoa… Jericho!"

Then Chenoa said it. "Jericho."

Imala followed a little louder, "Jericho."

"That's it! Jericho!" he said. "Imala… Chenoa… Jericho!" His excitement brought a sudden bout of violent coughing. Jericho wheezed and coughed, bringing stabbing pain from his broken rib. He gasped for air as he tried to quit the convulsions. It took several moments for the coughing to stop, and then several moments more to catch his breath. Tears streamed from his eyes as he regained composure. Finally, he spoke quietly, his voice hoarse. "But I don't know which is which," he said. He looked up to the woman cradling his head, meeting her eyes. "Chenoa?"

She smiled as she shook her head "no" and said. "Imala."

"Imala," he repeated then looked to the other woman and said, "Chenoa."

Chenoa nodded and smiled.

The wickiup flap pulled to the side and Crow Talks entered. "I hear you from outside," he said as he looked down at Jericho. "You are not dying today, I think."

"Reckon not, I'm hopin'," Jericho agreed. "Hungrier today. I take that as a good sign." Jericho frowned a moment then said, "I hope you don't take offense at me askin', but how is it you're the only one can speak English?"

Crow Talks glared and answered, "Perhaps I will tell you one day… but not this day. Tell me… is the thing you call mail the letters you carry?"

Jericho's eyes widened. "You have the letters? My mochila?"

"Yes," Crow Talks answered, "we have all your things. What is a mochila?"

"That's the saddlebag that holds the mail!… the letters! I have to get that mochila to Cold Springs Station! Those letters are for folks in California!" Jericho said excitedly then took to another bout of coughing. After a minute he stopped and breathed raggedly for a time, then spoke quietly again. "Please… keep my mochila safe. I'd be much obliged."

Crow Talks nodded, "All your things are safe. But you will not be ready to travel to this place you say, Cold Springs Station, for some time. And you have no horse. Yours is dead."

"I know," Jericho said. "Maybe I could buy one from you… or borrow one?"

"Maybe," Crow Talks said. "It is not for me to decide."

"How long I been here?" Jericho asked. "How many days?"

Crow Talks considered for a moment then answered, "Six days."

"Lordy… I don't remember hardly any of it," Jericho said, "just you, Imala, and Chenoa… and I reckon your chief one night… and his daughter another night… but I ain't sure I wasn't just dreamin' it. My head's been crazy. One thing certain… I sure got'a get that mail to Cold Springs."

Jericho began coughing again, then stopped, greatly fatigued from talking and coughing. His eyes drooped.

"You did not dream," Crow Talks said. "Our chief, Leaping Elk, sang over you. His daughter, Wyanet, also did. That is why you are healing. Rest now."

"Wyanet," Jericho said as if committing it to memory. Then he was asleep almost before Crow Talks finished his words.

****

He came awake with a start, feeling as if his bowels might explode. The bowl was beside him but he needed more. He needed to be outside and decided he would now find out if he could stand. Jericho threw the blanket off him and rolled to his side, surprised that he was wearing a breechcloth and wondering how it had been put on him without him knowing. Ignoring the pain, he rolled half again and pushed to his hands and knees then brought a leg up and pushed slowly. A moment later he was standing, a bit wobbly at first with lightheadedness, but then more stable as he took cautious steps toward the flap of the wickiup opening. A moment later he was outside in the night, under the full moon and stars, a cool breeze wrapping around him and invigorating his senses. The hour was late and all was still. He looked about at the encampment, taking stock of his wickiup's proximity to the rest. It was on the rear perimeter, near the faint sound of running water.

Jericho immediately began moving toward the river, lined by cottonwoods a hundred feet away. It was all he could do to move at a fast hobble and hold off his bowels for a few moments more. He was too weak to squat. Then he reached one of the trees near the bank and leaned his back against it, pulling up the rear flap of his breech cloth and moving his feet out from the tree's base. His thighs quivered as he fought to maintain the position and relieve himself. The waste shot out of him for a long moment. He panted, sucking hard for air and hoping his legs could hold on a few seconds more. Then it was over.

Sweat broke out on his forehead as he pushed himself off the tree and continued on to the bank of the river. He judged it was about thirty feet wide and a few feet deep, with a few large rocks clustered in the center, their presence diverting the flow and creating the rushing sound. He moved easy down the bank and stepped into the cold liquid, standing still for a moment. Then he took small, cautious steps, venturing farther out into deeper water. Suddenly, he stepped into a hole that submerged him up to his chest, causing him to lose his balance and flap his arms to keep upright. "Ohhhhh!" Jericho involuntarily exclaimed as he fought to get his feet down. The water flowed briskly, but not enough to float him away if he could get his feet planted. He moved a bit and found solid footing. Then he began to wash himself, dunking his head a few times and rubbing his hands easy over himself to clean what he could. The frigid water numbed his body and stung his burns, which had become mixtures of scab and pus.

Jericho quickly finished, then struggled to the riverbank and climbed out, leaving him exhausted. His strength gone, he trembled badly as he walked back to the wickiup, wondering if he would make it. Toward the end, he staggered badly but stayed on his feet and shuffled inside. His numbed fingers fumbled with the hide string of the breechcloth, straining to undo it. He finally managed it and threw the wet garment aside. Then he attempted to kneel down at his bed. His legs collapsed and he fell, thumping on the fur-covered ground and groaning with pain as he pulled the heavy blanket up tight around him. Jericho lay shivering uncontrollably, wishing that the fire pit was ablaze with warmth.

Moments later, a dark shadow entered the wickiup and moved toward him. Jericho made out the shape of a woman carrying something, but he was too cold to do anything other than shiver and hope. She kneeled down at the fire pit and let loose a load of wood to the ground. Then she placed her kindling of dry grass and twigs in the center of the ring, followed by several pieces of wood. She squeezed some more dry grass to a tight ball then knelt in close and flicked her striker flint to the chert several times rapidly, creating the spark to the grass ball, which she nurtured with controlled breath from her lips. Flame came alive and began to spread from the grass to the twigs and the wood. She stood up for a moment, looking down at him. The light revealed her face. It was Wyanet. She wore a buckskin top and a long, full, red and blue cotton skirt that hung down to just above her ankles, revealing her high-top moccasins. Her fine, black hair fell full to her neck where it braided into two long pigtails, one on either side continuing down her chest and ending at her waist. Her face was slender with high cheekbones, full lips, and large, almond eyes that gazed celestially at him.

Jericho's teeth chattered as he lay staring at her, entranced by her presence and beauty. The flames danced higher as warmth pierced the cold and began to comfort him. She held her pigtails against her body with one hand, then bent down and strategically placed several more pieces of wood on the fire. Within a minute it burned full, radiating heat and casting more light. She moved to Jericho and sat cross-legged next to him, producing a smile that warmed his heart while the fire warmed the rest. His teeth stopped chattering, and his body stopped shivering.

She talked to him for several moments, her soft tone inducing bliss upon him like a language of its own. Then she paused for a moment, so he quickly spoke.

"Wyanet… Wyanet," he said.

Her eyes widened at his declaration. She nodded her head and smiled again.

"I am Jericho," he said. Then he pulled his right arm out from beneath the blanket and pointed at himself. "Jericho… Jericho." Then he pointed from her to himself, saying, "You are Wyanet… I am Jericho."

"Jericho," she said.

"Yes, ma'am," he said, deeply satisfied that she had said his name.

Wyanet reached out and took his still-cold hand in hers and then began singing a song, her voice pure and resonant with an exquisite yet haunting melody. Jericho watched her intently for a few moments, but then fought to stay awake. With the warmth of the fire and the serenity of her song, his effort was futile. He drifted off like a baby rocked to sleep.

18

Jericho was awake when they came in. "Chenoa… Imala… good morning," he said.

They each gave a short response with his name attached at the end, then smiled and took their positions next to him. Chenoa pulled the blanket aside as Imala held the bota skin of water to his mouth. Jericho suddenly realized he was naked and felt embarrassed, mostly because he knew they had put the breechcloth on him and guessed it was because they didn't care to see his privates anymore while tending him.

"Oh… sorry. That getup I was wearin' was wet, so I took it off… over there," Jericho said then pointed to where he'd thrown it. He abruptly grunted and strained to sit up then pulled part of the blanket back over his privates. "You gals surely have been good to me… and I reckon I'm a sight better now 'cause of it. Still weak as can be, but I reckon I can feed and water myself now."

Chenoa and Imala looked confused by his words and what they might have meant, yet they knew his tone was declarative, and his physical action of sitting up and covering himself seemed akin to some sort of objection. Jericho took the bota from Imala and began to squeeze it and drink. Then he put it down and grabbed the food bowl, taking pieces of fresh rabbit meat and stuffing them in his mouth as Chenoa and Imala looked on.

The flap of the wickiup rustled and Crow Talks entered.

"Good morning," Jericho offered through a mouthful of rabbit and frybread.

"Yes, it is a good morning," Crow Talks agreed. "I am told you went to the river last night… and into the water."

Jericho frowned as he chewed and then swallowed. "Well, yes I did. Had to relieve myself, and felt like bathin'. How'd you know about that?"

"Our village has night eyes… always," Crow Talks replied. "That was cold bathing. You could have had heated water from Chenoa and Imala. They would have washed you, cleaned you well. You would not have been bitterly cold."

"Sometimes a mood strikes a man," Jericho said, "and it struck me that I wanted to see a night sky with the moon and stars… and take breath outside, standing on my feet… and do my personals somewhere other than in that bowl."

Crow Talks nodded, "Such is yours to decide. Leaping Elk is happy to hear you are able to stand and walk. He invites you to his wickiup for food and meeting, today when the sun sets."

"I'd be right honored," Jericho said. "Say, can I have my clothes and my boots? I ain't seen 'em in here. Don't mean to give offense but I ain't carin' to visit the chief naked… and that flappy thing they put on me ain't quite my style. I like a little more coverage."

"Yes," Crow Talks said. "They will be brought. They have been washed. Your top had much blood on it."

"I reckon so. Much obliged," Jericho said then abruptly lay down and pulled the blanket up all the way over him. "I get cold easy, and tired even easier."

"They will put more wood on the coals to build the fire and leave you to rest," Crow Talks said, then asked, "Wyanet came and made you a fire in the night?"

Jericho looked apprehensive for an instant, having no idea what might be proper or otherwise. "Yes… she did," he replied. "Lucky for me, too, 'cause that river set me to shakin' bad. The fire sure helped me get settled back down and off to sleep. Hope it weren't no trouble for anyone," Jericho said, looking at Crow Talks, trying to read his face. Jericho quickly decided that he might as well have been trying to read the backside of a hog. Crow Talks looked as blank as blue sky.

"Is Miss Wyanet spoken for?" Jericho asked. "I mean is she married?… or engaged?… or something other in your ways and customs?" Jericho understood the possible implication of his question just after he asked it. For a fleeting moment he thought Crow Talks might produce his knife again and send it hurtling through the air straight into his heart.

Crow Talks's eyes narrowed. "No," he answered. "She would not have come alone and built a fire if she was married. There are many who want her, but no one has won her heart, and her father has not yet ordered her to marry. Be careful, white boy. You are not yet ready for the cold water of the river… and you could lose your scalp in the night to one who loves her."

"Oh," Jericho said, wide-eyed. "Well, I ain't askin' save for I don't want somebody thinkin' I'm tryin' to horn in on his gal. Soon as I'm fit to ride, I'll be on my way."

Crow Talks squatted down next to Jericho and paused a moment as if gathering his thoughts. Then he spoke in a quiet tone: "Wyanet cares much for you. Is it only because you saved her? Or does she have other feelings for you? Perhaps the first has brought the second. I do not know what her feelings are, but it is clear to all that she favors you… and some will take it as a sign of swooning… of love, whether it is true or not. And though you have done this great thing in saving her, you are not one of us, so killing you is not defiance of our own customs. Leaping Elk has told our people of your great deed, which brings understanding that no harm should come to you. Anyone who would do so would bring the wrath of

Leaping Elk down upon them. But if it is done where nobody sees it, then it becomes bad medicine and is quickly forgotten."

"So I best be ready when I'm alone? Sleep with one eye open?" Jericho asked.

"No one would come for you in here," Crow Talks replied. "The wickiup is sacred ground by custom. But anywhere else that others are not present brings risk… such as the river… or a walk in the night."

"I'll be armed," said Jericho.

"If you kill one of ours, it will not matter if it is self defense. You will die… badly."

"Reckon I shouldn't walk around alone," Jericho quipped.

Crow Talks nodded. "Yes, but there is other danger as well. If you and Wyanet have feelings for each other and come together in love, then you must become her husband and tend your love. If you break her heart as an outsider, you will die badly. There is obligation in picking a beautiful flower."

Jericho looked at Imala and Chenoa who sat still, their faces blank in apparent oblivion to the conversation. But he knew they had heard Wyanet's name and wondered what they thought. He looked back at Crow Talks and said, "I'll be keepin' my feelings to myself. If any intentions grow on me, I'll make 'em known to those that's concerned. Me and Wyanet can't even understand each other… so can't see how that'd ever work."

"Love has its own understanding," Crow Talks said.

"Yeah, well, I understand I got a job to do. That's my obligation right now," Jericho said matter-of-factly. "I gotta get that mail to Cold Springs. No tellin' what important things are goin' unattended due to that mail not bein' where it's supposed to be. But I sure am obliged to Chenoa and Imala and Wyanet for all the good tendin'… and to you for the good counsel and advice."

Jericho suddenly looked woozy. "My eyelids feel like they got anvils hangin' from 'em… so they're likely gonna close any second now."

19

He woke up hours later to see his clothes, boots, and hat next to him, even his holster and shells, tobacco pouch, compass, money, canteen, and his knife. And his saddle and mochila were there, too. But his two revolvers were missing. Jericho struggled mightily to dress himself, finding ragged breathing and half a sweat in the process. Then he stuffed his tobacco pouch in his pocket and emerged from his wickiup into the early afternoon air, warm and bright with sunshine that caused him to squint. He pulled his hat lower. The Paiutes who were close by cast glances for a moment. The younger braves looked longer, sizing him up as they got their first look at him standing upright. He looked diminutive, but they knew he was fierce.

Jericho walked slowly out of camp toward a bush hedgerow near the river. His steps were methodical and guarded against weakened legs and unsteady balance. He glanced behind him just before he walked behind the bushes, disappearing from view. Then he positioned himself where he could see back to the village over the bush tops as he pissed, long and steady in relief.

He was out of breath by the time he returned but had no intention of going back into the wickiup. The medium boulder alongside it caught his eye, so he sat on the ground and leaned back against it, admiring the fine view it gave him of the village and the goings on. He reveled in enjoyment of the light breeze and vast sky as he sat there, outside, watching it all and being a man on the mend. He dug out his tobacco pouch and retrieved a paper and match, then tapped the tobacco to the trough, thinking that rolling a cigarette had never before been such a splendid thing. But it was *this* day. Like a signal of normal life again, he struck the match and put the fire to his smoke, inhaling cautiously of how it might hit him, yet ever anxious to find out. He didn't cough but became as lightheaded as a drifting balloon, worrying after a moment that he might topple over and pass out. When his head cleared, he began to take notice of the activity.

A few braves were moving about with rifles in hand. Jericho began to wonder where and how they got such fine armament. He figured any tribe would have some rifles for those who hunted, but he hadn't seen a man here without a rifle, though this was the first Indian camp he'd ever sat in. The fact of it took him and he chuckled a moment. They were good, expensive rifles the Paiute men had.

He took notice of the women who were cooking over fires with cast iron skillets and pots and other utensils. Where did they get such cook things? he wondered. And other women were fashioning clothes and blankets from cotton, denim, and wool. And there were tools around that were manufactured: shears and hatchets and axes and hammers and mallets. Jericho smoked and puzzled on how all of these things of the white world were here.

He saw the young warrior walking in his direction, lean, muscled and tough looking. Jericho watched with rising interest as it became apparent the brave was coming directly at him. The brave stopped ten feet away with rifle in hand and a serious expression. Then he began speaking mildly with a pleasant tone and friendly demeanor like an acquaintance. Twenty seconds later, the brave stopped talking and nodded his head with a faint smile, standing in place as if awaiting a reply.

"Yes, it is a fine day," Jericho said, giving a reciprocal nod. "I am most happy to be here… but I ain't exactly sure what day it is… or what month… reckon if I figured on it for a moment, it must be gettin' on to early June. Thank you for whatever it was you said to me."

Jericho gave a respectful nod then took another drag of his cigarette and watched as the brave turned and walked away. A moment later another brave approached. He was older, perhaps mid-thirties, Jericho thought. And he was shorter and thicker than the first brave, heavily muscled with more girth and a scar that started at the upper right corner of his forehead and traced deep in his flesh diagonally down across the bridge of his nose and on down his left cheek till it traced off the jawbone. He began speaking in a gruff voice that seemed to contain no malice or anger, just deep and rough like a wild animal that could do great harm in an instant if so inclined. Unlike the first brave, this one finished in a matter of seconds. Then like the other brave he nodded and stood looking for a moment.

Jericho nodded back. "I sure do appreciate your words. They sounded fine and strong. Wish I knew what they were… but I take 'em with the kind spirit that you said 'em. Much obliged."

The brave nodded at Jericho's reply then turned and walked away. One by one, they kept coming and delivering their short salutations, greetings, threats, warnings, or whatever it was they said. Jericho had no idea, but heard some of the same words over and over, so figured it was friendly and must have been some kind of custom.

After an hour and several cigarettes, Jericho guessed thirty men or so had come to him and offered words of a sentence or two before departing, though a few had spoken for nearly a minute or longer. Jericho had reciprocated with statements of his own in similar length to what he received, though most of it was just his ramblings of the weather, or his thanks for getting better and being able to enjoy the afternoon, and his thanks for whatever it was that each was saying.

Then Crow Talks appeared from nowhere and stood before Jericho with a contented look. "It is good to see you taking the day outside," he said. "By the will of the Great Spirit, you are getting stronger."

"Yes, sir," Jericho said. "Still weak as a day-old pup but I'm comin' along. Say, you got any notion of what these men been sayin' to me?"

Crow Talks answered, "They have been giving respect and thanks to you for saving our chief's daughter."

"Oh," Jericho said. "Well… I'm honored. Sight better'n hearin' they want to kill me."

"They would not tell you that," Crow Talks said flatly. "They would just do it."

20

Warmth of the day quickly yielded when the sun fell beneath the etched horizon of the western range. The deepening blue sky brought its chill and signaled that the appointed time had arrived.

"It's Jericho Buck," Jericho called, standing just outside the chief's wickiup.

"Come in," came the familiar voice in English that Jericho recognized as Crow Talks.

Jericho entered to see Chief Leaping Elk and Crow Talks sitting at the unlit fire ring.

"Welcome," the chief said in stilted English and then waved his arm to a spot by the ring, indicating where Jericho should sit. Jericho moved quickly to the spot and sat down cross-legged.

"Good evening," Jericho said, nodding to the chief who was on his left, and then to Crow Talks who was straight across.

The chief nodded at Jericho and looked at him, his black eyes calm yet intensely probing as if extracting all there was to know from Jericho's soul. Jericho stared back like it might be a respected custom, their eyes locked in a greeting akin to a visual handshake that was not to be relinquished until the chief let go. After a long, silent moment, Leaping Elk's eyes broke away to the task of preparing a pipe he had before him. His long, mostly gray hair spilled over powerfully muscled shoulders as his fingers kneaded the substance to be smoked.

Jericho watched the technique of the ritual but let his eyes sneak about, taking in his surroundings in the faint light. Leaping Elk's wickiup was bigger than Jericho's. There were pipes fashioned from antlers hanging from the branch wall in the small areas not covered by hide. And several ornate headdresses hung, too, along with a few articles of clothing, an assortment of knives, two rifles, and a heavy coat fashioned of buffalo hide. Jericho stared for a long moment at a hanging leather strip that contained a dozen or so tufts of hair running down it that varied in color. It was a moment more before he realized the dried, curled base of each tuft was the skin of a human scalp. On the ground at the back of the wickiup was Leaping Elk's bed made of bear skin, big enough for three and dressed with half a dozen rabbit-fur pillows. Directly next to the bed were several hide bags stuffed with more of the chief's possessions.

Leaping Elk leaned forward and struck the flint to the kindling beneath the wood, expertly flashing the spark to a flame, then nurturing it fuller with the bellows of his breath. The fire leapt alive, bringing light and warmth. Leaping Elk lit a stick from the fire and then fired the pipe, drawing deeply on it twice before passing it to Jericho. Jericho did as he had seen and smoked it deep. The smoke expanded in his lungs and sent him into a coughing fit, each convulsion firing bright pain in his broken rib. He passed the pipe over to Crow Talks and managed to stop coughing, but his breathing was labored and ragged. The pipe made two more trips around before Leaping Elk retired it and looked for a long moment at his guest. Jericho had partaken in all three passes of the pipe but had drawn much more lightly on the second and third times.

A faint smile showed on the chief's face as his words filled the air with a deep, rich tone. He spoke for about a minute and then stopped. Crow Talks immediately followed with the translation:

"Leaping Elk wants you to know he can speak and understand

some English, but to avoid any misunderstanding, he wants me to tell you his words, and also tell your words to him during this meeting. He says he is honored to have you here tonight and that he will give great thanks of you for as long as the wind shall blow. He says he is in your debt and will grant any requests that he can."

"I'm much obliged, Chief Leaping Elk… highly honored I am," Jericho said. "What I'm most concerned with now is getting my mochila to the Cold Springs Station as fast as I can."

Crow Talks translated Jericho's words to Leaping Elk, who nodded slowly with a thoughtful look on his face. Then the chief spoke again.

A moment later, Crow Talks translated. "Leaping Elk wants to know of Pony Express… what they do… where they go… what you do for Pony Express."

Jericho looked at the chief as he spoke. "The Pony Express hauls mail… letters and such and government business… two thousand miles in ten days from St. Joseph, Missouri, on the Missouri River, maybe fifteen hundred miles east of here… all the way to Sacramento, California, 'bout five hundred miles west of here. And then other mail from Sacramento back to St. Joseph in ten days goin' the other direction!"

Jericho stopped and gave Crow Talks time to translate what he'd said, then he continued: "Got about a hundred 'n fifty stations along that two-thousand-mile trail… every fifteen miles or so, where a rider changes horses so he can be gallopin' most all the time. And each rider goes about four or five stations… about sixty to seventy five miles 'fore they hand off the mochila… that's the letter bag… to the next rider. Got eighty riders or so, forty goin' each way all the time, day and night."

Jericho stopped and let Crow Talks tell what he'd said. A look of wonder and amazement came over Leaping Elk's face as he listened, occasionally interrupting with a question or comment to Crow

Talks which Jericho didn't understand. And then the chief listened intently as Crow Talks continued. Crow Talks finally stopped and looked at Jericho. "Tell us your path in the Pony Express. It pays you for taking this mail? From where to where?"

Jericho looked to the chief again. "Well, I take the westbound mail from Dry Creek Station over to Cold Springs Station, stopping four times along the way to change horses… at Simpson Park, Jacob's Spring, Smith's Creek, and Edwards Creek. Can't rightly say where those stations are from here, as I got no idea where I am now. The place where I came upon your daughter I'd reckon is about ten miles due east of Cold Springs, where my route ends." Jericho stopped and waited for Crow Talks to translate, then continued:"My route is one hundred miles… there ain't none longer… and yep, they pay me good money. I ride the hundred miles goin' west, then I get thirteen hours to rest, then I'm goin' and blowin' back east to Dry Creek. It takes me about eight hours each way. Every rider works every horse for all the speed he can get."

Leaping Elk listened intently, nodding his understanding as Crow Talks translated to him. When Crow Talks finished, Leaping Elk waxed thoughtful as he looked at Jericho. Then he spoke, his voice strong as his eyes danced.

Crow Talks began translating, "Leaping Elk is highly taken with the greatness of Pony Express and the courage and strength of the distance you ride, over and over again with little rest. He is surprised he has not heard of Pony Express before now."

"Only been goin' a year now… and maybe not much longer," Jericho said. "They say the telegraph's goin' to be finished all the way to California 'fore too long. Then the Pony Express'll be out'a business."

Crow Talks translated, and Leaping Elk immediately spoke.

"He wants to know what is this thing… telegraph?" said Crow Talks.

"Well, it's big poles stickin' up out'a the ground every rock's throw or so… and wire strung across the top from pole to pole, and…"

"Singing wire," Leaping Elk interrupted.

"Yes, sir… I heard it called that," said Jericho, surprised that the chief had not waited for Crow Talks to translate.

"Yes, we have heard of it," Crow Talks said. "It was told that signals travel over the wire… very fast."

"Yep," Jericho agreed. "They say them signals can travel a hundred miles in just a few seconds. I got no idea how… but it's so. The men on each end tap their finger on a thing called a telegraph key, in patterns that make up letters and spell out words. Damn thing'll be the end of the Pony Express. They say someday the railroad will be goin' clear cross the country from the Atlantic Ocean on the east to the Pacific Ocean on the west."

As Crow Talks translated to Leaping Elk, Jericho watched the chief's face grow heavy, his eyes moving over the wickiup interior as if seeing and hearing the end of his people's ways, their nomadic freedom choked as the country filled with the white man. Jericho suddenly wished he hadn't said anything about the railroad and its eventual paths. He only learned of it himself through the banter of Pony Express riders and station agents in the natural carrying on and conversations that occurred during their down time.

When Crow Talks finished, Jericho made a quick, declarative statement he hoped would ease the melancholy. "*Someday* will likely take fifty or a hundred years gettin' here. Heard many a man say as much."

While Crow Talks translated, Imala and Chenoa entered with bowls of meat and a platter of frybread. They placed a bowl before each man and the frybread in front of the chief. Chenoa unslung the bota skin and placed it to the chief's side. Leaping Elk nodded his approval and thanks to the women, then they flashed quick smiles to Jericho and were gone. Leaping Elk held the woven platter of frybread to Jericho who took two pieces, and then to Crow Talks who took three.

Leaping Elk and Crow Talks said nothing more as they began eating their food like starved men. Jericho began eating from his bowl, which had portions of roasted turkey, rabbit, and fish. He immediately got into the spirit of the feast, relishing the exotic seasoning and perfectly cooked meats. The frybread was hot, fresh, and sweet. For several minutes they devoured the food in silence, except for the lip smacking and grunting. And then it was over.

Leaping Elk took a long pull from the bota, drinking the same way he had eaten. Jericho wiped his hands on his pants and accepted the bota then drank heartily of the liquid. It was fermented, tasting something like beer and of about the same strength. Jericho quenched his thirst fully then handed the bota back to Leaping Elk, who handed it to Crow Talks.

As Crow Talks drank, the chief turned to Jericho and spoke stilted English. "You ride far… you see more Indians?"

Jericho nodded. "I seen some Indians now and again… farther east… Shoshones I reckon. Been chased a few times, but more like they was just tryin' to run me off. I change my route now and again so I'm not regular on one trail. That's what I was doin' when I came across your daughter. Don't ride that way much… it's a mite slower… but the scenery sure is fine. Glad I picked it that day."

Lost by Jericho's many words, the chief looked to Crow Talks for translation and received it, long and slow. Then the chief nodded and spoke in Paiute.

Crow Talks looked at Jericho and said, "He also is glad you picked that trail on that day. Wyanet tells that our warriors had no chance. The white men swiftly appeared in surprise from the thick brush on horseback with guns drawn and began firing. Then you came and kept her from being taken. Leaping Elk says that you are now a member of this Paiute tribe for all time, and you are welcome now and always for as long as you wish to stay. He has given you a tribal name… Nievi Karü'wa… Brave Rider."

Jericho's eyes widened and then just as fast they began to roll. His head began to teeter back and forth. Then he abruptly slumped over to the side, hitting the ground unconscious.

21

He was on his side when his eyes opened and naturally took in what fell into his line of sight, the leather strip hanging from the wickiup wall, adorned with scalps. It gave him a moment of pause as he tried to imagine who the original owners were, and the circumstances leading to the loss of their hair. Jericho grunted as he rolled to his back and tried to remember what had happened. It was daytime now and he was alone in the chief's quarters. The dot of blue sky above him showed a bright morning. He was lying just about where he had been sitting the night before. His head was sweat-soaked, and his body felt like it was roasting beneath the buffalo hide that someone had put over him. He pushed it off him. Jericho grunted and sat up slowly, looking around for water. There was none.

Chenoa and Imala entered as he was getting to his feet. They helped him steady himself as he staggered a moment, his head throbbing and his throat dry.

"Please… water. Can you give me some water," he said as he mimicked holding a cup and drinking.

Imala answered in Paiute and nodded her understanding as Jericho headed out of the wickiup with Chenoa in tow. A light breeze instantly cooled the sweat on his forehead. He turned his face up to catch all the wind he could and then began hobbling toward his wickiup. A moment later he stumbled in as Chenoa held the entrance hide to the side for him. Then she left to get her supplies.

Inside, Jericho immediately stripped down to his undershorts and fell down on his bed, weak, sick, and feverish. A moment later he rolled to his side and grabbed his big latrine bowl. He vomited into it several times then slid it an arm's distance away and lay back again, shaking.

Chenoa and Imala entered and took their customary positions. Jericho was so weak that he was relieved to be tended the way he had been in the beginning. Imala poured water from an olla into a cup then cradled his head and poured the water to his mouth as he thirstily gulped, swiftly drinking it all. She refilled the cup to give him more.

Chenoa checked his bullet wounds and saw that they were healing well. But she stared at some of the burns on his stomach and chest, knowing that infection was beginning to set in. She said a few words to Imala who immediately passed the olla to her. Chenoa slowly poured water over the burns and then produced the small pouch and untied the top. She carefully tapped out white powder onto the burns, giving care to thoroughly coat the areas of infection. Then she very gently massaged the powder with the water on his torso to create a paste, further smearing the coverage as Jericho grunted from the pain of her process.

"Jericho," Imala said, prompting him to open his eyes. He looked at her as she pointed to the food in the bowl she had.

"No… no, I can't eat right now," Jericho replied, shaking his head weakly and closing his eyes again.

A moment later, Crow Talks came in and looked at Jericho who was shaking, his torso swabbed in the white paste that Chenoa had finished applying. Crow Talks began speaking to the women, prompting Jericho's eyes to barely open. Imala answered Crow Talks and then Chenoa offered words, too. Jericho had little interest in what they were saying. He was overwhelmed by how poorly he felt. But then Crow Talks was speaking in English to him:

"You are not well, Brave Rider. You have taken steps backward on your path back to strength. Your burns are festering. You should rest. Do not think about taking your mail. You cannot ride."

"Brave Rider?" Jericho asked, his eyes opening wider as he remembered what the chief had said the night before.

"Yes," said Crow Talks. "Leaping Elk made you a member of our tribe and gave you the tribal name of Brave Rider. Then you fell over."

"I reckon I shouldn't'a smoked that pipe and drunk that head-buster," Jericho said. "Feel like I might die now."

"You might," Crow Talks agreed. "But it is not the pipe or the drink that would kill you. It is your festering burns. You must rest and let Imala use her potions."

Jericho nodded slowly then said, "The chief said he would grant any request he could. I got one."

"Tell me," said Crow Talks.

"I want someone to deliver my mochila of mail to the Cold Springs Station. I reckon I could tell 'im how to get there if you tell me where I am now… compared to where I met Wyanet."

Crow Talks pondered on it a moment, then said, "We are thirty miles north of the Valley of High Bloom. Last night you told that this place, Cold Springs Station, was ten miles west of the valley. How would you tell someone to get there from here… thirty miles north?"

Jericho tried to focus beyond his ragged condition. "Well, the other route I usually ride to Cold Springs would be about five miles north of that valley. Just have to figure what landmarks would lay out comin' from north to south. Ain't never seen it that way. But if your man can get to that valley, I sure could tell 'im how to finish from there… just be a mite longer. If I'm goin' to die, I'll feel better about it if my run gets finished."

Crow Talks nodded. "I understand, but what of the danger to

our brave. Will the men of this station not fire if they see a brave approaching?"

"Tie a white flag to a stick and have him hold it high when he gets close… high so they can see it. Nobody'll fire on him," said Jericho.

"And if we send several men? It is better to travel in numbers."

Jericho countered, "As long as they got that white flag held high. It's a sign that they come in peace. But I wouldn't send more'n three or four."

"I am sure Leaping Elk would grant your request," said Crow Talks.

Jericho broke to a grim smile. "I'll be much obliged. Say, do you have any graphite? or a quill and ink? I'd like to send a note along. Couldn't write it now… but maybe after a while when I stop shakin' and don't feel so poorly."

Crow Talks nodded, "I have graphite or quill and ink, and parchment, and Singing Water has brushes, some very fine, thin, and ink colors if you like."

Crow Talks sank gracefully to a cross-legged seated position next to Jericho. Chenoa and Imala stood to take their leave, Imala having fetched the large latrine bowl that Jericho had vomited into. She left the water olla and cup and they took their leave as Chenoa said a few words to Crow Talks on their way out. Crow Talks said something back to them, and they were gone.

"Imala will bring your bowl back in a few moments for when you need to relieve yourself. Chenoa says you should not leave the wickiup. They will be back each hour to see about your needs."

"I'll do what they say," Jericho said as he continued quivering. He pulled one of the cotton blankets up over him as if he'd caught a chill.

"You asked me how it is that I know English so well," said Crow Talks. "Now that you are Brave Rider of our tribe, I will tell you. In the year of 1830, when I was a boy of eight years, I was lost to my parents, and my tribe, when I fell into a swift-running river of springtime… maybe two hundred miles north of here. I was alone… so no one knew to track me. I bumped a small log that I grabbed and clung to. It saved me, but I traveled many miles, all of the day before the waters calmed enough for me to make it to shore. I fell out on the sand, blue with cold. When I woke, I was in the back of an Army wagon. We traveled for many days before we arrived at a fort by the Great Salt Lake. An English family named Lord… Gareth and Melanie Lord, took me in. They lived in the nearby settlement of Kingsley Bird, and operated a mercantile and livery with their six children. I worked in both, but I also went to school with the other children of Kingsley Bird. Over the years, I learned to speak English and also how to read and write. I did well. I read many books. I still do. They were good people… but they were not my people. When I was sixteen years I left with my horse to find my tribe. It took me many months… half of a year. They had come together with this tribe when the warrior Burning Sky was still Chief. He gave me the name Crow Talks because I knew the white man's language. Then the sickness came and took many… Chief Burning Sky, too… and Leaping Elk's wife and two sons… and my father and sister. Then Leaping Elk became chief, twenty years ago. He is a great warrior… a great chief. Our tribe has prospered. Now it is your tribe, too."

Jericho's eyes were at half mast but the awe of hearing the story was written on his face. He asked, "Is your mother still alive?"

"Yes," Crow Talks answered. "She is here, and also my two brothers. Chenoa is my wife. We have a son and two daughters."

"Well, I'll be hogtied!" Jericho said, his voice weak and raspy but excited. "Don't that churn the butter."

"Yes, life is forever churning something," Crow Talks deadpanned.

Imala came back in with the latrine bowl and set it next to Jericho.

"We will talk more later," Crow Talks said as he stood up to leave. "I will tell you many things… but you must live to hear them. Rest now and live."

"I'd damned sure like to," Jericho said as he took a deep breath and closed his eyes.

22

The night wind blew intemperately with gusts and howls followed by light breezes and momentary calm. Then the sound of distant treetops rustling violently signaled the next approaching round. Inside the wickiup, the hide-covered walls blocked the worst of it, yet the cold breeze ventilated the interior enough to make the fire bend and dance about. Jericho was asleep, fully covered in blankets, when she came in and sat down next to him, placing the pot she had brought down beside her.

Wyanet began to softly sing as the wind howled in accompaniment. Seeing the fingers on his right hand sticking out from under the blankets, Wyanet reached and took his hand, pulling it out and holding it in her hands as she continued singing, her gaze now looking up as if to the heavens. After a few minutes, Jericho's eyes opened. A smile came to his face. He listened to her song and let his hand begin to caress her hands, gently, minutely, not knowing how she might react. Her eyes came down from above to meet his, landing on him with tenderness that exuded all the love of the universe. She smiled at him as she sang, leaving Jericho feeling as if his heart might burst from his chest. A moment later she stopped singing.

"You're like a dream… the sweetest I ever had," Jericho said, knowing he could profess his love and she wouldn't have an idea of what he was saying. "And you're so beautiful… like an angel. I love you. You have my heart to do with as you will."

"What should I do with it?" Wyanet asked in clear English.

Jericho's eyes blinked rapidly as his face turned redder than just his fever. "You know English?" he asked, terrified that her answer would confirm that she understood all that he had said.

"Yes," she said with a giggle, "I know English. I can speak it… and also read and write it. Is this true… you love me?"

"Aww, now that ain't fair!" Jericho protested. "I didn't know you could understand what I was sayin'!"

"It would make a difference?" she asked sincerely.

"No… well yeah! I mean sure… it makes a difference! A man doesn't just go around spouting off love sayings to a girl he don't know well."

"You did," she said.

"Yeah… but I didn't know you understood!"

Wyanet frowned slightly. "Does that mean you did not speak the truth?"

"No!" Jericho answered, flustered. "It means I wouldn't say it to you… it might embarrass you… maybe make you uncomfortable… no, not until I knew you better and maybe thought you had feelings for me, too." Jericho grunted and sat up with his blanket wrapped around him. "I wasn't intendin' for you to hear it. It was like whisperin' to the sky… or making a wish." Jericho knew his mistake right after he said it.

"You wish to love me?" she asked.

"That didn't come out right," he quickly countered. "We ain't acquainted long enough for such talk. It was my mistake. I'm sorry for it."

"Do not be sorry. You did not know me but you saved my life. We are acquainted for all time. I will love you always… not as a wife loves a husband, but as a soul loves another because of kindness. Yours was the greatest kindness."

"Well, it ain't particularly kind in return to let someone think you don't understand when you really do," Jericho said.

"I am sorry," Wyanet said. "I was unsure about speaking to you last time. My feelings for you are strong. I was scared, I think, to talk to you, but I wanted to sing in prayer over you. I should not have let you think I did not know your words. That was *my* mistake. But now I am happy that you thought I did not know, because now I have heard what you whisper to the sky... and what you wish for... and it makes my heart full to know that you feel for me as I feel for you."

Jericho sat quietly for a long moment looking at her, their eyes locked. "Well, I reckon our feelings ain't quite the same 'cause mine may run a mite closer to the way a husband loves a wife."

"Mine might, too," she said, smiling, "but I will not tell you such things yet."

"Well, how about tellin' me who else around here knows English," Jericho said, "so I don't step in it again."

Wyanet laughed and answered, "My father knows some... and an elder named Singing Water knows a little more, but Crow Talks and I are the only ones that know it well. He taught me from the time I was a young girl. My father wanted me to learn so I could advise him and translate in any business dealings with the white man. Crow Talks does most of that now, but I am also present."

"Crow Talks didn't teach his family?... Chenoa?" Jericho asked.

"All of them know some words, but his brothers do not care. Chenoa does not care, his son does not care. The white man is a creeping threat to us. Our people do not care to learn the language of the people who threaten our homelands... our way of life. Crow Talks is very respected and high in our tribe, part of my father's council and inner circle, but his name 'Crow Talks' tells of his ability to speak as the white man... as the crow. It is not a name of majesty to him or others."

"Oh," Jericho said, not wanting to venture anything further on that subject. Jericho reached and grabbed two pieces of wood then fed the fire ring.

"Would you like some sweet chicory root tea?" asked Wyanet. "My friend Star Woman says it has healing powers and will bring good sleep."

"Sure will try it," Jericho said.

Wyanet produced two small cups from a pocket in her skirt and filled them, then handed one to Jericho.

"Oh, and this is a celebration drink as well," she said. "Today, my father told us all that you are a Benjepo and your tribal name is Nievi Karü'wa… Brave Rider."

"What's a Benjepo?" Jericho asked.

"It is a tribe member who is not a Paiute but becomes one because of a great thing."

"I hope your tea can do a great thing and get me feelin' better," Jericho said, then reached his cup over and clinked on hers in a toast. "That's my custom," he said, knowing she wondered about the clinking. "It's called a toast… a drink in celebration of something or someone. I'm toasting to us. May we always be a light on each other's path."

She smiled at him and they drank. "That's a mighty fine drink," he said after draining it. "Can I have another?"

They drank and talked about his years and travels as she asked questions of him through two more cups. Then she saw the fatigue of his fever and knew he should rest.

"I must go," she said.

He nodded, knowing he was at the end of his rope. "Thank you, Wyanet, for liftin' my spirits and bringin' your fine tea. I surely am lookin' forward to seein' you again."

"Be well, Brave Rider. I will come tomorrow," she said, then disappeared into the night as the wind continued and the heavens twinkled brightly upon the moonless, cloudless evening.

Jericho was tempted to go outside to relieve his tea-filled bladder but thought better of it. He put more wood on the fire then pissed in his latrine bowl and slid it away to a safe distance. Then he hunkered in under his blankets and thought about her until he fell asleep.

****

In the morning, Crow Talks came with parchment and quill and ink. Jericho wrote his letter slowly, his mind confused by the persisting fever and an accompanying nausea. He had slept well enough but felt weak and shaky now, making his penning of words most difficult. With the letter done, Jericho carefully told Crow Talks the way to Cold Springs Station via the west end of the lake in the Valley of High Bloom. Jericho's abundant description of the route prompted Crow Talks to write it down in Paiute, stopping frequently to ask Jericho questions for further clarification. It took an hour, as Jericho vomited twice and gasped for air afterwards, needing several minutes before he could continue. Crow Talks wondered silently if Jericho would survive another day, but felt more hopeful when Jericho declared it was the breakfast Imala had brought earlier and that he'd eaten too much. When Crow Talks finally left with the mochila and parchments, Jericho collapsed back to a full prone position and pulled his blankets up tight, praying to survive another day.

23

Chuck McCarter was in the round pen trying to get aboard a hot-tempered mustang that was newly arrived and unbroken. "Dammit! Hold still, you flea-bitten, ornery, sack'a hot peppers!" he yelled as the horse kept pivoting when he moved into position to mount.

Skinner sat on the top rail smoking a cigarette and enjoying the show, but figured McCarter might be accepting of help at this point. "You want me to pin his flank, Mac?"

McCarter shot a hot look at Skinner. "Not likely! Ain't a two-man affair when he's broke! Can't be that way breaking him either!"

"Yep," Skinner agreed then took another drag. "Have at 'im, Mac!"

McCarter pulled the lead rope in tight and looked the horse in the eye while giving it a few soft pats on the jaw. He spoke soft and easy to it: "My ma learned me to be polite… so I'll just act like I got nothing but good feelings for you as I mosey down this way…"

McCarter had taken two steps down the horse's side, hugging tight to the neck, but then flashed to full speed, leaping and grabbing the saddle horn and pulling his body around in a half turn, landing in the saddle. The horse had tried to pivot away but was too late. McCarter was aboard. Then the horse jumped and began violently bucking as though there was a wasps' nest tucked up under its tail.

McCarter hung on as the mustang thrashed in cyclonic turns

one way and then another, simultaneously ripping up and down. But McCarter stayed aboard and the horse soon tired and settled to a run around the pen, then slowed to a fast trot.

"You got 'im, Mac!" Skinner yelled. The sound of the clanging bell cut clearly in the light breeze. Skinner swung his legs around to the outside of the pen and jumped down. "Grub's on!" he called as he strode toward the station a hundred feet away.

McCarter worked the horse for another few minutes then reined him to a stop and jumped down. "I'll be back directly after supper. Don't you forget what you just learned," he said to the horse as he hitched it to a rail. A moment later, McCarter turned the corner to the front side of Cold Springs Station and headed for the door. He caught sight of the rising dust and stopped for a good look. The dust finally drifted apart and he guessed it was two riders. McCarter continued on in the front door and headed to get his plate.

"Riders coming," he said to no one in particular. "Maybe two miles out."

Stan glanced at the clock. "Did you say riders? Two?" Stan asked.

"Yeah, looked like two," McCarter said, grabbing a plate and preparing to scoop from the pot.

Hags and Skinner were just getting started on their plates but Stan was finished and had his pipe in his hand. He walked outside and sat on the porch rocker, then fired the pipe as he watched the faint dust trail. Stan knew it wasn't any of the Express riders; nothing due from the east for a while yet, and whoever it was had an easy gait which wasn't how any of the company riders finished a run. He savored the flavor of his pipe tobacco, smooth with a cherry wood aroma that satisfied nicely after the fine stew he'd made and eaten his fill of before he clanged the bell for the rest of the vultures.

They were at a mile and a half out now, Stan figured. But there was something else, something he caught a glimpse of just overhead of them, a flag maybe? He wondered. The dust picked up a bit like they were at a lope now, coming faster. Stan was comfortable rocking himself lightly. "Hey… Danny!" Stan called loudly. "Bring the field glasses!"

Young Danny popped out the door and handed Stan the glasses, then looked out to the east where the afternoon sun cast the riders in shimmering light on the arid, flat approach.

"They look like Indians," Danny said.

"How could you tell that from here?" Stan asked skeptically, then looked through the glasses. "Damn if you ain't right!" Stan declared. "They're holding up a white flag and they sure as hell are Indians!"

Stan bolted up out of his chair and scanned the other directions he could see, knowing that those with bad intentions could send a few men in the easiest line of sight to distract from others coming from the rear or a different direction.

"Get a rifle, Danny," Stan said as he threw open the door. "You boys get your guns! There's two Indians coming from the east holding a white flag. Let's make sure there ain't more somewhere else. Skinner, you and Mac get around back. Hags, you and Danny post out front with me."

"Should I go wake up Pooch?" Danny asked.

"No," Stan shot back. "He'll be up fast enough if the shooting starts."

A rumble of chairs on the wood floor ensued as the men flew for their gunbelts and the rifle rack. Stan grabbed his gun belt and a Sharps rifle. "Hags! Bring that shotgun, too!" Stan yelled as he walked briskly out the front door. The approaching riders were less than a mile out now. Stan put the glasses on them again, watching as they came on at an easy lope. He put the glasses down. "Skinner! Anything out back?" Stan called out.

"Nope! Nothin' here!" Skinner yelled.

"All right! Stay put! You hear any shootin'... come runnin'!" declared Stan. He relit his pipe and stood smoking it as he watched the Indians close the last of the distance.

They came to a stop fifty feet in front of the porch where Stan stood flanked by Hags and Danny, all three men holding their rifles with the barrels down. Stan saw the mochila on one Paiute's horse and stepped forward off the porch, putting up his right palm in a sign of peace.

"What is it you want?" Stan said, calmly.

The Paiute with the mochila leapt from his horse, hitting the ground like a feather. He pulled the mochila from the horse and opened one of the pouches, retrieving the marked parchment. Then he walked slowly to Stan and held out the mochila and parchment for him to take. Stan took them and asked, "Where did you get this?" nodding to the mochila.

The Paiute shook his head with his fingers to his lips.

"It don't seem he knows what you're sayin'," Danny said.

Hags chuckled, "Well there's the revelation of the day."

"Take this," Stan said to Hags, holding the mochila back to him. Hags took a few quick steps forward and took it from Stan.

"Lord Almighty," Hags said, "you reckon this could be Jericho's?"

"Maybe. Let's see what this parchment says," Stan replied as he untied and unrolled the parchment and started to read it. His expression quickly turned to amazement.

"Well! What's it say?" Hags asked impatiently.

"It's from Jericho!" Stan said gleefully. "He's alive! Says he got shot up by some desperadoes while saving an Indian girl! Says he's in bad shape but he's in an Indian camp about thirty miles north and they're taking care of him. Says it will be some time before he's able to ride so these braves are bringing his mochila... finishing my run! Say hello to the boys for me… hope I still got a job when I get back. Signed Jericho Buck!"

"Skinner! Mac!" Stan yelled. "Come on around! We're all right here!"

Stan flashed a big smile at the Indians. "I don't know where you boys came from but I'm guessin' you're hungry!" Stan mimicked putting food in his mouth and chewing. "We got water, too. Come on and get some stew and coffee! Water your horses!"

The other Paiute dismounted as Skinner and Mac rounded the corner.

"Jericho's alive!" Danny immediately yelled to them, anxious to break the news. "These fellas brung his mochila!"

"Well, why ain't he here?" Skinner asked.

"You'll hear about it inside," Hags said. "My plate's gettin' cold and I ain't ate but half of it."

The men piled into the station as Stan showed the Paiute braves to the hitching rail at the water trough. When they'd hitched their horses, Stan walked with them to the open door and waved them in, but the Paiutes stopped, unsure and unwilling to enter the station. Stan nodded knowingly to them and waved them to the row of rockers on the porch.

"Sit down right here and I'll bring you your plates," said Stan, leading them to the chairs. The Paiutes moved cautiously to the rocking chairs and sat down, still unsure. But then they started rocking and smiled at the sensation of it as Stan chuckled, "That's right… nice to sit in and rock. You boys just relax. I'll be back with your plates."

Stan got them set up with stew and coffee and then sat down with a piece of flat board, paper, and pencil, and began writing as he smoked his pipe again. "I know you boys ain't sure what I'm doin'," he said as the Paiutes ate, "but I'm writing a letter for you to take back to Jericho."

Minutes later, Hags, Danny, McCarter, and Skinner drifted out and found their spots, sitting and standing around Stan and the Paiutes. The boys commenced to smoking or chewing, fascinated to be in the company of two Paiute braves. The Paiutes were equally awed to be in the company of white men at this lone place in the middle of nowhere. While the Paiutes ate, the boys talked as they smoked or spit, speculating on Jericho and all the circumstances that might have beset him, knowing they wouldn't get any confirmation from the Paiutes but talking it up just the same.

"You fellas want some more?" Danny asked the Paiutes as he pointed to their empty plates and nodded. The Paiutes nodded back. Danny collected their plates and went for more.

"Hags, you'll be carrying extra weight on your westbound tonight," said Stan. "Jericho's mochila weighs fifteen to twenty… heavy one. Better not have seconds on supper tonight."

"I'd have to be carryin' four extra mochilas to weigh what most of our boys weigh!" Hags said with a chuckle.

"True enough," Skinner chimed. "Yer 'bout knee high to a horse's ass and the skinniest thing I ever saw. Why, I reckon the after-supper gas I blow weighs more 'n you."

All the boys broke out laughing which caused the Paiutes to look around wondering, and then they laughed, too, thinking it might be a custom. Danny walked out and handed the plates to the Paiutes. "Got the Indians laughing, too," Danny quipped. "Must have been a good one."

****

Three more hours of daylight remained when the Paiutes rode away to the northeast at a lope in possession of Stan's letter for Jericho. Hags stood leaning against a porch timber, watching them fade into the horizon as he troubled on his thinking.

"You reckon it was all on the straight?" he asked Stan who was still in a rocker with a month-old edition of a Sacramento newspaper.

Stan looked up. "What do you mean?"

"Just the whole story with Jericho," Hags said. "Him bein' cared for by the Paiutes. Seems any Indians I ever come across start ta chasin' me… and it ain't 'cause they want to be friendly. You reckon they could be holdin' Jericho? Maybe they made him write that letter."

Stan relit his pipe and blew out a slow stream of smoke. "Nope, that doesn't figure. I suspect it's just what he said in his letter. Why would they bring his mochila here? If they meant to kill him… or hold him prisoner, they wouldn't have brought his mochila. Hell, they wouldn't have ever known where to go with it unless he asked them to deliver it. If he got shot up saving an Indian girl from desperadoes, they'd sure be grateful… grateful enough to take care of him and honor his request to finish his run. I can't see it any other way. Sure be worth a few rounds of whiskey to hear all the details of what happened to him."

"Yeah, I reckon you're right with that figurin'," Hags agreed. "But why didn't they just bring 'im here… on a travois or a wagon if they got one… let us care for 'im? He's been gone better'n a fortnight."

Stan frowned. "Well, that's a more interesting question. He could still be teetering on dying… not strong enough to move that distance. Letter said it was thirty miles or so. No telling what kind of shape he's in."

"We could tell if we seen him," Hags said. "Maybe we should send someone. Mac's a hell of a tracker. He could get on their trail fresh right now. They're sure to bed somewhere tonight… horses are played out. We can get by with one wrangler for a few days. Danny can handle it."

Stan blew out another slow stream of smoke and looked to the northeast where the Paiutes were no longer visible. "He could get killed doing that."

24

Jericho emerged from his wickiup at the first trace of light, shuffling slowly toward the thick bushes near the river. He found his spot and did his business and then continued on along the path of the river to the far end of the camp where two corrals held upward of twenty horses each. Several dozen travois and mount carriers fashioned of hide and timber frame sat in rows just outside the corrals. And there were four wagons and a buckboard with rigging and harnesses. The sprawling meadow beyond stood high in seasonal grass where another sixty horses wearing front hobbles occupied little of the hundred or so acres, dotted with occasional pine and cottonwood trees. Jericho took it all in, marveling at the beauty and majesty of the land that seemed secretly tucked away from the vast and stark surroundings of the region. He wondered where exactly he was, not having been conscious for most of the trip from what the Paiutes had called the Valley of High Bloom. But this place was lower in elevation than the valley. A good spot to winter, Jericho thought.

Jericho looked back at the encampment of sixty or seventy wickiups that housed the two hundred or so Paiutes of the tribe. There were more horses tethered near many of the wickiups, prompting Jericho's consideration of all the work there was in maintaining the animals and everything else of the encampment. He figured there were maybe fifty warriors, and the rest were other men, women, and children. He looked to the wood cutting area where a wall of stacked wood stood five feet high and forty feet long. Six chopping stumps and a log bracket for crosscut sawing showed that a dozen men could be hard at it all at the same time. But for the moment, all was quiet in the faint gray light of dawn.

"Brave Rider, you should be in your bed," Wyanet said, having slipped up behind him without his awareness.

He turned quickly with a blanket draped over his shoulders and hanging down far enough to cover all but the bottom of his bare legs. "I brought my bed with me," he said. "And I think my fever's a little better… don't feel so poorly this mornin'."

She felt his forehead. "You still have fever… but maybe not as bad. I will walk back with you. Imala and Chenoa will be coming soon with food and treatment."

"Yes, ma'am," he said as he started his slow shuffle back. Wyanet walked close beside him, occasionally glancing at him. Jericho sensed it and looked at her, his eyes holding her as he slowed even more. "This is the first time I ever seen you outside the wickiup. Never imagined you could look more lovely than before… but you surely do in the morning light."

"Lovely?" she asked with a smile.

"Yep! That might be the first time in my life I ever used that word. Don't even know how I came up with it. Truth flows easiest, I reckon."

"Like the other night when you said you love me?" she asked.

Jericho chuckled, then stopped. Wyanet stopped, too, and looked at him, their eyes locking with intent and excitement. He scanned the area, looking to see if anybody was around and watching them. The camp was beginning to come to life with a few people outside. But nobody was looking at them. For good measure, he pulled her behind the big cottonwood they had stopped next to. And then he drew her close and kissed her, long and full as she embraced him with her own passion. Their lips lingered in discovery for several long moments as they held each other tightly. Then they came apart as each backed up half a step, shocked but excited and entranced by what had just happened.

Jericho spoke just above a whisper: "That night… waking up to see you there, I loved the vision of you. Your beauty takes my breath… makes my head spin… like somethin' from a dream. But we don't know each other much, so I ain't sure what to make of it."

She stepped to him and kissed him again with another embrace that lasted sweet moments. Then she looked into his brown eyes and ran her hand in his blond hair as she spoke: "Our paths coming together was as a lightning strike from the Great Spirit. When I first saw you, the sun fell upon you in a light that gave me hope from the darkness of certain death. You were destiny… a man alone in a lonely place at the very moment of my greatest need. Such a thing is not by chance. And you think I am lovely… and I think you are handsome. What becomes of this, and us, is not yet told, but I have never felt for a man as I do for you. And perhaps your feelings for me are the same. But you are white and I am brown. Our peoples are different… and adversarial."

"What's that mean… adversarial?" Jericho asked.

"It means we are in conflict… that there has been trouble before, and we will become greater enemies as more whites come into our lands and move us out. Our people were here long before the white man, yet they take over wherever they please, with their great armies and people that are many more than ours. It means that if we love each other, there will always be those who condemn us because we are not the same. But I cannot help how I feel for you."

"Nor I for you," said Jericho. "If we were to take up, I reckon it's a good thing your father made me Brave Rider… a member of your tribe."

"It is your tribe, too, now," she said.

"And I am deeply honored," he said as he began his slow shuffle again with Wyanet by his side, both of them silent in thought at the burst of passion and the obstacles of its continuing.

When they arrived at the wickiup, he kept his distance from her as he knew some of the braves were watching. "Would you come for another visit soon?" he asked.

"Yes... tonight when the many eyes see only the inside of their wickiups," she replied. Then she smiled before turning away to a brisk walk.

25

The afternoon warmth permeated the wickiup as Jericho slept peacefully, his bare torso exposed with the paste that Chenoa washed away and recreated daily. Crow Talks entered quietly and stood looking at him a moment before turning to leave, deciding he would not wake him.

"Wait," Jericho said, opening his eyes to see Crow Talks departing. "I'm up… or maybe just awake. You have word of your braves?" he asked, anxious to know.

"Yes, they have returned," Crow Talks answered as he sat down next to Jericho. "Your mochila has been delivered, and this letter came from one of the men at the station."

Jericho accepted the letter and grunted as he sat up to a cross-legged position. "That's a great piece of news!" he said, smiling. "I'm deeply obliged to you and the chief for granting my request. My run is finished!"

Crow Talks was taken with Jericho's happiness at the news, so he added, "Our braves tell that your men were kind to them… giving them food and letting them rest in rocking chairs, and watering their horses."

"Well, sure!" Jericho declared, "that's a good bunch'a men there… all of 'em hard workin' and always willin' to help. Glad to hear it went well! Now, let's see what this letter's all about!"

Jericho unfolded the paper and began reading it, his face growing a smile as his eyes burned with intensity, taking it all in. "It's from Stan, the Station Keeper at Cold Springs. He says they sure were happy to hear I'm alive… can't wait to hear the story. Ha! I can't wait to tell it! Wup! Wup!" Jericho declared with a laugh as he read more. "They pulled Pooch off his westbound from Cold Springs… put 'im as my replacement and got a temporary to ride Cold Springs westbound. I'll bet that put the hornet 'tween his ass cheeks! He hates my route… it's the longest! Hahaha! Ole Pooch is missin' his soft sixty-mile westbound! Ain't that too bad! Hahaha! Peckerweed!"

Crow Talks didn't really have much thought on what Jericho was talking about but could certainly see he delighted in it. "I am happy to see this has lifted your spirits!" he said, smiling at Jericho. "It is good for your healing!"

"Oh yeah! Don't ya know it!" Jericho exclaimed jubilantly. "Why, I'd take a good drink of that headknocker if ya got any!"

"Headknocker?" Crow Talks queried.

"Yeah, mister! Some shine!… firewater!… liquor!"

"Oh… yes," Crow Talks said, "I will get some for us!"

"Good! Splendipity!" Jericho chimed. "I feel good all of the sudden… feel like celebratin'! My run's finished and Stan says I still got a job! Hell, let's have us a few drinks! Then I might just go jump in that river! Ain't nothin' could kill me now!"

Crow Talks was back inside of two minutes with cups and a jug. He spoke as he poured: "Chenoa says your burns look as if they are no longer festering, and your fever is less."

"Yep, my head ain't as hot as it was. Can't say about my burns with all this white stuff covering me. Who could tell what they're doin'. But I reckon they must be gettin' better if they's what's causing my fever. I'll drink to my prospects!" Jericho said, taking one of the cups and taking a pull from it. "Whoaaa… that's stronger'n what we had with the chief."

"That was drink to have with food," Crow Talks said. "This is drink for howling with the coyotes. Chenoa says you should not be having this yet, but she smiled when I told her of your lifted spirits. She made this spirit. I told her it could only lift you more!"

Jericho laughed, "Bless her heart, she sure has taken good care of me. Imala too. Kind of wonder why she didn't start out with that white powder on my burns from the first. She had poultice for my bullet holes and some sort'a liniment that she rubbed on my legs, but nothin' for the burns."

"The leg oil is to keep good blood flow and ease pain when you are not using your legs for a time," Crow Talks said as he refilled their cups. "She told that burns usually heal best left alone with only daily water, but yours turned worse with festering, so she made up the powder treatment."

Jericho clinked cups with Crow Talks. "Here's to the powder treatment!" he said, then threw back his drink as Crow Talks did the same. "Oh, I like this headbuster!" Jericho said with a hoarse voice.

"It is good!" Crow Talks agreed. "We should have at least one more!"

"At least," Jericho seconded.

As Crow Talks poured them another one, Jericho felt lubricated enough to venture a question: "I been noticin' all the good things you got here… rifles, wagons, tools, crosscut saws, axes, cookin' utensils, cotton and wool… and more. Costs a lot'a money… valuable things. Where do you get all that stuff?"

Crow Talks shot him a surprised look as his head swayed just a bit. "You have seen such things?" he asked.

"Well, it don't take an overly keen eye," Jericho replied, chuckling.

"There are many more things we also get from the white man. I will tell you, Brave Rider! But first we drink!"

"That's fine thinkin', Crow Talks!… First we drink!"

They drank the shot-worth in their cups and then Jericho fished in his belongings and pulled out a rolled cigarette. "I surely like a smoke with good headbuster. You want one?"

"Yes, I would like to try one," Crow Talks answered.

Jericho pulled out another rolled one and fired a match, lighting his own and then Crow Talks's.

Crow Talks took a drag and exhaled. "It is good tobacco… I like it."

"Surely is," Jericho said. "I reckon you could get a good store of it from the same place you get the rest of the stuff I just asked you about. Where is it? Might want to get some more myself."

Crow Talks's eyes narrowed. "You are persistent with your craftiness of direction, Brave Rider."

"Persistent… craftiness?" Jericho puzzled. "You and Wyanet know more English words than I do! She said the word 'adversarial' to me this morning. Had to ask her the meanin'."

"She is a very smart girl… woman," Crow Talks said. "She has read all the books I have… and I have many. She also has a dictionary that tells the meaning of each word."

Jericho nodded as the thought of her invaded his mind again. "I care for her very much," Jericho admitted.

"She cares for you also," Crow Talks nodded back. "All our people know. Be careful. There is one named Liwanu… Growling Bear. He is dangerous… and he loves Wyanet. You are of our tribe now, Brave Rider, but watch for him. He could break tribal law and come for you."

Jericho took a drag and exhaled slowly, coolly, seemingly unaffected by the warning. "Then I reckon I better have one more drink… while I can," he said, smiling.

Crow Talks nodded and poured another one for each of them. He held up his cup and clinked it on Jericho's. "Here is to having one more drink while you can."

"And enjoyin' it like it might be your last," Jericho added. They threw back the shots and looked at each other, each knowing the other was drunk, and each taking a drag on their cigarettes as if they'd achieved the perfect routine and timing.

"There is a town, two days ride north," Crow Talks began, his enunciation sounding challenged. "It is called Cavendish West… perhaps a hundred people. There is a man there… a merchant who can order many things that come by freight wagon. Twice we have bought things in the last two years, the things that you noticed, and more."

"How far is two days' ride? How many miles?" Jericho asked.

Crow Talks considered it a moment. "Perhaps seventy miles."

"Hell, that's only a pinch more'n half a day's ride for me!"

"We do not get a fresh horse every hour," Crow Talks retorted.

Jericho chuckled. "I know… I'm just funnin' ya. So they let you come in and place an order?"

"The others wait out of town. I go in wearing white man's clothes… my hair up under a hat. No one bothers me. The orders take several months to arrive. I give him gold to cover the order with the promise of a thousand dollars more when it is delivered to Elephant Rocks, fifteen miles north of here. I go back once a month to see if it has arrived. When it does, we set a date for delivery at Elephant Rocks. He must get men to help with the delivery, driving wagons and guarding. I give gold for the horses and wagons and the thousand more when it reaches Elephant Rocks."

Jericho had wide eyes. He took a final drag and flicked his butt into the fire ring. "Lord Alive!… he brought all that stuff to a place fifteen miles away? That would take some doing. But them boys would likely take it all to California for what you're payin'. That's a lot'a money!"

Crow Talks leveled his gaze on Jericho, his face absent of all but seriousness. "We have always reaped enough from the land to survive… but we were a poor people until two years ago. We are no longer poor."

"I'm no longer sober," Jericho declared, his body suddenly swaying as if he might go down. "It ain't my place to ask about such."

"I trust you, Brave Rider. Do you still wish to go in the river?"

"I surely do," Jericho said as his eyes came alive with anticipation. "Take my lye bar and wash up. Wake up, too!"

"Let us go to the river," Crow Talks said. "I will tell you how we came to such money."

"I'll drink to that," Jericho said.

Crow Talks poured again.

****

An owl hooted his night song from a nearby perch as Jericho slept. Wyanet slipped in like a ghost, silent and stealthily. She carried several pieces of wood and promptly placed them on the remaining coals of the evening's fire. A few breaths to the coals brought flames to life and rendered a soft glow of light to the interior. Jericho lay sleeping with a book next to him. She recognized the title, *Walden: or, Life In The Woods* by Henry D. Thoreau. She also recognized the smell of alcohol that hung near Jericho in a cloud, being fed with each of his exhales. A nearby bowl held the scant remnants of his evening meal.

"Your afternoon with Crow Talks has brought an evening of sleep," she whispered, doubting that he would awaken. Jericho didn't stir but began to snore.

"Rest well, Nievi Karü'wa. I will see you tomorrow," said Wyanet. And then she was gone.

26

He awoke with the dawn, his head thick and dull with throbbing from his celebratory indulgence. Jericho reached for the olla and swigged heartily, draining all the water that remained. Then he got up slowly and donned his pants before taking the walk to the bush hedgerow where he relieved himself.

The first crack of sunlight showed over the eastern foothills casting him in full light. He began to take stock of himself. His rib hurt with motion, yet a sneeze or a cough brought the worst of it. Still, the pain of it had slowly diminished to much more tolerable levels. His gaze turned to his bullet holes which had closed and scarred over nicely. Jericho could not see his forehead where the thrown gun had hit him or the side of his head where he'd been clubbed, but his finger detected no more open wounds. Then he examined his chest and abdomen in the sunlight. The white powder was gone from the previous day's bathing in the river. His burns were no longer excreting yellow pus. They had a start on scabbing over, and the redness appeared to be receding. But he knew he still had some fever. Jericho suddenly felt lightheaded.

Gettin' better but ain't quite there yet, he thought.

The camp had come to life. Many Paiutes were out and moving toward an area that Jericho knew was used as a latrine. Then he saw Wyanet coming his way. In the distance behind her a brave stood still, watching her as she walked toward Jericho.

"Good morning," she said as she arrived.

Jericho nodded, "Looks to be a fine day ahead. Did I miss you last night?"

"Yes, I came late but you were sleeping. I did not want to wake you after your howling spirit had finished."

Jericho frowned with an understanding smile. "That might be the best I've ever heard that put. Crow Talks said that drink was for howling with the coyotes. Never did hear any but I howled anyway… 'specially when I hit that river!"

Wyanet's lips tightened. "Chenoa says that it is not wise to do such things and to drink howling spirits when you are at the edge of healing. Taking one step forward then two steps back by your own actions is foolhardy, Brave Rider."

"I reckon," Jericho agreed. "Some might say pullin' iron on four men… two of 'em already sighted on ya… is foolhardy, too. What would you say?"

"I would say… I love you," she answered.

"I love you, too… in every way," he said, his eyes softening. He wanted to hold her and kiss her. She wanted the same, but they knew there were too many eyes watching.

"Got a little carried away yesterday, is all," Jericho said. "I was so happy to hear my mochila made it to Cold Springs that I just felt like celebratin'. My run got finished! It meant a lot to me. Felt the best I have in a while so I tore loose."

"Tore loose?" Wyanet said. "Perhaps good for the spirit, but you should do what is best for your healing now. Sometimes spirit lifting is best for healing… sometimes not. This time, not."

"Likely not," Jericho said, abruptly feeling worse. "What else did Chenoa say? She had orders for what I ought'a be doin'?"

Wyanet nodded. "She said you should rest for several more days. No howling spirit… no river washing. Stay in your bed. I saw that Crow Talks brought you a book. You can read books and rest. We have many good ones."

"Yep… okay," Jericho said, with a look like he was being herded to a corral. "Anything else?"

"That was all she said… but you can ask her. She is waiting with treatment. I will tell you what she says."

"Ahh… teamwork," Jericho muttered as he started back toward the wickiup with Wyanet at his side. Jericho caught sight again of the brave watching them from the camp. "Say, who is that brave looking at us?" he asked.

Wyanet glanced up and frowned. "That is Growling Bear. He wants me to be his wife."

"Oh? Well, what do you think about that?"

"I do not love him. My heart belongs to another."

"Who!?" Jericho fired back.

Wyanet looked at him. "You need rest… your mind is not working. Perhaps it is pickled."

"Oh… oh," Jericho said with lame realization. "Well, that lifts my spirits. You lift my spirits." Jericho took her hand and softly squeezed it then looked to the brave who was still watching. "Crow Talks told me to watch out for him. Least I know who he is now."

27

Jericho stayed in his bed for a week, only leaving it to make his way to his latrine in the hedgerows near the river. Chenoa had continued to come and apply the white powder, and Imala brought his meals He slept and ate and then slept some more and ate some more. Then he visited with Wyanet who came twice daily, and Crow Talks who dropped in for a visit every other day. And Leaping Elk had come by once as well.

When he wasn't sleeping or eating or visiting, he read the book by Thoreau, slowly and deliberately, rereading passages in appreciation of how it reflected his own beliefs or experiences. It was the first book he'd ever read. It took him a week to read it, but at the end of the book his fever broke. He saw it as a sign that he should read more and asked Crow Talks if he could borrow another book. Crow Talks brought him *Eldorado* by Bayard Taylor. Jericho liked it from the start but he was restless now and needed movement.

He emerged from the wickiup at first light with a water bota slung over his shoulder, dressed in his pants and the new shirt and moccasins she had made for him. Wyanet was waiting for him, having told him the day before that she would walk with him and show him some of her favorite spots nearby.

"I'm ready to get these legs workin' again," he said. "I feel better'n I've felt since I got here."

"The overlook I want to show you is two miles… with some uphill walking at the end," Wyanet said as if she were reconsidering whether it was too much for him. "Perhaps we should do a shorter walk this first day."

"I'd like to see that overlook," Jericho said. "I'll be all right… and if I ain't, we'll turn back."

She smiled. "I have food for us, too."

"Sounds just right! Lead the way."

Off they walked at an easy pace, following the course of the river for the first mile in the bright sun of early June. Then the river turned to the north and Wyanet led them on a meadow trail continuing east. A herd of whitetail deer fed in the deeper grass of the meadow's edge.

"Sometimes buffalo are here… and sometimes elk," Wyanet said. There is very good hunting in this area, good fishing, too."

"Do you move your camp to other places in different seasons?" Jericho asked.

"We did," Wyanet replied, "but we stopped about two years ago. When I was growing up, we would move two or three times a year, changing camps with the seasons and rotating between a dozen, all within a hundred miles of this place. Now we only move between here for winter and the Valley of High Bloom for summer. That is where you saved me… and it is where my mother is buried. That is why I was there that day."

Jericho nodded, "It's a beautiful valley… got a lake, good timber, good huntin' and fishin' to boot, I reckon. And this place is mighty fine, too. Warmer in winter here… cooler in summer there. Don't see how you could come on two finer places."

"Yes," Wyanet agreed. "We call this camp Swift River. There is no need to move as much. And my father does not wish to be far from the source of our security."

"The gold?" Jericho asked. "Well, that makes sense. Best to stay close."

"You know?" Wyanet asked, surprised.

Jericho nodded. "Crow Talks told me… says he trusts me… swore me to secrecy and silence. I don't know where it is. Didn't ask, and he didn't say. I'll never speak of it outside the tribe."

"It is here… near this camp. My father came upon it by chance, finding a gold nugget at the base of a hill… just a tiny glint with the sun in the right position to show it. He dismounted and dug it from the earth. It was half the size of his fist. We began a digging party that found more nuggets. Then Crow Talks sent for books on gold mining and assaying, and the tools and chemicals necessary. We bought many picks and shovels and dug a shaft into the hill, girded with logs. Our braves hit a vein that is rich with gold. There has been no end to it."

Jericho was breathing harder as the path began to gain incline. He huffed a bit as he spoke: "Hope that merchant Crow Talks dealt with ain't partial to runnin' his mouth. Folks hear about an Indian payin' with sacks of gold and there'll be those who'll be bustin' their wit's end with inclination of murder to find out where that gold came from… and how they can get it for themselves!"

"Crow Talks has said much the same and spoke of being as careful in his dealings as he could be. He trusts the merchant, but others have eyes and ears. He bought many things… thousands of dollars. Such things do not go unnoticed."

Jericho stopped and caught his breath for a moment. "Well, I got no idea where we are other'n what Crow Talks told me… thirty miles north of the Valley of High Bloom. Got mountains all around, and this place ain't near any stage line or settlement or town. I'm guessin' you got to know a way in here… right pass to the right basin, or blind luck. You ever seen any white men come through here—ever?"

"No."

"What about the Valley of High Bloom?"

Wyanet considered it a moment. "Once, a few years ago when our camp was there, four or five men with mules and tools."

"Prospectors, sounds like," Jericho said. "Bet they skedaddled when they caught sight of your camp."

"They did!" Wyanet said, smiling. "Some of our men chased them for a while."

Jericho smiled, then turned serious. "Well, sure as the sun rises every day, there'll be men huntin' where this tribe is livin' if they suspect a gold strike. Lot'a Indians in this territory though… be a dangerous chore sortin' out who's got what. But I reckon there'll be a few on the lookout for an Indian dressed like a white man showin' up again to place an order in that town Cavendish West."

"Yes. I think Crow Talks worries on that," Wyanet said. "Did you speak to him about these thoughts you are having?"

"No… too drunk when he told me. These past days while I was restin', he didn't say anything about it again, so I didn't, neither."

"Do you feel strong enough to go the rest of the way?" she asked.

He stepped to her and kissed her long and deep then gazed into her eyes. "I'm strong enough," he said.

****

Jericho sucked for air as his legs burned walking up a short, steep grade the last hundred feet. Then they hit the flat and rounded a bend that gave way to the sweeping view of the river valley below, ringed by foothills and the high peaks of the distant range behind. Wyanet led the way another fifty feet to a flat rock shelf that cantilevered out from the steep face as a perfect observation platform. She walked out to the end of it.

"Whoa!" Jericho said as he cautiously followed her to within inches of the edge. The drop-off was straight down to a wide pool below where the river turned and the water slowed. Jericho figured it was a hundred feet down.

"It is beautiful, yes?" Wyanet asked.

"Yes," Jericho said, "but I reckon I'll back up a step or two. I'm a bit light in the head right now and don't figure toppling off here would be good for full healin'."

"No, no!" she said, "we can sit back here and eat and drink. This place is called Moosejaw Shelf. Sapphire Woman found a moose jaw bone here many years ago. She is the oldest woman of our tribe."

Jericho waxed curious. "Wonder what happened to the rest of the moose?"

"No one knows," Wyanet answered, "but Sapphire woman considered it a good omen."

They moved ten feet back into a hollow of shade where they could still see all the magnificence. The morning was warm and Jericho was sweating. He stripped his shirt off and took a long pull on the water bota. "Say, that pool below is dark," he said. "Is it deep?"

Wyanet nodded an affirmation. "Very deep! It is the deepest part of the river that we know of. Many of us come to swim and dive here, as the water is still."

"You mean people jump off this ledge?" Jericho asked, incredulous.

"Oh no… no. They jump or dive from the rocks below, around the edges. Nobody has ever jumped from here."

"Kill you, I reckon!" Jericho opined. "Glad you cleared that up… thought I was gettin' soft! Well, come to think on it, I have gotten soft! Breathin' hard with quiverin' legs gettin' up here… like I was climbin' some big mountain for hours on end. This ain't much bigger'n a Texas anthill."

"But you did it!" she said, happily. "You could not have made it halfway here only a week ago, yet you are here today."

"Yep… stronger every day," Jericho said. Then his expression turned solemn. He contemplated a moment on his words that could find no soft edge. "I will have to leave soon… get back to my job," he said, his tone tinged with regret.

"When?" she asked, taken by the news she knew would one day come.

"Another week, maybe two. Ain't no sense in gettin' back until I can work. I'm not close to being able to ride a hundred miles a day yet. It's hard enough just thinkin' I won't see you. I love you, Wyanet."

"Ohh," she said as tears welled in her eyes. "I cannot bear to think of your absence. Hold me tight, my love."

They embraced and kissed and held each other as a cooling breeze swirled about them.

28

Over the next days, Wyanet and Jericho hiked through different parts of the expansive basin that seemed an oasis unto itself, surrounded by high ranges and barren hills that locked the land away. They took food and drink for picnicking and spent blissful moments together as she showed him the beauty of her favorite places. They talked for hours about all there was to the heavens and their lives and their experiences, all the while their hearts growing closer in the unstoppable bloom of love.

Then one morning Jericho set out alone for the Moosejaw Shelf at daylight. Wearing moccasins, trousers, and a light cotton shirt, he walked out of camp and broke to a run, something he rarely did, but did now to strengthen his legs and improve his wind. The morning was cool. He felt stiff as he ran along the river trail with rays of sun streaming through the trees. Then he emerged into full sunshine as he entered the long meadow, his limbs warming and his stride loosening as his rhythm soaked in the heat. A half mile later the terrain started to climb. Jericho slowed to a walk, breathing hard but knowing this was his strongest day yet. The steepest terrain came at the very end as he once again made his way up to the Moosejaw Shelf.

He walked cautiously to the edge and gazed on the magnificence of the land and the pool of water far below. As he caught his breath and took in all there was to see, his thoughts turned to danger for the Paiutes. He knew if ambitious men or government officials got word of a Paiute gold strike in this yet undiscovered basin, there would be hordes descending upon it without any regard for Indians who had lived in the region for generations. The area was generally thought to be barren and desolate, an arid land that held none of the allure of California's gold with landscapes of milk and honey. Word of a strike in this largely uninhabited region would bring them running though, Jericho knew. And he knew that some were already looking. It was only a matter of time now.

Soft, fast steps from behind interrupted his thoughts at the last instant. Jericho quickly jumped back from the edge as he turned and saw the Indian with knife in hand coming for him. Jericho darted frantically to the side as Growling Bear swung his knife, the tip slashing across Jericho's shoulder, opening up an eight-inch gash. Growling Bear lunged with a straight thrust, trying to stab Jericho in the chest. Jericho sidestepped the thrust and grabbed Growling Bear's arm, clamping down on it with both hands to keep the Indian's knife hand from doing what Jericho knew he intended to do. The brave who loved Wyanet meant to kill him here and now. Growling Bear struggled to get his knife hand free as the two men wrestled for advantage. Then Growling Bear began punching Jericho in the head with his free hand. Jericho hung on to Growling Bear's knife hand until the Indian's fist caught him flush on the chin, stunning Jericho for only an instant. But it was long enough. The knife was up for an overhand plunge when Jericho charged and made a desperate grab for Growling Bear's wrist. Jericho took Growling Bear through the chest with his shoulder, the impact causing an involuntary grunt from Growling Bear as the wind was knocked out of him.

And then the two men were untangled and free in space, having gone off the ledge. They were no longer concerned with each other as they plummeted toward the water, gaining deadly speed with each passing instant. Jericho had the presence of mind to turn vertical, pulling his legs together and his arms in tight just before he hit the water. The impact came like a brutal slap to his entire body, and just as quickly was dismissed as he slammed the river bottom twelve feet below the surface. But his knees were bent and his adrenaline pumped with the instinct for survival. Jericho pushed off the bottom and swam quickly up, breaking the surface and gasping for air while he took in his surroundings. His nose was bleeding and Growling Bear was gone.

Jericho took a deep breath and immediately dove down again, his eyes open in the cold, clear water that was only slightly obscured from his earlier disturbance of the sandy bottom. He saw the shadow beneath and swam for it, recognizing the limp body as he got closer. But Growling Bear was drifting in the current and Jericho wouldn't catch him before he ran out of air. Jericho shot up to the surface and swam as fast as he could to get ahead of where Growling Bear was drifting beneath him. When he had covered enough distance, Jericho took a few deep breaths then dove again. Growling Bear had drifted in a slightly different line, leaving tough distance between them, but Jericho knew time was running out. He swam for the limp body, his shoulder throbbing and his lungs feeling as if they would burst. Jericho reached Growling Bear and grabbed him by the hair then yanked as he kicked his legs to move upward.

The breath shot out of Jericho's lungs just before he reached the surface. He broke the water line but drew breath too soon, sucking in water that caused him to cough and hack violently as he fought to stay afloat. Jericho paddled with his left arm and wildly kicked his legs, hanging on to Growling Bear's hair with a death grip.

After a minute of excruciating effort, his feet finally touched bottom near the shoreline. Jericho gained his footing and pulled Growling Bear's head above water, then made the last lunges onto the shore. He laid Growling Bear on his back and sat on his stomach, immediately beginning a rhythmic two-handed thrusting on the Indian's chest but Growling Bear did not respond.

Moments later, Jericho jumped up and rolled Growling Bear over onto his stomach with his head turned to the side. Jericho started brutally pushing both palms on Growling Bear's back with all the strength he had left. Water flooded from Growling Bear's nose and mouth. The Indian began to gag. Jericho kept at it a while longer, pushing more water out as Growling Bear sputtered for breath.

Jericho stood up and walked away coughing, catching his own breath and trying to get the remaining water out of his own lungs. He turned and walked back to Growling Bear. The Indian's lower leg was badly broken and his shoulder was dislocated. Jericho rolled him over on his back again and grabbed the arm of the dislocated shoulder. Growling Bear's eyes opened wide as Jericho put his right foot in the Indian's armpit and suddenly yanked with brute force. Growling Bear screamed for a brief moment before the loud pop sounded, returning the shoulder to the socket.

Jericho looked at his own shoulder for the first time. It was laid open wide and bleeding steadily, though the cut wasn't deep. He looked back at Growling Bear like he just remembered the Indian had tried to kill him.

"You damn sure better not try that ever again… or I'll kill ya!" Jericho shouted. "Don't even know why I saved you! Should'a let ya drown!"

Jericho looked around a moment then back at Growling Bear. "You got a horse somewheres near?" Jericho asked as he scooted his feet like the gait of a horse and mimicked holding reins.

Growling bear pointed down the river toward a turn and waved his arm to the side, indicating a left turn around the end of the hill. Jericho knew where the trail picked up and where the horse would likely be.

"I got'a get 'im," Jericho said. "You're busted up to hell. Leg's bad broke… and your side's turnin' color… busted ribs, likely. I can't carry ya… barely walk myself now! I ought'a tie a rock to ya and throw you back in the river! Crazy son of a bitch!"

Growling Bear lay still, his chest heaving as he drew breath, his eyes stoically passive as he took in the figure of Jericho Buck standing before him.

"Guess you'll be here when I get back!" Jericho said with disgust. Then he turned and strode off like he had a hornet in his pants.

****

White billowing clouds rolled along on a sea of blue, their pace bringing moments of intense morning sun followed by equal bouts of cooling shade. The camp was alive with activity. Children carried logs from the wood-cutting area, delivering them to each wickiup for the cooking fires. The older boys carried the largest loads in competition with each other. But the girls and younger children carried wood as well, girls with fewer logs, and the youngest carrying twigs and chips for kindling.

One of the girls caught sight first, pointing at the distant walking man, staggering a bit as he led a horse with a mounted brave. The brave was leaning forward, resting or passed out on the horse's neck. And one of his legs stuck out farther from the horse, splinted with birch branches. The camp began to take notice, and then several braves took off running toward them, recognizing one of their own and Brave Rider. When they reached Jericho and Growling Bear, Jericho handed the lead rope to the first.

"Take 'im," Jericho said. "I got'a lay down. My head's spinnin'."

Jericho walked unsteadily for his wickiup, ignoring the few inquiries that he couldn't understand from those who had arrived running. His shirt was dry now, but was cut at the shoulder and blood-soaked down the sleeve. A dull ache hung like a fog in his head and soreness like a blanket over every inch of his body. And his vision was blurred. Jericho made his way into the wickiup then fell to his bed and drank from the olla before closing his eyes and instantly being out.

29

The pain invaded his dreamless sleep, permeating the darkness with a persistent nuisance that demanded he awaken. Chenoa came into his focus, sitting by his shoulder looking carefully at what she was doing. Jericho felt the pinch again as she made another pass with the crude needle, attached to a long, thin piece of animal sinew. He craned his head to see his shoulder. The cut was almost completely closed now with neat uniform rows of sinew going back and forth, side by side, cinched tight. She pushed the needle through the skin again, and then through the other side of the cut, pulling more of the fibrous material tight and closing the cut a fraction further. Jericho guessed she only needed two more passes to be finished.

"Thank you, Chenoa," Jericho said. "You've taken such good care of me."

Chenoa smiled and continued with her work.

"What happened, Brave Rider?" came the question from his other side.

Jericho turned his head to see Wyanet sitting next to him, holding his hand. He hadn't even realized her presence but now felt the soothing comfort of her touch. Her face held worry.

"Damn Growling Bear was tryin' to tell me he'd like me gone sooner rather than later," Jericho drawled with a half smile.

"I do not see the humor in it," Wyanet said.

"Yeah, neither did I… but I'm happy for the blessing of being able to speak of it."

Wyanet frowned. "He told that he tried to kill you… that you both fell from Moosejaw Shelf. He told that you saved his life, pulling him from the water and giving back his breath."

"Well, I'll be," Jericho said, surprised. "How is he?"

"Imala says you did a good job with the splint. Still, it is a bad break and its healing is uncertain. She says he has broken ribs also… and his breathing is much labored. He may die, she thinks."

"I hope not," Jericho said.

****

Jericho rested in his bed for four days, shocked at how sore he was from head to toe, and how long it stuck to him. But it did. His head hurt and the fog on his thinking held for three days, then finally cleared like a storm passed. His body continued to ache through the fourth day. Then, in the calm beauty of a clear morning on the fifth day, he felt better and walked with Wyanet along the river, his stiffness letting up as they walked another mile to the stand of cottonwoods at the end of a meadow. She told him of Growling Bear's condition, as Jericho had asked each day.

"He is alive still, so it is thought he may escape death," Wyanet said. "But he is very sick… like you once were. It will take many, many days… a new moon or two perhaps."

Jericho nodded. "Hittin' the water at that speed felt like gettin' trampled by a herd'a buffalo. Almost had that happen once. Now I know how I'd'a felt if I'd lived through it. Growling Bear will be a long time on the mend. I reckon he didn't land near as forgiving on that water as I did."

She took his hand and squeezed it. "I thank the Great Spirit every day that you have lived through all that has befallen you since we met."

Jericho smiled, “I been mendin’ from one thing or another ever since I got here. But my heart’s been full with you. I’d’a tried to run off long ago if you hadn’t been here. Now I can’t hardly leave ’cause you *are* here.” Jericho stopped and turned to her. “I’m ridin’ out in a few more days… got business that needs attention. Then I’ll be back. Your father said he’d give me a horse. Tonight I will ask him if he’ll give me his daughter too. I will ask him if I can marry you.”

Wyanet showed a sly smile. “Do you not think you should ask me first? His answer will make no difference if I say ‘no’.”

“That’s why I’m askin’ you first!” Jericho quickly retorted. “Wyanet, will you marry me? Will you be my wife? I love you so much my heart might bust out’a my chest.”

She stepped into his arms, pressing against him as she looked up into his eyes with her lips just inches from his. “I will marry you, Jericho Buck, my Brave Rider. I will love you and be a good wife always. You will be my loving, good husband always. Our passion will burn hot, and our love will carry us a lifetime.”

He kissed her and she bore her weight on him as they melted to the ground beneath the shade of a cottonwood, alone to themselves.

30

Leaping Elk smiled when Jericho entered his wickiup. Crow Talks sat to the chief's left and spoke as Jericho seated himself on the chief's right.

"He wants you to know that your legend grows ever greater. Our tribe bows with respect and thanks. Leaping Elk is glad of heart and certain that he chose well with the name of Nievi Karü'wa. You are most rightly Brave Rider."

Jericho nodded to Crow Talks then looked to Leaping Elk. "Thank you, Chief… I'm much obliged for the kindness you've shown me. I hope you'll feel the same about me after I tell you why I wanted to see you tonight."

Leaping Elk gave Jericho his penetrating stare as Crow Talks translated Jericho's words.

"First, we smoke… eat… drink," Leaping Elk said in his stilted English.

"You're the chief," Jericho said, waxing slight trepidation about his own indulgence.

The pipe made its customary three rounds, though Jericho only partook on the first pass as courtesy and then feigned queasiness on the next two passes. They took a meal of roasted fish and sweet cornmeal biscuits during which the chief insisted that Jericho recount his fight with Growling Bear and how he had saved him. Leaping Elk wanted to hear each and every detail of the encounter including the great fall from Moosejaw Shelf to the water, and how

Jericho had managed to pull Growling Bear from the bottom of the river. But Leaping Elk's greatest curiosity came with how Jericho had purged the water from Growling Bear and gotten him to begin breathing again. Jericho explained how as a boy he had seen men pulled from the Seedskeedee River unconscious and drowned, but then brought back by bargemen who knew to push the chest rhythmically, like a heartbeat, and flip the victim over to push on the back too if needed.

"Sometimes it worked and sometimes it didn't," Jericho concluded. "Never done it myself before, but seeing it done before was fixed in my mind… recollected right to me when I got 'im out'a the water. Sure glad it worked."

Crow Talks translated to Leaping Elk. Then Leaping Elk spoke for a minute and Crow Talks translated back to Jericho: "Leaping Elk says you had no obligation to save him after he tried to kill you. But he is grateful that you saw him as a tribal brother in life's struggle… the journey that weighs on every man in different ways. Growling Bear's love for Wyanet drove him to try and take you. He had not hate in his heart for you, but love for her that blinded all else."

Jericho paused for a moment and decided the moment had arrived. "Well, I reckon it's time for me to tell you that I love Wyanet, too," he said, staring at the chief. "I have come here tonight to ask your permission… to marry your daughter, Wyanet. I asked her to marry me and she said 'yes.' But I will not marry her without your blessing and permission."

Crow Talks's eyes widened at Jericho's revelation. He turned to Leaping Elk to translate but Jericho sensed that the chief already knew what he had said as his eyes had also widened. Jericho sat still watching as Crow Talks translated. An imagination of the chief pulling his knife and cutting his throat went through Jericho's mind for a brief instant, but then subsided as a smile slowly grew on Leaping Elk's brown, age-lined and weather-beaten face.

"Good!" Leaping Elk declared at the end of the translation. "When?" he asked, and then answered it himself with, "Soon!"

"Soon… yes," Jericho said. "But I need to go back to where I work… Cold Springs and Dry Creek Stations… settle up on my pay and let 'em know I'm movin' on. Got'a get my horse from Dry Creek Station. He's been there gettin' fat for quite a spell. And there's one more thing, too…"

Jericho paused as Crow Talks translated. Leaping Elk's face took on a look of concern and then he spoke, sticking to Paiute.

Crow Talks translated: "Leaping Elk is not happy that you would leave right after this great announcement of marriage. He says you could take care of your dealings after the ceremony. And he wants to know where you plan to live. Would you stay here? Or would you take Wyanet away from her people? Leaping Elk prefers that you would live with, or very near to our tribe. But if you want to live somewhere else, he would not stop the marriage if Wyanet agrees to it."

Leaping Elk grabbed his bota skin and handed it to Jericho. "Drink! Tell me!" the chief declared with iron in his tone.

Jericho squeezed the bota which yielded a strong stream of clear fluid into his open mouth, about four ounces that he swallowed in one take. The burn was instant. Jericho coughed violently and imagined flame might come out.

"Could'a warned me!" he said in a hoarse voice. "That's some straight-up, thump-ya-down shine!"

Leaping Elk laughed which started Crow Talks laughing. Jericho continued to cough for a minute more, noting he'd never drunk anything stronger. The warmth of intoxication flooded through him and he began to laugh between his hacking coughs.

"You tell me now!" Leaping Elk declared.

"No!" Jericho retorted. "You ain't drunk squat yet! First you drink… then Crow Talks drinks… then I tell you!"

Leaping Elk took the bota and squeezed off a good amount, swallowing without coughing, though it hadn't been as much as Jericho had taken. The chief handed it on to Crow Talks who took a good squeeze and coughed once.

"I'll tell you now," Jericho said. "First off, me and Wyanet reckon it would be better to get married after I get back so we could be together… proper… without me leavin' just after we's married. I got to check in, get my money, get my horse… and I been thinkin' I should find out about claim laws for your mines… 'fore the white men show up to take it from you. I reckon you got a right to live here on this land, but maybe you could make a claim on it, legal like. Anyway I got some ideas about that. I need to talk to some people who know without tipping them off about your mines." Jericho looked at Crow Talks and said, "Tell 'im that, then I'll tell the rest."

Crow Talks began translating slowly, deliberately while the chief listened, his eyes moving about as if considering the contingencies and unknowns. Jericho knew what he had just spilled would require implicit trust from Leaping Elk; the kind reserved for a son, not some white man he'd known for little more than a month.

Crow Talks finished the translation and Leaping Elk fixed his eyes on Jericho, assessing, searching for anything false or contrived, and summing up the young man who sat before him, the young man who already held knowledge that could bring about his tribe's demise.

"I know I'm asking you to trust me," Jericho said, holding his own eyes firmly on Leaping Elk's. "I love your daughter and I will be a good husband to her… and a good son to you. I think I can help you with this. We'll be happy to live here. It's good land. I been driftin' a long time now. Happy to settle in here with my wife… but I'd build a cabin for us. Nothin' against your wickiups, but I want my own cabin."

Crow Talks began translating again as Leaping Elk listened with rapt attention, nodding his head as the words found his understanding. Then Leaping Elk spoke, once more pinning his eyes to Jericho as he did so.

Crow Talks spoke: "Our chief says when you saved Wyanet's life, you saved *his* life as well, and for this he owes you his trust. He knows that as a white man, you would be better able to find answers to the questions you have raised without arousing suspicion… and he trusts in your ability to be guarded wisely in your approach so as not to betray your true purpose. He knows that even knowing the language, I could not manage these things without suspicion… and he knows that to buy things with gold is to invite others to our discovery, which would mean the loss of our land and our lives. Leaping Elk welcomes your help in this. He trusts you with his life, with our lives. He says to go and tend your affairs and ours as well. He will meet with you again before you leave, to talk of your plans and to offer guidance. His heart is full in you becoming his son and Wyanet's husband."

31

The first gray of light showed the tears on Wyanet's face as she stood watching Jericho tighten his saddle cinch. The horse was a good one but flinched with movement, unaccustomed to a saddle and the heavy hide saddlebags. Jericho fed it a piece of hard, peppermint candy and rubbed its neck, momentarily calming the animal. He turned to Wyanet and hugged her.

"I'll be back as fast as I can… a month maybe," he said. "I love you. Be well, stay strong." He kissed her tenderly near her ear and whispered in it, "My heart aches until we're together again." Then he found her lips and kissed her fully for a moment.

"Come back to me, my love," she said.

He nodded with a warm smile then turned and sprang to his saddle like a cat, awake and alive with the excitement of good health and a mission ahead. With both Navy Colts holstered at his hips and his Bowie knife sheathed, Jericho gave light heels to his horse and it jumped to a trot. He waved to her and then turned straight in the saddle, minding his bearings as he left the encampment, looking forward to discovering the path that would lead from this fertile, vibrant basin back to the arid and mostly stark region between Cold Springs and Dry Creek that he'd ridden so many times.

With detailed instructions from Crow Talks, Jericho believed he was riding due south toward the Valley of High Bloom, but it seemed he was meandering a little east as well.

"Won't be gettin' a fresh mount anytime soon… it's all on you, boy," Jericho said to his horse as the morning began to wane.

For two hours more, he rode on at a slow pace paying close attention to the landmarks he'd been told of. He finally came to a point where he looked boxed in by steeply ascending butte faces all around him, just as Crow Talks had described. Then he saw the jutting rocks with a lone birch tree to the north. Jericho reined his horse toward it and within minutes detected the fold-back of one butte to another. He found the corridor and rode through it for two miles, awed at the steep cliffs on both sides that were swirled with shades from deep mocha to beige, in patterns that looked painted on by giant brushes. The ground was sand and the corridor was perhaps a hundred feet across at its widest point. But when he came to the end, the width choked down to twenty feet and emptied out onto an open, arid plain.

He recognized the hills that were a few miles in front of him, surprised to find he was closer to Edwards Creek Station than Cold Springs. His Paiute pony had developed a hitch in his gait and storm clouds were rolling up fast from the west. Jericho decided to make for Edwards Creek.

"Looks like we'll be arrivin' wet," he said for the benefit of his horse. A mile farther south, he intersected the Pony Express trail he knew so well. Then he looked back at the butte wall, knowing where he'd come through the corridor. It seemed to have vanished.

"I'll be hornswoggled… can't see it… never know it was there," he said to the darkening sky. Jericho jumped the trail for Edwards Creek. It was only a relay station but it had a barn with good feed and water for the animals, and a good cot for him. He broke to a lope, knowing he wouldn't beat the storm.

****

Brandon and Russ were playing checkers. Frank was watching with keen interest, unsure of which man he might be playing next. It still looked like anybody's game after being twenty minutes in. Russ had been considering his move for nearly two minutes.

"Let's go!" Brandon declared, nearly shouting to be heard over the pounding rain and rumbling thunder. "The hair on my nuts is turnin' gray waitin' on you!"

"You ain't got no nuts," Russ said as he made his move.

"Doggies," Frank said, looking at Russ's move.

Brandon's eyes widened as he chuckled, "And you ain't got no brains," he said, moving his piece in a zig-zag triple jump. Brandon gleefully picked up Russ's pieces.

Lightning cracked right overhead with a deafening boom that made the three men reflexively duck. The door flew open and Jericho hustled inside, soaking wet. Brandon, Russ, and Frank stared in disbelief for a moment as if Jericho had been thrust through the door by the god of lightning.

"Jericho?" Brandon asked, still unsure of the wet face beneath the hat.

"Hello, Brandon! Russ! Frank!" Jericho said as he pulled his lid and slapped it against his leg to get the worst of the water off. "Can ya put me up for the night?"

"Jericho! What on God's green earth are you doing here! We heard tell you were hole up with some Paiutes who were nursing you back from death's doorstep!"

"You heard right," Jericho said. "Got shot up savin' an Indian girl from some desperadoes. Paiutes seen me through it… caring for me 'bout two months. But I'm right as rain now, and soaked down with it too. Can I bunk here tonight… dry out my clothes by the cookstove?"

"Sure you can!" Brandon chimed. "Say, where'd you come from?"

"Left the Paiute camp this morning for the first time," Jericho answered.

"And you came straight here?" Russ asked.

"Yep... bound for Cold Springs tomorrow. Draw my pay... send word to Dry Creek 'bout lookin' after my horse."

"Your horse? How'd you get here?" Brandon asked.

"Got a Paiute pony. Put 'im up in the barn already."

"Couldn't tell nobody was even around with all the noise this storm's making," Brandon said. "Good thing you wasn't a war party come to get us or we'd have been throwing checkers at you!"

"Hey, ya got anything I could put on while my clothes is dryin'?" Jericho asked.

"Yep," Brandon said and went to a cabinet against the far wall.

Jericho stripped off his shirt and was kicking his boots off when Frank caught sight of his bare torso and the burn scars and sewed-up gash across his shoulder.

"Lord be! Those desperadoes shot you and burned and cut you, too?" Frank hooted.

"No... the Paiutes burned me. Dropped hot coals on me while I was staked to the ground."

"What in the hell are you talking about?" Frank asked. "I thought you said the Paiutes was caring for you!"

"They was," Jericho said. "But before they was carin', they was fixin' to kill me. One tried to kill me 'bout a fortnight ago," Jericho said, pointing to the sewed slash across his shoulder.

Frank shook his head in confusion and looked at Russ and Brandon who looked equally confused.

Jericho smiled. "You give me a drink'a whiskey and some supper tonight and I'll tell you the whole story. It's entertainin'... I swear."

Brandon looked unsure. "Well, we'd be breaking the oath if we have a drink."

"You got any whiskey?" Jericho asked.

"Yeah, I do," Brandon said.

"Well then just give it to me! One drink… maybe two. I'm sore as a boil," Jericho said. "I ain't ridin' for the Pony Express no more. I'm gettin' married to the Paiute girl I saved!"

"Oh hell!" Brandon said, "I gotta hear this. Sounds like a whiskey story. I'll have a drink, too. Stormy weather is drinkin' weather." Brandon looked at Frank and Russ. "You boys better not say shit! Right?"

"As long as we're all drinking together… we don't say shit," Frank declared.

Russ looked around. "Let's have it! We ain't riders anyhow… save for emergencies. Nobody due through for three more hours… I'm sick of checkers."

"I'll get the bottle," Brandon said.

32

Jericho slept late at Edwards Creek, then rose and ate and examined his Paiute pony's hooves. The horse had a bad stone bruise on his left front sole. "This ought'a take the hurt away," Jericho told the horse as he nailed shoes on it, putting the last one on the sore sole. Then he gave his thanks and said his goodbyes and trailed on west toward Cold Springs Station, opting for the slower route through the Valley of High Bloom just to see it again and remember where he and Wyanet had first laid eyes on each other. When he came to the spot in the valley where they'd met, the violence of the events played through his mind again, as did the vision of Wyanet who had seared his heart even in the life and death intensity of the moment. Jericho looked around the ground, remembering where the dead men lay, their bodies now gone and the ground undisturbed, replaced by a serenity of time gone by. Only the remnant carcasses of his and Wyanet's horses remained. The wolves and coyotes had thrived. Jericho continued on through the valley, wondering where the grave of Wyanet's mother was.

An hour and a half later, he was on the plains again, riding the last leg to Cold Creek. Jericho pulled his timepiece out and looked. It was nearly 2 p.m. He turned and scanned to his right rear where the more common Pony Express trail came from. The dust of a rider was visible behind him and Cold Springs Station came into view ahead. Jericho could make out two men and a horse standing in the yard. He guessed the tender to be Danny and the new westbound rider was likely Purdy.

Jericho held his horse to a trot and soon heard the pounding gallop coming up fast behind him. He chuckled at the coincidence, arriving at the same time as the 2 p.m. westbound rider. Normally, he would have put his horse to a run just to beat the man coming up from behind, but his horse was carrying weight and his days of "taking up the run" were over. A slight feeling of melancholy overcame him when Pooch smoked by him, thirty feet wide on his right side, giving a quick glance and shouting out loudly, "Jerichooooooo!" as he passed at top speed. The rider and tender in the yard were staring out at Jericho until Pooch arrived, and then their attention turned to speed the handoff.

Jericho watched with respect as Pooch flew out of his saddle and the mochila was quickly transferred to the fresh horse. The new rider was aboard an instant later and made dust in a gallop to the west as the run continued. The tender began to walk the horse back to the corral and barn where he would strip the tack, then water and feed the pony. Jericho knew from the man's gait that it was Danny tending the horse. Pooch stood where he had dismounted, smoking a cigarette and staring at Jericho who was coming on at a trot from a quarter mile away.

"Ole Frank told me you was through there last night!" Pooch called out as Jericho trotted in the last hundred feet. "Couldn't hardly believe it! Good to hear!... and now good to see! You know I couldn't stop to hear any of the story. Hope you're not tired of telling it. Stan and whoever's awake are gonna wanna hear it!"

Jericho reined up and dismounted. He shook Pooch's hand. "No, I ain't tired'a tellin' it yet. Good to see you, Pooch!" Jericho put his hands on his hips and stretched backwards. "Man, I'm stiff as one'a Willie's flapjacks. Not in very good ridin' shape."

Pooch smiled. "Must not be if you're stiff only coming from

Edwards Creek. Your horse is loaded down good. Are those Indian saddlebags?" Pooch asked, looking at the deer-hide pack bags on Jericho's horse.

"Yes, sir… Paiute," Jericho replied, as he began leading the horse away. "I'll get 'im stripped and watered and see ya inside."

****

"Hello Danny!" Jericho called as he entered the barn.

Danny was turning Pooch's mount to a stall. He turned and looked at Jericho with a toothy grin. "Hey Jericho!… heard you was comin'! You look fine, but we all heard you been through it bad."

"Yeah, rough days. Better now," Jericho said. "I'm damn happy to be here and see ya. I'll tell ya the whole guts of it when I get inside."

Danny looked at Jericho's horse. "He ain't one of ours? You want me to strip him and turn him out?… Happy to."

"No, I'll do it. He's a Paiute pony… damn good horse."

"Okay," Danny said as he left.

Jericho un-cinched the hide packs and stashed them under the root bin then pulled the tack and racked it.

"Looks like that foot ain't botherin' you anymore," Jericho said as he fed him a peppermint. "We got a lot'a ridin' comin' up. Get your rest… I need all ya got." Jericho rubbed the horse's neck, then turned him to the stall with feed and water before heading to the station.

"Mister Jericho Buck… what a fine surprise!" Stan called from an easy chair where he sat with an old newspaper.

"Mister Stan Brock!" Jericho sang out, returning the address of respect. "May I inquire of today's dining choices?"

Pooch looked up from his plate of pintos and pork like he

thought Stan might announce some other choices that he hadn't been privy to.

Stan chuckled at Jericho's show of formal vernacular. "Why, it's the best braised hog and seasoned pintos anywhere north of the Pecos. We got lots of it, too!"

Danny was planted on the settee with his feet up on the rough-hewn table in front. "It's splendid fare, I will attest," Danny said, showing his own aptitude for finer speak. He continued, "And the biscuits are particularly nascent."

"Nascent?" Jericho quipped. "I ain't heard that one."

"Me neither," Danny admitted. "I heard a dude over to Redmon say it while talking about some such or the other. Sounded like it could go with biscuits. Who knows? Nascent biscuits could be the best. Purdy and Sinkhole ate a bushel of 'em before they took their leave. They might say the pork and pintos is nascent, too."

"Who's Sinkhole?" Jericho asked.

Stan frowned, "He's been a fill-in for Pooch on the westbound… an alternate over from Carson Sink Station. But anytime you're ready to take up the run, we'll send him back and put Pooch back on his regular run."

"Keep 'im if ya want," Jericho said. "I'm not comin' back… I'm gettin' married to a Paiute girl… the chief's daughter. She stole my heart like a thief in the night… plum beautiful she is."

Pooch stopped eating, and Danny and Stan sat up straighter as if making sure they'd heard right.

"I reckon we're gonna get the whole story right now," Danny said.

"I believe you're right," Stan agreed.

Jericho nodded, "All right… just let me fill up a plate with all them nascent delectables and I'll talk while I'm eatin'!"

With big eyes and burning ears, the men listened as if Moses were speaking. Jericho ate his way through three plates and told all that he cared for them to hear, livening it up with vivid description and nuanced detail that lasted over an hour. Then Pooch and Danny left for the bunkroom. Jericho knew the other tender, Garrett, and Pooch's replacement, Sinkhole, would be up soon.

"How 'bout a smoke on the front porch, Stan," Jericho said. "Like to ask you 'bout a few things."

Stan nodded, "Sure."

The late afternoon showed clear sky and the sun blazing over the western range. Stan lit his pipe and Jericho his smoke as the two men sat in rockers, swaying easy while they smoked and looked north where a herd of antelope streaked across a wide, crested ridge. The silence was peaceful for a long, lingering moment in homage to another day.

Then Jericho asked, "Do you know anything about Indians and land rights? Can they make claims to land… like preempters?"

"No they can't. Indians ain't citizens. Only citizens can make land claims," Stan said. "Kind of peculiar, I know, seeing as how they say Indians were here long before people from overseas in England and Europe started showing up. But that ain't to say Indians don't have the right to live on whatever land they're living on. They can live there right up till the time the government says they can't. Easy to see why they don't like the white man. I hear a lot of them back east already been run off their land."

"What about buyin' land?" Jericho asked. "You think they could pay for land and get a deed, legal like?"

"Nope… least not any land the government owns. Same deal… they're not citizens. Might be able to buy land privately from a citizen… don't know for sure about that situation. Lots of charlatans willing to sell whatever they don't have rights for to whoever's willing to pay for it."

Jericho looked riled-up and asked indignantly, “Hey, what the hell makes someone a citizen?”

Stan pulled on his pipe deep in thought then exhaled a long slow stream of smoke. “Well, it ain’t just about being born here or they’d all be citizens… slaves and Chinamen, too. As I recall, you have to be a free white man and have been born here. If you came from a different country, you have to be a free white man who’s been living here for fourteen years, and then you must pledge an oath of loyalty to this country over wherever you came from.”

Jericho took a drag from his smoke as he considered what he’d just heard. “Must’a made them Mormons madder’n hornets when all this became Nevada Territory. But I heard some of ’em been runnin’ Indian slaves… blacks, too. Got some comeuppance for it.”

Stan nodded, “Maybe. War going now… mostly back east. I believe it will settle the question of slavery. It’s a bloody, vicious affair. Good time to be living in the West.”

“I reckon it’s always a good time to be livin’ in the West,” Jericho agreed. “Hey, where’s the government for Nevada Territory… how far?”

“Genoa,” Stan said. “West of here another dozen stations or so… maybe a hundred, eighty miles.”

Jericho waxed thoughtful. “That’s where a man would go to find out about land claims or buyin’ government land?”

“Yes, sir,” Stan replied then looked at the concern on Jericho’s face. “You worried about the Paiutes losing their land?”

“Yeah,” Jericho said. “They made me part’a their tribe, and I’m marryin’ the chief’s daughter. Tryin’ to look out for them.”

Stan gazed skyward as he spoke: “That’s mostly barren, dry land where the Paiutes and Shoshones move abouts. They make a go of it, but I don’t suspect anybody’s going to be in a hurry to run them out. Couldn’t be much for farming or otherwise.”

"Some of it's fine land," Jericho said. "Wouldn't even guess it's there unless you just stumbled on it… and ain't many likely to do so, what with the east-west trails bein' farther north or south, clear of the ranges that look the most inhospitable."

"Well, I hope you find the best of the best with the gal you're marrying," Stan said with ringing sincerity. "We're just about washed up now anyways. Word is, Western Union is only a few months away from having the transcontinental telegraph finished… up Salt Lake way … spanning across the whole country. Then the Pony Express will be out of business and we'll all be looking for the next great adventure to carve out a living… keep us fed and sheltered."

"Ridin' for the Pony Express has been my greatest adventure so far… a true honor. I sure am obliged to your brother Willie for giving me the chance," Jericho said. "My next adventure will be findin' my way to Genoa. I'm leaving tomorrow. Goin' to find out what I can find out. I'd sure appreciate any information you can give me on trailin' there."

"Won't be hard. There's Pony Express stations all the way there," said Stan. "Got a map inside shows all of 'em… settlements too. Now, when you get to Genoa, you'll be inquiring about Millard County of old Utah Territory. That's what all this area is, from here to Camp Station east, and all the way to Genoa going west. To hell and gone going north and south, too. It's all Millard County, over six thousand square miles. Biggest damn county you ever saw. None bigger in the old Utah Territory. I haven't heard about the Nevada government naming their counties yet, so you can use Millard for a reference if you're talking about land anywhere in these parts."

Jericho nodded, "Obliged."

Jericho and Stan fell silent again, smoking and gazing out over the vast plains and distant ranges. A few moments later, Jericho asked, "Hey, how'd this fella Sinkhole get that name?"

Stan chuckled, "That's his real name… his surname. Sinkhole… Jamison Sinkhole. Says he's Irish. I believe he's tired of being asked about it, what with most figuring it's a nickname with a good story behind it. He knows a lot about the ground west of here though. Rode a run west from Carson Sink to Fort Churchill. Churchill is eight stations west of here."

"That'll help. Never been west of Carson Sink. I'll ask him about the country," Jericho said, "but I won't ask him 'bout his name."

****

Before Jericho turned in for the night, he talked with Sinkhole who had awakened for his 7 p.m. westbound run.

"Genoa, huh? You can cut ten miles off between Williams and Fort Churchhill going the way of Sandy Pass," Sinkhole said with a clear Irish accent. "A wee bit risky skipping two stations… Hooten Wells and Buckland… but there's a good spring at the start of Sandy Pass. It's the first water you'll find going that way, nigh on to thirty miles after you leave Williams. That's why the Pony Express didn't route that way. Only rode it once… on my time off. Lass I knew in Fort Churchill."

"I like savin' ten miles," Jericho said. "How 'bout the pass… what's that like?"

"Four miles getting over… hard-packed sand… mostly even ground, tough climb for some of it, and likely hot as the devil right now," Sinkhole said. "Water your horse before you start. Fort Churchill is another twenty-five miles once you're out. There's a station there… town too."

The two men talked on for a few more minutes as Sinkhole

described the headings and landmarks to reach the spring at Sandy Pass, and then on beyond to Fort Churchill.

"Obliged," Jericho said, shaking hands. "Best to ya."

"You as well," Sinkhole cheerily offered.

Jericho made for a cot, weary from all the action of late.

33

The yard was fresh with faint light as the three men stood in front of the station. "Good luck, Jericho! Take care of yourself!" Danny said as they shook hands.

"Best to you, Danny!" Jericho said.

Jericho turned to Stan. "Thank you, Mister Brock… it's been grand! Say hello to Willie for me. I sent a letter and some money to him with the eastbound to care for my horse Buddy and my personals. Hope the wind keeps at your back and prosperity rains on your trail."

"Thank you, son… Been a true pleasure working with you. I hope you can stop in on your way back through."

Jericho mounted up. His horse was a ball of restless energy and jumped to a lope at the lightest prompt. "So long!" he called. He'd ridden the westbound a few times out of necessity and knew the way as far as the Carson Sink Station. But this day he would only make it to West Gate Station, the second station west of Cold Springs, and a thirty-two-mile ride. It was a relay station with a keeper and two tenders, but they knew Jericho by face and reputation and happily put him up for the night.

The next day he stopped briefly at the relay station of Sand Springs, then skipped the home station of Carson Sink and made for the relay station of Williams. The day's ride had been forty-four miles in ten hours with water stops, leaving his horse played out. Two young men came out as Jericho tied up to the rail.

"Hello!" he called. "I'm Jericho Buck. I rode the run between Dry Creek and Cold Springs for three months... but I'm finished now. On my way to Genoa. Could I put up here for the night? Feed and water my horse? I'll pay for the feed."

"I heard of you," said the shorter one. "You made a few runs between from Cold Springs to Carson Sink, didn't you?"

"Yes, sir... when they was in a pickle for riders."

"Happy to know you. I'm Lee Tumes... they call me Tombstone."

"Wayne Carlisi," the second man said.

They smiled and shook hands with Jericho like they were all brothers in the cause.

"Sure you can bunk here," Tombstone said. "We got extra. Water and plenty of oats, too. Your horse looks done in. You can stall him... Got some ornery ones in the corral right now."

"I'm makin' for Sandy Pass tomorrow. Heard it cuts ten miles off the ride to Fort Churchill," Jericho said.

"That's what they say. Never done it myself," said Tombstone. "But you have, ain't ya, Wayne?"

"Yeah, it will save you some miles. Ten sounds about right. There's a spring at the pass... real good water. You best plan on camping there... it's better than thirty miles making it that far, then another twenty or so over to Fort Churchill with no water. Keep a sharp eye... Indians can be about."

Jericho nodded, "Another rider I talked to said just about the same things."

****

The next morning he was in the saddle at first light, his belly full with biscuits and strong, hot coffee, compliments of Tombstone and the fraternity of the Pony Express. His horse broke strong but Jericho held him to a brisk walk, knowing the coming toll of the day. The rising sun warmed Jericho's back and cast his shadow thirty feet ahead, a dark image of rider and horse undulating over the occasional low brush and ragged ground that played out across the plain. It was all new territory for Jericho and enlivened his senses. Soon he would be in Genoa, the capital of Nevada Territory. He figured another five days getting there, not wanting to push his horse too hard under the weight he had on him.

Tonight he would camp. He was well provisioned with food and necessities and would be able to feed his horse from oats he had on hand. With two canteens, Jericho could water him once during the day. Still, he had to find the spring that Sinkhole and Tombstone had told him of. It was more than thirty miles ahead through the July heat that could range from oppressive to deadly. His horse would need water.

The morning grew long and hot. At noon, he cleared another grade and reined up a moment. He dismounted and took another compass heading. From his elevated position he could see the V in the range with a clear depression in front and several acres of pine to the north side. It was the landmark for the spring just as Sinkhole had described it, and it was no more than five miles from where he stood.

"There you go… can see it now. You ready for that, boy?"

His horse was lathered of sweat and his head hung in fatigue. Jericho untied the large canteen and took a long pull, then took off his hat and poured the remainder in it. He held it to the horse's snout, which had come up quickly with the scent of water. "Hurry up, boy, before it leaks out." His horse obliged him and sucked quickly for what he could get.

Jericho heard them before he saw them. His head snapped left to see the rising dust of the galloping horses a half mile away. Four Shoshones began yipping loudly at the air as they held a line right at him. His horse drank the last of the water from the hat just as a rifle shot rang out and spit up dust fifty feet in front of Jericho.

"Son of a bitch!" Jericho exclaimed. He jammed his water-cooled hat on his head and jumped to the saddle. "I know you're played out, boy, but we got'a git!"

Jericho kicked his horse a quick, hard shot, calling out, "Hyah! Hyah!" The horse hit top speed an instant later. Jericho reined toward the distant V and tucked tight and low to his animal's neck, hearing the wild sucking and exhaling of his horse giving everything as it pounded over the hard-packed earth. Jericho kept him running hard for a half mile, knowing the luck of having just watered him in a brief respite. He expected to hear more rifle shots from behind. They never came. Instead, he heard his horse's breathing quickly becoming ragged, accompanied by the feel of it tightening up with muscle fatigue. Jericho turned and looked over his shoulder. The Shoshones had broken off the chase toward a few wild mustangs that had abruptly appeared over a ridge to the north. He slowed his horse to a trot then a brisk walk.

"They wouldn't'a quit on us if they'd known how worn we are," Jericho said toward his horse's upright ears. "But they weren't passin' up those wild horses. That was a bit of good luck! And you sure ran, boy! Discouraged 'em, you did." He patted the horse's sweat-soaked neck.

An hour later, they approached the spring. Jericho looked carefully about before he stopped and dismounted. Predators, human and otherwise, sometimes held to such places in hiding, knowing something would be along in time.

The pool of water was wide and deep and clear, encircled by smooth granite shoreline. It butted up against a rock face at the base of a mountain, giving the appearance of being fed by a waterfall. Yet Jericho quickly discounted it, deciding it rose from underground. Jericho squatted down at the water's edge and cupped some to his mouth, expecting a brackish taste. But it tasted just like it looked, like good spring water.

He turned his horse loose to drink. Then he stripped down naked and put his revolvers and knife right at the shoreline before walking into the water and submerging for several seconds. The hottest time of the day vanished in the bound of water. Jericho swam the sixty-foot span of it, across and back, submerging and swimming underwater several times then breaking up like the creature of the spring,swimming the surface with a fast, powerful overarm stroke that he'd perfected as a boy. He'd spent many summer hours in the swimming holes of the Seedskeedee.

"We're puttin' up in the pines there… done for today," Jericho said as he dressed. His horse didn't look taken with the announcement but walked happily as Jericho led him a quarter mile on foot to the small forest of spruce and ponderosa. Jericho found the high ground with the best view then stripped the animal clean and gave him a ration of oats in the shade of the evergreens. Jericho stretched out on his bedroll with the last book Crow Talks had given him, *The Confidence Man*, by Herman Melville.

He read for half an hour before falling asleep in the shade of the hot afternoon. Wyanet came in a dream, calling to him from his wickiup with lures of good food and lovemaking, and then she vanished. Two hours later he was awake, eating more biscuits that Tombstone had provided, along with some jerked venison from his own food provisions. Then he read the afternoon away until he could glimpse the first star. The book was nearly finished so he put it down, deciding to keep the ending for another time. Sleep came easily as the evening began to cool.

****

It was black within the trees, requiring his full attention as he weaved his horse through the evergreens until they emerged from the forest. Then he could see ahead in the moonlight to the area where the spring resided. They trailed to it once again. Jericho dismounted at the shoreline and topped off a canteen while the horse drank. A half hour later, Jericho turned up into Sandy Pass and watched carefully as he held his horse to a walk, content with the pace until first light would offer better vision. It came shortly, giving Jericho his first look at the expanse of the pass. Its ground was pure sand and the walls sloped away from each other in a rocky ascent that had presented the V image from five miles away the day before.

The pass grew steeper as the morning came fuller. Jericho let the horse set his own pace up the steepest part of the climb to the crest. When the worst of the incline began to fade, his horse picked up the pace, knowing the hardest work was over. The ground finally flattened along the summit prompting his horse to a brisk walk.

Two riders came into view, approaching from the opposite direction around a bend on the pass. Jericho sized them up from a hundred feet. They were young men who didn't have the look of cowhands or anything other than unsavory, vagabond types. They wore two pistols each, white men who were brown with dirt and grime, dressed like outlaws and keenly watching him now. One said something to the other that Jericho could not hear from the distance. He zeroed in on their hands as they drew closer, waiting for any movement that might come. Jericho reined his horse to the right, wanting to give a wide berth and determine if they would try to make any play on him. They immediately reined in his direction and fanned out from each other flanking each side.

"Hold on, mister!" one of them called genially. "Just wanna ask you a question about the trail ahead."

Jericho took the reins with his left hand and dropped his right onto the butt of his pistol. They meant to stop him with their position as they drew closer. Jericho reined his horse to a stop then dropped his left hand alongside his other Navy Colt.

"What is it?" Jericho asked.

They stopped in front of him, one to his left and one to his right, both of them taking notice of his mild demeanor and posture to draw both guns. They moved their hands close to their guns.

"Well now, no need to get jumpy, mister. Just needin' to know if you passed a spring near where the pass commences?" the swarthier one asked.

"Yep," Jericho replied easy. "Two miles down… but I reckon you already know that."

The other man spoke up: "You're awful puny to be breakin' smart. Those pack bags look loaded heavy. Watcha got in there, smart boy?"

"I got nothin' in there," Jericho said, "and I'll be keepin' every bit of it."

In a flash of movement Jericho had pistols in each hand as they attempted to draw theirs but were way too late and froze at Jericho's advantage.

"Whup!" Jericho said with one gun trained on each man. "Get your hands off your pistols or I'll kill you both in one more second."

The men slowly moved their hands away from their guns. Jericho nodded his head to the left where they could clearly ride around him at a distance.

"Go on… get around there, nice and wide. Haul yourselves clear'a me and keep movin'. You look back… I'll be shootin' 'fore you lay eyes on me. Now git!"

"You made a bad mistake bracin' us, mister," the swarthy one said as they trotted their horses wide. "We'll be comin' for you."

Jericho fired a rapid burst, twice from each pistol, peppering the feet of the men's horses and causing the animals to jump to a momentary run. The diversion of the men's attention to their horses was long enough for Jericho to holster his pistols and skin his rifle to his shoulder. He drew a bead in their direction.

"I don't take to threats. You best shut your mouth and keep ridin'…'fore I split your heads like melons."

Jericho watched them trail away quickly and silently till they were gone from his vision several hundred feet down the pass.

34

Danny and Skinner rocked easy on the porch of the Cold Springs Station, smoking cigarettes and watching the northeastern horizon for the dust that would show when the 2 p.m. westbound was close. Skinner's fresh mount was tethered to the nearby hitching post. A light wind was afoot and thick clouds blocked the sun, keeping the warm afternoon from becoming blistering hot.

"You got an idea about what you'll do when the run gets shut down?" Danny asked Skinner.

"Hope we don't get shut down," Skinner said. "It ain't over till it's over. This is a damn good job… good money, open spaces, suits me good. I ain't leavin' till they run me out, and I reckon they won't do that unless they do. Then I'll believe it… not before."

Danny laughed. "Well, I don't want to believe it neither… but just supposin' that you was to do somethin' else?"

"I can cowboy good," Skinner said. "Might could give that a turn again. Know how to build some, too… framing and such. Maybe soldierin' now that war's brewin', North agin the South. Do they pay for soldierin'?"

Danny frowned in thought. "I don't know. They must pay somethin'. What side would you join?"

"Ain't got an idea about that," Skinner said.

"Well, where you from… North or South?" Danny asked.

"Kansas land… was a territory but I heard it's a state now."

"Hmm… that North or South?"

"Middle, I reckon," Skinner said. "Saw it on a map once… looked like the middle. Ain't you from Colorado Territory?"

"Yes, sir."

"That North or South?"

"West, I'm thinkin'," Danny said.

"Might be they wouldn't let us join either side," Skinner speculated. "I ain't got the first idea what they're fightin' about anyways."

"Abe Lincoln was just elected President," Danny proclaimed. "Stan told me he's on the side of the slaves… wants to free them. The South don't want to do that."

"Well, they ain't right!" Skinner declared. "One man should never be able to have another as a slave. Reckon I wouldn't take up for the South."

"Then you'll just have to take up the run… he's comin," Danny said, eyeing the rider that was a mile out, coming on at a gallop.

Skinner flicked his cigarette away and stood up, stretching a moment as he looked around. "What in hell is that?" he said, surprised by a large dust cloud that was rising in the west.

Danny stared. "Might be a herd… buffalo or somethin'. Not runnin' though. Comin' right from the direction you'll be goin' lickety split. You should get a good look at whatever it is."

"Then I best hope it ain't half the Indian nation," Skinner quipped.

Moments later, Hambone galloped into the yard and reined hard as he pushed off the saddlehorn and landed on the ground, running for a few steps to keep from tumbling.

"Hello boys!" Hambone sang out like he'd just arrived at a party.

Skinner already had the mochila off Hambone's mount and was walking briskly with it to his own. "Right on time, Hambone! Some good brisket and taters waitin'."

"I never keep women or brisket and taters waiting," Hambone

insisted jovially. "So what in creation is that?" he asked, looking to the rising dust in the west.

"That's the puzzlement of the moment," Skinner replied as he mounted up. "If you see me go down out there, come fetch my body!"

Skinner juiced his horse to an instant gallop out of the yard, on a direct line toward the rising dust. Danny walked Hambone's worn-out mount toward the barn to turn him out. Hambone suddenly figured he'd better keep watch on Skinner's progress, having taken his words about fetching his body half-seriously. Hambone opened the station door and fetched the spyglass hanging on the wall just inside. Then he stepped out to the edge of the porch and trained the glass on the dust, guessing it was perhaps three miles away. It was a mass of men on horses, riding in formation and dressed in the same colors. They were soldiers, maybe fifty or so, he figured. And they were riding toward the station at a trot. Skinner was still better than two miles away from them but probably knew they were men on horses by now, Hambone thought.

"You got something in your sights there, Hambone?" Stan asked as he and Hags came out the door.

"Bunch of soldiers comin' this way!"

"Yeah?" Hags asked.

"Give me that glass," Stan said, taking the single-eye telescope from Hambone.

"Can't tell what kind of soldiers they are," Hambone said.

"Have to be Union boys," Stan said as he began observing. "I don't believe there are any Rebs in this country."

"Rebs?… they the South?" Hambone asked.

"Yes… Confederate troops… Rebels," Stan said. "None around here yet, I don't believe."

"Whoever it is, Skinner ain't interested in seeing 'em up close… he's ridin' wide," Hags observed.

Hambone walked for the door. "I'm gettin' me some brisket and taters before any damn hungry soldiers show up."

Hags followed Hambone. "I'm gettin' some more shuteye before someone wants my cot."

Stan pulled out his pipe and took a seat in one of the rockers, taking up smoking and watching as the formation of men came on at a trot. Ten minutes later, sixty men arrived. Fifty-five of them were on horseback, another two drove wagons, and three more were mounted and led two pack-mules each. A sergeant at the front gave the command to halt at a hundred feet out. Then the leader trotted his horse up within ten feet of where Stan stood waiting a few feet off the porch. He wore a sword and a holster with a pistol, and his coat was lashed just in front of his saddle pommel. His eyes held intensely on Stan from underneath the brim of his hat.

"Good day, sir. I am Major Daniel Adams of the Second Regiment Cavalry, currently on orders out of Fort Churchill. This is Cold Springs Pony Express Station?"

"It is. I'm Stan Brock, the Station Keeper. What can I do for you?"

"Paiutes… any around these parts?" the major asked.

"Yes, sir," Stan said. "Paiutes… Shoshones… they travel this country from time to time, though they've been scarcer since Pyramid Lake. Shoshones seem to stay farther east… Paiutes more north or west."

Major Adams nodded. "Seen any Paiutes of late? I am looking for a particular tribe, maybe north of here a ways… or east."

"Particular tribe, eh?" Stan said. "No, can't say I've seen any lately. Some kind of trouble?"

"Maybe… maybe not. We just want to find their encampment and talk to them about their means. Do you know where any encampments are, past or present?"

Stan looked to the east then pointed at the mountains. "Desatoya

Mountains… there's a valley with a lake about eight miles there, then a couple more up a pass you'll find once you get closer. Our riders trail around the north end of the range… it's faster gettin' over to Edwards Creek Station… but we've had one or two that have trailed straight through ahead of schedule so took the slower route through the range. Plum beautiful I hear. They say the Indians call it The Valley of High Bloom and camp there from time to time. Don't know if they're Shoshones or Paiutes. Abundant game and a lake, they say."

Major Adams pulled a spyglass from his saddle bag and trained it on the range for a moment. He spoke as he kept looking through the glass. "What about encampments to the north?"

"Sure would be some north of here, but I don't know where," Stan said.

"What about your riders? Would any of them know?"

Stan shrugged. "Well, if they do, they haven't said anything to me about it. You can talk to them if you like. Got one sleepin' and one eatin'. Same with our tenders."

Major Adams lowered his spyglass and returned it to his saddle bag, staring at Stan as he did so. "We stopped in at Carson Sink yesterday. They said there was a Pony Express rider over this way that spent two months with a Paiute tribe healing up after getting shot by bandits who were trying to take a Paiute woman. A man named Jericho Buck? He rode for you?"

Stan held steady and relaxed. "His home station was Dry Creek, a hundred miles east of here."

"Was?" Adams asked, staring hard.

"That's right. He's not riding for us anymore."

Major Adams smirked cynically. "Is that because he's marrying the Paiute woman?"

"Maybe… maybe not," Stan dryly replied.

"Was he through here after he left the Paiutes?" the major asked.

"Yep, just for a night. Left for Genoa a week ago."

"Genoa? Did he say where the Paiute encampment was that he was healing up at?"

Stan shot a look of thought. "The scrape he got into saving the woman happened in the Valley of High Bloom… there in the Desatoyas. He said he was mostly unconscious going from there to wherever the encampment was, but he said it was northwest, toward the Augusta range."

Major Adams looked incredulous. "Hell! He was a Pony Express rider… knows direction… landmarks! He has to know where he came from when he rode out!"

"Likely does," Stan said. "But he didn't tell the specifics and we wasn't askin'. Could be he wouldn't say anyway."

"Why not?" Adams demanded.

"A man's business is his own," Stan said. "But I'd say he's partial to them, especially the woman. Likely doesn't care to make their whereabouts public knowledge. You could ask him yourself, but knowing Jericho, you might not get a polite answer."

"I *will* ask him!" Adams declared. "Why'd he go to Genoa?"

"There you go again," Stan said with a light air.

Major Adams cracked to a look of anger. "I am the United States Army. You tell me what you know when I ask you a question. That's an order, mister."

Stan nodded calmly. "You don't give orders here, Major. We're the United States Pony Express, carrying United States mail and vital government communications. If Union armies out here receive orders from the president, we'll be the ones delivering them. I don't answer to you unless I care to, which I am happy to do unless you start ordering me."

Major Adams grimaced and nodded his understanding.

Stan struck a match and relit his pipe. "Jericho's got relations in

Genoa. Said he wanted to do a little more wandering, too. See the Sierras… maybe California."

Adams looked around in thought for a moment then looked to Stan. "You can direct my men as to how to find that pass up to the Valley of High Bloom?"

"Got a man inside who can," Stan replied.

"Good. We would like to water our horses and camp a night here… out of your way."

"You're welcome to. The spring is around back. Camp wherever you want… just clear of the yard on the side there where our riders and horses switch out," Stan said.

"Sergeant Cooper!" Adams called out to his men.

A stout-looking man put his horse to a lope and arrived in front of Adams seconds later.

"Yes, sir?" the sergeant said.

Major Adams pointed to the Desatoyas. "There's a valley in those mountains that has a lake. Take Corporal Dunn and ten men and a night's provisions and go scout it for any Indian encampments. If you find any, do not approach, do not engage except in defense of retreat, but determine through a glass or otherwise whether they're Shoshones or Paiutes. Be back in the morning. We'll camp here. Shouldn't be but a two-hour ride. A man will be out in a minute to tell you how to find the pass."

"Yes, sir."

35

The trail into Carson City showed the grandeur of the Sierra Nevada range as a backdrop, just miles to the west, towering above all in evergreen and jagged peaks that beckoned to the land of milk and honey beyond in California. Jericho turned onto Main Street as afternoon fingers of sunlight stretched up alleys and divided the shadows on the thoroughfare, busy with people and commerce. The banner that spanned the street immediately caught his eye: *Carson City, Capital of Nevada Territory!* Jericho abruptly reined up at a mercantile where a few men sat upon benches and barrels on the boardwalk in front, watching the action of the street. He didn't dismount but reined close enough to be heard.

"Hey! Is this the capital city?" he asked toward the street-watching men.

One old coot drawing on his pipe chuckled and pointed to the banner. "That's what it says, sonny!"

Jericho smiled, "Yes, sir, I can see that. I was told the capital was Genoa!"

"Was till a month ago," another old-timer replied.

"Obliged," Jericho said then put his horse to a walk up the street.

He took it all in, excited by the action. There were stores of every kind, clothes and leather goods, mercantiles with sundries, furniture, a gunsmith, a butcher, a bathhouse, a barber, foodstuffs, an undertaker, saloons and gambling, dining halls, an assayer, a bank, a hotel, a sheriff's office, a courthouse, a land office, and much more. He rode the length of the street and meandered up side streets just to see it all. Then he reined into the livery where the sign at the entrance said, *David Perkins, Proprietor.* A man sat in a rocker just inside the barn door while two teenage boys brushed out horses in different stalls.

"Mister Perkins?" Jericho asked.

"Yep," Perkins replied as he stood up.

"Can ya care for my horse?"

"Yep… four bits a day, water, oat feed, and brush. How long you staying?"

"Don't know that yet but I reckon it could be upwards of a week… or more. I'll pay in advance for a week."

"Then you got a stall, mister," Perkins replied. "You want to leave him now?"

"Yes, sir. Hey, does the Sierra Hotel have good beds?" Jericho asked excitedly.

"They'll do. The Warm Springs Hotel is better… mile east of town. Twice as much though."

"I'd rather be in town," Jericho replied as he dismounted.

Perkins stared at the saddle a moment. "You Pony Express?"

"I was. Movin' on now."

Perkins gave a look as if unsure why Jericho would still have the saddle. "You know there's a station here, behind Davis Mercantile," Perkins offered.

"I know there's a station here… didn't know it's behind a mercantile. My run was from Dry Creek, west to Cold Springs. Cold Springs is a dozen stations east of here. Hey, you know if the bank's still open?"

"It closed at three o'clock. Opens at seven."

Jericho slung the pack bags onto his shoulder and grabbed his rifle from the scabbard. He fished in his pocket and brought out his silver. "Here's for six nights," he said, handing three silver dollars to Perkins. "What are your hours?"

"Five a.m. to six p.m. Sunday morning from six to seven only."

Jericho nodded and extended his hand. "Thank you, Mister Perkins. I'll be around. My name is Jericho Buck."

"Good to know you, Jericho," Perkins said as he shook Jericho's hand. "Clay, come get Mister Buck's horse and strip him. Put him in the end stall."

Jericho crossed the street and walked along the boardwalk, nodding to folks and taking in the storefronts, getting an up-close look at all the fine things for sale. He liked the shirt in the window of a clothing store, so he ducked in and bought it, and a pair of pants, socks, and underwear, too. The merchants were intrigued with the young man who was heavily laden with pack bags, twin holsters, and a Sharps rifle in his left hand. But he managed the purchase inside of five minutes and left with both hands now occupied.

The Sierra Hotel was two stories with a double-door entrance. Farther on down the boardwalk from where Jericho was about to enter, Sadie McDown and Becky Harper caught sight of him for the last twenty feet before he turned in.

"Ain't he the handsome one," Sadie said.

"Yes he is!" Becky agreed. "Not of much stature, but he's put together and looks to be all man. He could stand a bath and some clean clothes."

"He's carrying new duds in his hand. I'll give him the bath," said Sadie.

Becky laughed. "Maybe he'd cook you a meal. Those bags look like they're weighted with iron skillets."

Jericho registered at the hotel desk then climbed the stairs to his room. Inside, he put the pack bags down easy and slid them under the bed. Then he lay down just to consider the mattress.

"Ahhh, that's a fine feel. Been a long time waitin' on this again," he said in a state of bliss. But a moment later he was up collecting his new clothes and a few personals before he left and locked his door, heading for the bathhouse half a block away.

A deep red sunset painted the western sky when Jericho emerged from the bathhouse an hour later, clean and shaved with combed hair that was still wet. He carried his hat and dropped his dirty clothes off at the hotel laundry, wondering why they had a laundry service but not their own baths. "Bet that Warm Springs Hotel out'a town has their own baths," he mumbled to himself. Then he realized how hungry he was.

"I'll have the biggest steak you got and whatever comes with it," he told the waitress before she could say anything.

"Okay darlin'," she said.

Jericho waxed realization. "Oh, almost forgot! Your sign out front said cold beer. Is it really cold?"

She smiled seductively. "It'll make you wanna put on a coat, sweet pea."

"Well then, bring the biggest one'a those you got, too. And if you see it empty, you just go ahead and bring another!"

"I'll do that little thing," she said.

Jericho ate it all, aided by two beers and a piece of apple pie for good measure. Then as twilight faded toward darkness, he walked the street again, passing the land office and the assayer's office and taking notice of their respective hours. When he came upon the Silver Strike Saloon, the piano music and rollicking sounds drew him in for a look. He was tired and figured watching the festivities for awhile with a whiskey and a smoke would cap the evening nicely.

Sadie was sitting in the corner with a man when she saw Jericho walk in. Her eyes immediately went to him, recognizing him from earlier on the boardwalk. She watched him walk to the end of the bar and order.

Jericho had just lit his smoke and taken a sip from his double-shot glass when she nudged him from his blind side, pushing her breast against his arm and brushing his thigh with her hand. He quickly turned to see her pretty young face just inches from his own.

"Hi cowboy," she cooed. "I saw you earlier going into the hotel… before your bath and clean clothes. You looked good then. You look better now."

Jericho stood stunned a moment, just staring at her, taken by her painted beauty. She pressed in a little harder.

"I'm not a cowboy, ma'am," he finally said.

Sadie shrugged, "It doesn't matter… buy me a drink?"

"Yes, ma'am, whatever you like."

"My, you're handsome *and* polite. I'll have what you're having. My name's Sadie… what's yours?"

"Jericho," he replied then called to the bartender. "A whiskey for the lady."

The bartender brought the bottle and a glass and poured as Jericho dug in his pocket for silver. But he brought out a few twenty-dollar gold pieces in his search, and also inadvertently pulled out his room key with the tag on it that identified his room as number 7. Sadie's eyes took it all in. Jericho found the two bits for the drink and put it on the bar.

"You should have him leave the bottle," said Sadie.

Jericho glanced at her then looked at the half-full bottle. "How much for the rest of the bottle?" he asked the bartender.

"Dollar and a half," the barkeep replied.

Jericho put the silver on the bar then turned to Sadie with a smile. "I'll have one more with ya, and that'll be it for me. I got business in the morning. The bottle's yours."

She took a drink and nudged against him again. "Why don't we take that bottle and go to your room. For two dollars I'll turn you inside-out for as long as you can take it… and I got an idea you can take it all night."

Jericho laughed and nodded. "With a girl as pretty as you, I believe I could! But my heart belongs to another… so I'll just have a drink with ya."

Sadie frowned. "It's not your heart I want. You're handsome enough I might give it to you for free."

Jericho smiled. "You're pretty enough I'd'a given you five dollars."

She laughed and they drank and talked for another quarter hour as she kept at it with her cooing and touching, hoping she could rope him. But he wasn't having it.

"I sure thank ya for makin' this the best time I've had today… but I'm done in. Good night," Jericho said.

"Wait!" she exclaimed. "I think I'll go home, too. I live close by… would you walk me?"

"Sure will, Sadie," Jericho said.

As they headed for the exit, Sadie's friend Becky walked in. Sadie didn't want to stop and visit, but Becky did. She remembered Jericho from when she and Sadie had seen him earlier. Becky stopped directly in front of them, giving Jericho an appraisingly seductive once-over from head to toe.

"Did you give him his bath?" Becky asked Sadie musingly, "'cause he sure cleaned up sweeter than honey."

"No, Becky!" Sadie answered, irritated.

Becky smiled at Jericho. "If you still got a hankering later, come see me, cowboy. I'm Becky… and I'm better."

"I'm not a cowboy, ma'am," Jericho said as Sadie took his arm and pulled Jericho around Becky and out the door.

The moon had not yet risen in the cloudless sky, yielding a night that was black and brilliant with stars. They slowly walked a block, her arm hooked to his in escort fashion.

"My place is at the end of this alley," said Sadie. She gently guided him off Main Street into the narrow lane that showed faint window light from the end, but deep darkness in between. Sadie began talking incessantly about the recent onset of hot weather as they entered the darkest part of the alley, all the while holding tightly to Jericho's arm. Jericho could no longer see the ground in front of him.

"A man could walk right off a cliff here if he didn't know there was ground ahead," Jericho said. He reached for his pocket. "I'll light a match so we can..."

The club came from behind with brutal force, hitting Jericho directly on the back-top of his head. He collapsed in the darkness.

"He's got a lot of money in his pockets," Sadie said. "Get his hotel key, too. He carried heavy-lookin' bags when he checked in... might be money or such in his room... if we got time to look."

"We got time. I hit 'im hard," said Petey Jenkins. "Killed 'im maybe."

"Jesus, Petey! We better get shut of this town tonight!"

"Suits me," Petey said. "A month here's been long enough."

36

Jericho gained consciousness in the dark alley where he lay face down. He groaned and rolled over, remembering he had been walking with Sadie. His head hurt. He felt the wet, sticky matting of his hair and knew he'd been hit and had bled. "Sadie!" he called, wondering if she was lying nearby. His eyes were better adjusted now and he saw nothing around him except his hat. He grabbed it then got to his feet and continued to the end of the alley where Sadie said her place was. He glanced in the faintly lit window and took in what seemed to be a clockmaker's living quarters and workshop. The man sat in an easy chair reading by lamplight, surrounded by numerous clocks on the walls and counter that all showed 10 o'clock. Jericho remembered the saloon clock had read 9:20 when he'd left with Sadie. He reached in his pockets. They were empty.

Jericho ran to his hotel and found the front desk vacant. He bounded up the stairs and ran to his room. The door was unlocked. His heart sank as he entered and saw the window open and the lantern lit. His rifle was gone from the bureau. Jericho immediately fell to the floor and looked under the bed. His pack bags were gone.

"Goddammit!" he yelled, feeling a rage welling up in him. He turned his head the other direction and looked under the bureau. They hadn't seen his gunbelt. He grabbed it then jumped to his feet and looked out the window, guessing his pack bags had been dropped to the alley below. Jericho strapped on his two Navy Colts and felt his knife in his belt sheath. He poured water in the bowl then wet the washcloth and quickly cleaned the blood from where it had run onto his ears and face from the back of his head. The swollen lump on his head had stopped bleeding. He put his hat on, then checked the inside top of his boot for his emergency pouch. It was there. He took half the coins from it and left the rest in his boot. And then he was gone.

Jericho strode into the Silver Strike Saloon like a bull on the prod. He saw Becky sitting toward the back with an older dude who was dressed and mannered like a banker. Jericho walked right to the table.

"Hey, girl… how 'bout that invite? I'm ready and able," Jericho said like a man who wouldn't be denied.

The dude immediately spoke up: "See here young man! This lady and I…"

"Shut up, mister, or you'll need a new suit," Jericho said.

The dude cowered in the face of Jericho's stare that appeared crazed.

"C'mon Becky, let's go," Jericho said, holding his hand out to her.

She took his hand and they walked out the door.

"I guess you been thinkin' about me," Becky said as they turned up the boardwalk. "I like it when I have that effect on a man… especially one as handsome as you. It's gonna be good, honey."

Jericho stopped at the end of the block and turned to her. "Where's your friend Sadie live?"

"Hey, what is this?" Becky asked.

Jericho spoke coolly. "She set me up… robbed me with help from someone else. I can't abide that. You're her friend. Where's she live?"

"Look, I only known her a month or so. She showed up here

with her manager boyfriend, Petey Jenkins. He's a bad one… cut me up if I spilled on her."

"Don't trouble your mind with Petey Jenkins. His number's up," Jericho said. Then he put a twenty-dollar gold piece in her hand. "Tell me where she lives… and don't you lie, girl, or you'll never see me comin'."

She looked at him, suddenly more fearful of what he might be capable of. "You promise you won't ever tell?" Becky asked, nearly in tears.

"Never."

Becky forced a pained smile, resigned to the notion that she had to tell. "I only been there once. They got a cabin about a mile out the Berdon Trail. Leave the south end of town on the trail to Genoa. Half a mile out, turn west where an old burned-out wagon sits… you'll see the trail… it's well worn and that wagon's just a marker for it. Go another half mile and it'll be on your left, back in the trees… little frame cabin painted red."

Jericho ran for the livery, knowing either the proprietor, David Perkins, or one of his employees lived behind the livery barn. Jericho figured that one way or another he would get his horse in a hot minute.

****

Petey had just seen what was in the pack bags but hadn't told Sadie yet. They had been so jubilant with finding over eighty dollars in Jericho's pockets that Petey hadn't even bothered to start going through the packs in Jericho's room. They were lashed closed with some kind of special knots that Petey didn't want to mess with right then. He just wanted to get out of the hotel and would see what all the heavy contents were back at the cabin. But now he was in a hot dash. Sadie was gathering her things.

"Hurry up, Sadie. We gotta light a shuck. I mean right now!" Petey said, anxious.

Sadie stopped packing her bag and turned to look at Petey. She'd never seen him quite so rattled. "You said we had time… you said you killed him likely!"

"Well, I hit him hard! But if he ain't dead, he'll be lookin'! Sure fire he's got partners, too! You was stopped by the door, jawin' with Becky when I left the Silver Strike. She's been here before! She could tell 'im!"

"What are you sayin'?" Sadie pressed. "Did you look in those bags yet?"

"Just now!" Petey blurted out. "Put a lantern to 'em loading the buckboard. Under his personals there's a gunnysack full of gold in each pack… gold, Sadie! Thousands of dollars' worth! There's more than just him on this! They'll be others lookin'! That's what I'm saying! We got to make a run for it right now! Sacramento or San Francisco… we can get lost in crowds that big! Let's go!"

Sadie was stunned at the news. But most of all, she knew Petey was scared about how soon someone might be coming, and just who, or how many, it might be. She immediately pulled her bag shut, not bothering with another thought other than getting gone.

"I'm ready!" she yelled as she ran for the door.

The moon was up now and nearly full as Petey drove the buckboard out of the trees and onto the trail. They had to get back to the junction where the burned-out wagon marked the turn for Genoa. Petey put the two-horse team to a gallop in the bright moonlight as Sadie gripped the seat handle with all her might, fighting to remain on the seat as they bumped and jerked at high speed. Then they saw the junction ahead and continued at a gallop until they got close. Petey slowed the team for the turn, feeling a measure of relief as he reined the horses onto the Genoa trail.

"Someone on a horse!" Sadie cried with panic, looking back up the trail from Carson City.

Petey craned his head around and saw the rider behind, coming on at a gallop. The rider did not turn on to Berdon Trail but kept straight on the Genoa Trail behind them. And he was gaining on them.

"Take the reins!" Petey yelled.

Sadie took the reins and began flapping them hard, yelling "Get now! Get now!"

Petey reached down to the floorboard and grabbed the Sharps rifle under his feet. It was Jericho's rifle and it was loaded. But Petey had no ammo for it, so one shot was all he'd get and then it would be his pistol and knife. Petey turned and kneeled on the floorboard, resting the rifle over the seatback as he tried to draw a bead. The buckboard bumped about, bringing panic to Petey as he realized his slim chances of hitting the rider. He'd never been a very good shot anyway. Petey had never been much good at anything other than thievery and graft and mistreating women.

He cocked the rifle and aimed the best he could as a fleeting sense of his life played in a lingering moment. Then he fired. The black powder explosion of the misfire took half of Petey's face off and sent him tumbling across Sadie's lap. She involuntarily pulled the reins to the right as she screamed at Petey's black, bloody head before her eyes. She continued screaming as the buckboard left the trail at high speed. Then the rear left wheel hit the tall rock, sending the buckboard airborne in a side flip over rocky ground. Sadie and Petey took flight from the seat, being thrown clear of where the wagon crashed upside down. But their landings were head-first amongst a patch of rocks that took Sadie's life and merely confirmed the end of Petey Jenkins.

Jericho reined up and dismounted, quickly determining there was nothing to be done for Sadie and Petey. He cut the harness straps of the team and freed the horses, then searched the site and found his pack bags and other personals, pitched about when the wagon flipped. He collected his money from Petey's pockets, just as Petey had collected it from his.

Jericho mounted up and headed back to town, shaking from the bad ending for Sadie and the fact that he'd almost blown his whole mission.

37

Milton Summerdill opened the back door of the assay office at 7 a.m. sharp and let the guards in. A minute later he unlocked the front door from inside and poked his head out.

"Do you have business, young man?" Milton asked Jericho, who was sitting on a bench just outside the front door.

Jericho stood up with the packs. "Yes, sir, I do."

Milton eyed the packs with intrigue. "I am Milton Summerdill, the assayer. Come in."

Jericho entered and walked past the two heavily-armed guards who looked like they knew their business well. He arrived at the counter where Milton had already taken up position on the other side. Jericho hoisted the packs up onto the counter and pulled the flap open on one. He untied the top of the gunnysack and pulled out a handful of nuggets, holding them open-palmed in front of Milton.

"I need to know the grade and value of this," Jericho said.

Milton stared at the nuggets then peered in the pack at the top of the gunnysack filled with more of the same. "You have more in the other bag, too?" Milton asked.

"Yep," Jericho said, noting the surprise on Milton's face.

Milton nodded. He looked past Jericho to the guards by the front door and said, "Bill, put the 'back soon' sign out and lock the door."

The guard nodded.

"Bring your bags and follow me," Milton said. He led Jericho through a door to a back room where several narrow, high transom windows let in enough morning light to clearly see the large vault, work counters, and shelves that held scales and a variety of tools, small and large, as well as a few dozen bottles, jars, and cans of various chemicals and compounds. Milton walked to a freight scale.

"Put your sacks on the scale please, Mister…?"

"Buck… Jericho Buck."

Jericho pulled the gunnysacks from the packs and placed them on the scale then watched as Milton tapped the weight along the balance arm until it dropped off the top-stop and suspended just above the bottom-stop.

Milton turned to Jericho with wide eyes, his spectacles magnifying their size to that of small peaches. "Mister Buck, you have eighty-three and a half pounds here," Milton said. "I can ascertain a preliminary karat rating with a few samples, but in order to certificate it for money conversion I'll have to test all of it. That will take some time… a week maybe. The charge will be significant… perhaps two hundred dollars with materials used."

"Go ahead on then," Jericho said.

Milton nodded and took a few nuggets from one of the gunnysacks. "It looks to be good ore by the naked eye," he said. Then he poured solution to a pan and began inspecting one of the nuggets with an eyepiece.

Ten minutes later, Milton announced, "Those nuggets are all ninety-two-percent pure and rate as twenty-two karat… good enough to mint coins. If it all holds up to that purity, your gold will have a worth of approximately twenty-seven thousand dollars."

Jericho swallowed hard, trying to remain calm at the verdict of such a fortune. "Well, if it takes a week to get this figured out, will it be safe here or do I need to haul it back and forth from the bank every day?"

Milton answered, "Of course, it is your choice, Mister Buck, but I would not advise moving it back and forth, lest it become known what you have… and your fortune and life become imperiled by those who would have it. I am sworn to secrecy. If no one else yet knows, no one *will* know unless you inform them. I have never been robbed. My iron chest weighs four thousand pounds. This building had to be built around it. There are no guarantees in life beyond death and taxes, but I believe it would be safest to leave it here until my work is done. Then I will make you an offer to buy your gold, and you can decide what you wish to do. I'm the largest and most reputable assayer in the territory… backed by Carson City Bank here, and San Francisco City Bank. I've been here since the founding in '58 and I've assayed more of the Comstock Lode than anyone. In any event, I will provide you a certificate of appraisal and valuation at the completion, and a receipt right now for the weight and preliminary assay result. You can trust me, son."

"Yes, sir, it seems I'll have to," said Jericho. "Tell me, what happens if someone just puts a gun to your head and tells you to open your four-thousand-pound iron chest?"

Milton's eyebrows hiked. "My guards are ex-army, decorated fighting men. They work by particular rules. We are on Main Street in the middle of town. The sheriff has two full-time deputies… hardened men… and there's a town militia that responds to any disturbance anywhere in town faster than you can imagine. Since '58, sixteen men have been shot dead here for trying one thing or another. But as I said, there are no guarantees… except for my own integrity. That, I pledge."

Jericho nodded his approval. "All right, Mister Summerdill… let's get 'er goin'."

****

The young man wore spectacles and had his hair perfectly parted and slicked across his head with hair tonic. But it was his string bowtie worn on a white shirt that gave him an official appearance as he sat at his desk reviewing a survey map. He looked up when Jericho walked through the door at 7:45 a.m., having come directly from the assayer's office.

"Good morning, sir. May I help you?" he asked Jericho.

"I surely do hope so," Jericho replied. "The sign out front says this is the Federal Land Office. Is this where I find out about buyin' government land in Nevada Territory?"

"Yes, sir."

Jericho waxed a bit uncertain as he looked at the proper young man before him whom he guessed to be a year or two younger than himself. It seemed a far departure from the likes of middle-aged, professionally sagacious Milton Summerdill, but Jericho pressed on: "Well, I'd like to find out about buyin' land in what used to be Millard County of Utah Territory. I don't know what the county name is now that it's Nevada Territory."

The young man sat up a little straighter. "Well, sir, county names for Nevada Territory have not yet been established, so we would reference anything that falls within the new Nevada Territory to its previous Utah Territory county name. It would still be called Millard County. If you will wait just a moment, I will see if Mister Riley is free to see you."

"Much obliged," Jericho said, duly impressed.

A moment later, Jericho was escorted into another office where an older, fatter, cigar-smoking man stood from behind his desk and extended his hand to shake Jericho's.

"I'm Barney Riley... pleased to make your acquaintance."

Jericho shook his hand. "Jericho Buck... good to know ya."

Barney spoke and puffed his cigar as he sat back down. "My clerk tells me you're interested in land of Millard County. There's plenty of it. It's as big and vast as counties come. The Nevada Territory east line of it ends at the hundred and sixteenth meridian. If what you want is east of that you'll have to talk to the land office of Utah Territory in Salt Lake City. If you can identify the area you're interested in on the big map there, we'll know if you're in the right office or not."

"I'm sure as the sun comin' up… the land I'm interested in is Nevada Territory," Jericho said, staring at the Nevada Territory map that Barney was referring to. It took up most of one wall at eight feet wide, showing the location of known towns and settlements, rivers, lakes, mountain ranges, forests, and other topographical features, all transected by meridians and base lines. But there amongst it all were the tiny features that caught Jericho's eye and arrested his attention, the Pony Express stations of the territory. "I reckon that's the biggest, finest map I ever saw!" Jericho declared as he walked up to it for closer inspection.

"Yes, it's quite a map," Barney agreed. "It took the cartographer a month to draw it, using interpretive and actual surveys. Are you seeking a hundred and sixty acres through the Preemption Act? You can claim unsurveyed government land and occupy and improve it, guaranteeing a price of a dollar and twenty-five cents per acre. Or, it is said that a new act is coming, called the Homestead Act. It will provide one hundred and sixty acres with the same requirements as the Preemption Act… except for money… none needed, the land is free."

"Sure sounds like a good deal for someone… but I'm interested in more land than that," Jericho said.

"Well then, young man, circumstances are in your favor. The federal government is eager to sell land and promote western expansion. Tell me what you have in mind."

Jericho had found the Cold Creek Pony Express Station on the map and was looking at the mountain range directly to the north. He knew it held the basin where his Paiute tribe was encamped.

Wyanet had called it Swift River Valley, though the rendering of the mountain range on the map showed no river or valley. Jericho knew the interior of the range had never been surveyed. And he knew he was right because of where it sat in relation to the Valley of High Bloom and Cold Springs Station, both of which were on the map in proper proximity to each other.

"I reckon these lines goin' up and down and side to side make up the borders. How big is each one'a these boxes?" Jericho asked.

Barney rose from his desk and walked to the map. "Yes, the meridians are going up and down and the ones side to side are baselines… or ranges. Meridians are six miles apart as are the baselines, so each box is six miles wide by six miles high, or thirty-six square miles. The boxes are known as townships, and each has twenty-three thousand and forty acres. That's the easiest explanation… but they're numbered as township and range, indicating their relationship to prime meridians for the sake of identifying each of those boxes. And each township is further subdivided into sections. A section is one square mile. So there's thirty-six sections in each township, and each section is six hundred and forty acres. Then each section is subdivided into quarters… four quarters per section that are one hundred and sixty acres each. Are you confused yet?"

Jericho nodded, "Like a goat in a chicken coop."

"Why don't you show me where the land is you're interested in," Barney said.

Jericho put his finger on the box that he knew would include the Swift River Valley and the Paiute gold mine. "Right there," Jericho declared.

"You'd like a section, or maybe half a section of that township?" Barney asked.

"No, I'd like the whole box… the township."

Barney's cigar tip glowed red as he drew deeply on the stogie.

Then he blew out a long, thin stream of smoke and looked at Jericho with a frown. "Son, a township is thirty-six sections. That's thirty-six square miles."

"Yes," Jericho said, "that was the only part I wasn't confused about."

Barney smiled. "Well, the government usually gets a dollar and a quarter per acre. Maybe you could get it for less because it's barren mountain wilderness to hell and gone away from everything. But that would still be many thousands of dollars. Why would you want to buy that country? Have you ever seen it?"

"Sure have," Jericho said, pointing to Cold Springs Station on the map. "I rode for the Pony Express… from Cold Springs over to Dry Creek." Jericho traced his finger east to the final Pony Express Station on the Nevada Territory map. "I know all that land, and I know that box! Good huntin'… good water… a place where a mountain man could be left alone to live out his days in peace."

"Well, that township is unsurveyed," said Barney. "Normally it would have to be surveyed before it's sold, but a buyer could waive that requirement at their own risk if they were confident of what's there. Surveying a mountain township is a big, big job."

"How do I buy that township if I want to?" Jericho asked.

"You would have to prove that you have at least half the funds for the size parcel you want, based on a dollar and twenty-five cents per acre. For a township, you would have to document by bank letter or other means, that you have at least fourteen thousand, four hundred dollars. Can you do that?"

"Yes, sir, I can."

"Then I would schedule an auction with one week's notice, and a description of the parcel being auctioned," said Barney. "Those interested can come here and see the location of the parcel on this map. Then if you win the auction, the sale must be approved by the territorial legislature. But since we don't have one yet, all sales are approved by the governor of the territory, Brad Danforth. Once approved, the sale is recorded and a quit claim deed is issued by the recorder, and signed by the governor."

"I'll bring proof of the money tomorrow," Jericho said.

38

Pooch galloped into the Cold Springs Station yard and threw down hard on a dime, dismounting in a cloud of dust. "Man alive… glad to be here!" he said, happy to be done with his run.

Billy took the reins of Pooch's horse as Hambone stripped the mochila and headed for his own horse.

"Looks like you outrode that storm," Billy opined, looking toward the western dark clouds from where Pooch had just come.

"Either that or he got wind-dried already," Hambone speculated as he put the mochila on his horse.

"Damned if you ain't right, Hambone," Pooch said. "Got rained on a while back but already dried up. Now I'm gonna feed up."

"One of your great talents!" Hambone said as he mounted up and then juiced his horse to a gallop heading east.

Pooch walked in the station and got himself a plate as Hags sat in one of the easy chairs reading an old newspaper.

"Where is everybody?" Pooch asked.

"They're all sleepin'," Hags answered. "Stan, Clyde, and Sinkhole."

"I'll be joinin' 'em shortly," Pooch chuckled. "Say, what happened with all them Army boys?"

Hags shrugged. "That posse they sent up the Desatoyas didn't find nothin' of Paiutes… so that major headed north with the whole soldier outfit. They're hard up to find 'em… Jericho too. They know he could lead 'em to that Paiute camp."

"It'll be hard to find Jericho up north when he's gone to Genoa," said Pooch.

"Yep, they'll have some Army boys lookin' for 'im there. Stan says that major sent a letter with our westbound... orders for somebody back that way to find Jericho in Genoa."

"You figure they'd drag Jericho back here just to show them where those Paiutes are hole up?" Pooch asked.

"That's what it looks like."

"Meanwhile that major just keeps lookin'? Wonder why they're so fired up over them Paiutes? Nobody said anything about them killin' or robbin' lately, did they?" Pooch asked.

Hags shrugged again. "Nope... just something about their 'means'... anybody's guess as to what that means."

****

Barney Riley walked into Diamond Jim's Saloon and Steak House and scanned the room. He saw the back of a balding head in a booth at the rear corner of the room.

"Greetings, Governor," Barney announced as he came to a stop at the booth where Governor Danforth was presently devouring a T-bone steak. The town's most popular harlot, nicknamed Legs Wrappin', sat across from him, leaning a bit forward with sumptuous cleavage that beckoned like a side dish to his steak and trimmings.

"Good day, Barney," the governor replied, looking up with stuffed cheeks and a busy mouth that continued working the present bite. "What can I do for you?"

"A word?" Barney said.

The governor continued chewing and nodded at Legs, who took the cue and exited the booth. Barney sat down opposite the governor, knowing he'd be competing with the steak for attention to the issue at hand.

"I've got a live one," Barney began, "a young man who wants to buy a township in a mountain range a hundred and fifty miles or so east of here."

The governor looked up from cutting his next bite. "A township? That's a hell of a lot of land, Barney. Does he have the money?"

"Enough for me to schedule an auction. The notices are up. He brought me a letter of credit today from Carson City Bank saying he had the requisite funds."

"How much is that?"

"Fourteen thousand, four hundred dollars… half of the dollar twenty-five per acre on a township."

"What about this land?" the governor asked.

"Unremarkable in every sense," Barney said. "Part of the Augusta Range… arid mountain range that's likely two day's ride south of the California Trail… and the same north of the Old Spanish Trail. It's desolate. This kid rode for the Pony Express between Cold Springs and Dry Creek. That's how he knows it… or came to find it. He says there's a valley up in there with good water and game where a mountain man could live out his days in peace."

The governor frowned. "You believe that shit? The Virginia Mountains were unremarkable, too, till Henry Comstock happened along."

"Well, why would this kid buy a whole township? Twenty-three thousand acres?" Barney quipped. "Hell, he could just file a mining claim for virtually nothing. Even if he *was* a dumb bastard, every dumb bastard west of the Mississippi knows that much after Sutter's Mill and Henry Comstock. He ain't quite that dumb."

"All right… point taken. But where'd he get that kind of money?" the governor asked. "He didn't make it riding for the Pony Express."

"You know I couldn't ask him that… but he did offer that it

was family money left to him by a grandfather in Texas who made a fortune in beef."

"Has he got more than the fourteen four?"

It was Barney's turn to frown. "Well, if he offered that up, we'd know he was a dumb bastard. And J.C. Bibble wouldn't tell me if I held a branding iron to his forehead. He wouldn't risk an ethics violation for his bank. Maybe *you* could squeeze that information out of him."

"That prig son of a bitch wouldn't tell me what day of the week it is," the governor said and then stuffed another bite in his mouth, chewing it like it was the banker's throat.

"Well, I think the kid is just what he says he is… a man who's found his piece of heaven and wants to buy it," Barney said. "I'd be surprised if anybody else shows up for the auction. A few will drop in during the week for a look at it on the map… but it's too big, too unknown, too far away and too much money even at half price. We don't know what he's able to pay or willing to pay, but we sure don't want to lose him."

"That's a fact, Barney," the governor said. "We need that kind of money. Still, perhaps we should survey it first so we know what we're selling."

"A survey like that would take a hell of a long time at substantial costs."

The governor chewed his bite and looked up at the ceiling in thought. "Even fourteen-four is a lot of money. We need it! Start the bidding at a dollar twenty-five an acre. Maybe he'll pay the twenty-eight, eight. If not, drop the price in increments of a thousand. I'll have someone there to bid in at twenty… if it gets that low. See if we can spur him."

Barney's eyebrows went up. "We could lose him."

"No… we won't lose him. And twenty-one is much sweeter than fourteen-four."

Barney nodded, "All right... The auction is a week from tomorrow, at my office, 10 a.m."

39

Jericho lay low the next few days. He stayed out of the saloons and rested up, reading two dime novels he bought at the mercantile. One was about mountain men and the other about gunfighters. He loved the sensationalism of each and was thoroughly entertained, quickly deciding he would buy every dime novel they had just before he left. The mercantile stocked at least a dozen of them. *Crow Talks and Wyanet will find these a hoot,* he thought to himself.

After two days of napping and reading while laid out in bed, he was plenty rested and itchy to move. He'd heard about the lake and knew where the trail was, so he set out to see it early on a new day. The trail led through towering pines thick enough to keep the sun off a man for near all of the five miles to the lake. Then he came out of the forest to view the entire expanse of Lake Tahoe, shimmering blue for miles, with shoreline of evergreens, and the massive, beautifully imposing Sierra Nevada Mountains to the west.

"Lord Almighty!" Jericho uttered to himself. "That's the biggest lake I ever saw. Most beautiful, too."

He dismounted and lit a cigarette then sat on a large rock at the water's edge and took in all the sights. There were a few rowboats a quarter mile out occupied with fishermen. A dozen or so more people were trying their luck spread out along the shoreline. Jericho saw the building down the shore a few hundred feet. It had four docks with rowboats tied at each that he guessed were for rent.

There were also several hitching posts and a small yard with a corral and a place to park buggies.

"I believe I'd like to row one of those boats on this lake… maybe take a swim," Jericho said to his horse. He took a last drag and climbed off the rock. A moment later he had his horse at a trot toward the building down the shore.

****

"I need to see the governor… it's important," Barney said to the clerk in the outer office.

"I'll see if he's available, Mister Riley," the clerk replied, then disappeared around a corner. "Go right in," the clerk said as he returned a moment later.

Barney entered and pulled the door shut behind him. The office was simple with a few bookshelves and a massive oak desk upon a Persian rug in the center of the room. Governor Danforth was chewing his cigar while reviewing some paperwork. He looked up as Barney took a seat.

"You look piqued, Barney," Danforth said flatly. "What is it?"

Barney shifted nervously in his chair. "There's a man called Horace Sipe who came to see me an hour ago. He's a federal auditor for Christ's sake… just happens to be passing through and saw the notice for the auction."

"So what? He doesn't pull any weight around here," Danforth immediately fired back.

"He said he's coming to the auction and will perform an auction audit… registrants, sale price, and some other lantern up our rectum requirements. I have to comply… I'm just a land agent."

"So, comply."

"Well, if I do, you better forget about a ringer at that auction unless you're prepared to buy that land yourself," Barney declared. "If the kid doesn't take the bait, you'll own it."

Governor Danforth nodded. "I'm working on another angle… just a day or two more. You don't have to hold an auction if nobody but the kid registers for it, do you?"

"No… but I have to keep the registration open till twenty-four hours before the event."

"All right," the governor said. "I'll get back to you with a plan when I know more. I don't believe anybody else will register."

"I'd bet a double sawbuck not," Barney agreed. "Hell, there's been nobody by yet to even look at the location on the map. Those posters tell 'em all they need to know… a township in the Augusta range… five days east. Nobody's interested."

"Good," Danforth said. "You can cancel the auction and that auditor can go shine boots. As governor I can sanction and approve the sale… and he can't compel me to state my name. By the way, did Mister Sipe show you credentials?"

"Yep."

****

Jericho rowed for nearly two hours, staying within a half mile of the shoreline and reveling in the work and sweat, and how it eased the weight on his mind. The morning had grown hot and he was far from anybody's eye, so he stripped and dove over the side of the boat. Clear and cold was the water, prompting him to swim hard for quick acclimation. He backstroked, side-stroked and breast-stroked for a few minutes each. Then he easily pulled up over the bow of the boat and lit a cigarette before lying stretched out, naked, soaking in the warmth of the sun.

The lodge where he'd rented the boat had a small saloon and dining room. When he returned, he had a meal of lake fish and roasted potatoes along with a beer and two whiskeys. Jericho floated out the door, well fed and painless. The trip back through the forest proved sublime as he smoked and drifted in and out of thought about Wyanet and their soon-to-be life together, all of it made more wonderful by his surroundings and his perfectly satiated state of relaxation. He resolved on having a nap when he returned to his hotel.

Jericho turned onto the main trail of Carson City just a few hundred feet south of town and immediately took notice of the two soldiers riding toward him. They wore sky-blue trousers, faded red undershirts, and black Union caps. And they were staring hard at Jericho who'd never seen a Union soldier before and wasn't sure what they were. But he was abruptly on guard. As he drew close, he nodded to them. They didn't nod back but continued to stare. Then just as they came abreast of each other, one of the soldiers said, "Jericho Buck?"

Jericho passed by without saying anything. The voice came in a menacing tone from behind, "Are you Jericho Buck?"

Jericho reined his horse around to face the soldiers who were stopped and facing him thirty feet away. "Are you talkin' to me?" Jericho asked. "I thought you were talkin' to each other."

The tougher looking one in his early thirties with a stripe down the side of each pant leg stared unkindly. "I'm speakin' to you. What about it, boy? Are you Jericho Buck?"

"No," Jericho answered and reined his horse back toward Carson City's Main Street.

"Don't you turn your back on me! I'm not done with you, boy!" the soldier shouted.

A few people at the south end of Main Street heard the soldier shout and now were watching. Jericho reined around again and spoke as calm as the devil.

"You're done with me unless you and your partner want'a lay dead in the dirt there. I ain't the fella you want… so you can leave me be, or die shuckin' your rifles."

The tough one stared silently a moment, taking more notice of the twin Navy Colts Jericho wore. "C'mon," he said to the other. They reined their horses around and continued on down the trail toward Genoa.

Jericho dropped his horse at the livery and headed toward the hotel, all the while wondering why soldiers were hunting him. There was nothing friendly about their inquiry. They had braced him. And they were heading toward Genoa, his original destination. His worry turned to Wyanet and the tribe.

40

The rap on the door woke him. Jericho climbed out of bed, his pants still on, and headed for the door as the late afternoon sun pierced the window. He'd been asleep for a few hours.

Jericho opened the door to a bigger man in his forties. He wore a star.

"Are you Jericho Buck?"

Jericho nodded, "I am… what can I do for you?"

"I'm Sheriff Horton. Do you know a gal named Sadie and a man called Petey Jenkins?"

"I know of 'em both… they're dead now," Jericho said.

"How do you happen to know that?" the sheriff asked.

"Well, I had a drink with that gal Sadie… then she asked me to walk her home. She led me up an alley and that hombre Petey clubbed me. They robbed me. Her friend Becky told me where they lived so I went out there. They was makin' a break for it when I came upon 'em. That Petey character shot at me with my own rifle. Reckon he didn't know to tamp that powder 'fore he pulled the trigger. It misfired and they flipped that buckboard. Hit the rocks and that was it for them. I collected my personals and left."

"All right then," the sheriff said like he'd heard enough. "Becky told the same about the robbery part. The rest of it fits the way you told it… and it don't surprise me or anyone else that no-account Petey met his end. Just needed to know the facts." The sheriff turned to leave, then stopped and asked, "You got business here?"

"Yes, sir… a few more days is all."

Sheriff Horton cracked a half-smile. "Well, if you're the only one around when somebody else gets killed, come tell me about it… right?"

"Yeah… right," Jericho said. "I should'a let you know… sorry."

After the sheriff left, Jericho threw on a shirt and his boots and hat and quickly made for the assayer's office, hoping it hadn't yet closed. His timepiece showed two minutes to spare as he walked in and got the evil eye from the guards who didn't want late business to delay their departure.

"Come to the back," Milton Summerdill said to Jericho, waving for him to follow. Milton had his coat on and also looked ready to leave for the day.

"Sorry to show up just as you're leavin'," Jericho said when they were alone in the back room. "Just wanted to see how your work was comin' on my bags."

"I'm finished, Mister Buck… about an hour ago. I was hoping you might drop in. Please sit down," Milton said as he seated himself behind his desk.

Milton produced a document from a drawer. "This is your assay report that gives all the specific information regarding your gold. It contains technical information that we can go over at a later time if you like… but to get to the point, your gold contains a median karat grade of twenty-two, point four… very fine indeed. It has a value of twenty-seven thousand and seventy-five dollars. Based on that, I'd like to offer you twenty-six thousand, five hundred and twenty dollars for it. That would include a one-and-a-half-percent brokerage fee with the rest being my assay fee. I do not believe you will find a better offer… and you would have to travel quite a distance to find out. In any event, if you do not judge that as satisfactory, you can pay my assay fee of one hundred fifty dollars and try your luck elsewhere."

Jericho broke to a broad smile. “No need for that, Mister Summerdill… I accept your offer.”

“Good! Good!” Milton declared, smiling back and offering his hand to shake Jericho’s. “Would you like the check now? Or I can simply deliver it to J.C. Bibble at the bank in the morning, now that you have established an account there.”

“I reckon I’d be happiest just havin’ it turn up in my account in the mornin’!”

****

Jericho went directly to the livery and collected his horse, then returned to his hotel and settled up. “I’m headed for the hills!” he conspicuously announced to the desk clerk. Moments later, he cleared town on the trail east and broke to a gallop. At nearly a mile out Jericho turned on the small, private trail that led a third of a mile north to the exclusive Warm Springs Hotel.

He checked in as Bill Mallory, not caring about it being double the rate of the Sierra Hotel. After trying his new bed and seeing the amenities of a stables, laundry, bath service, hot springs, and a top notch saloon and dining room, Jericho figured he would have been happy paying three times more. But mostly he just wanted to be unseen and unknown in town. He figured the soldiers from earlier in the day might return after not finding him in Genoa. They might search in earnest for the man named Jericho Buck. And after the Sadie and Petey episode, followed by a visit from the sheriff, there might be a number of folks that could say they’d heard of a man named Jericho Buck having been in town. He decided he’d hole up right there at the Warm Springs Hotel.

The next morning, Jericho headed for the bank. He stayed off Main Street and instead rode the back lanes and alleys. Banker Biddle was delighted to see him, informing Jericho that his money was on deposit and immediately available.

"Rest assured, Mister Buck, the details of you and your account are completely confidential," J.C. Biddle told him. Then Mister Biddle presented him with a book of checks and offered services reserved for VIPs. Jericho didn't have the heart to tell Biddle that his funds on account would soon be whittled down in a big way.

Next, Jericho went by the land office. "Hello, Mister Riley. Just checkin' to see how many's signed up for the auction."

Barney's eyebrows hiked. "Nobody else has registered yet, Mister Buck."

"Well, it's the day after tomorrow," Jericho said. "Can you have an auction with just one person biddin'?"

"You could… but if no one else has registered by tomorrow at 10 a.m., I'll cancel the auction and we'll enter into negotiations on a price. How does that sound?"

Jericho nodded, "Fine. I'm stayin' out'a town now, so I'll check back tomorrow at noon. I'd be obliged if you keep me and our business unknown to anybody who might ask."

"Oh, of course!" Barney said. "You can rely on my discretion."

"That's good to know," said Jericho, as he looked at the big wall map and the particular township he had picked. He looked closely, like a man who wanted to make certain he was getting it right. Then he left.

Jericho dropped by the mercantile and bought out all the dime novels they had and headed for the hotel.

41

The day broke cold with low clouds, light winds, and a drop in temperature of 25 degrees from the day before. By 7a.m. an intermittent drizzle cooled things even more as the front continued in from over the Sierra Nevada, shrouded in fog.

Jericho was happy to lie reading on the most comfortable bed he ever imagined. At mid-morning he grew hungry and restless so availed himself of the biscuits and sausage gravy in the dining room. Then he went to the hot springs bath house and rented a bathing suit. The woman at the counter was young and pretty.

"You picked the right day for the springs," she said, smiling. "We haven't had hardly anybody for a week, except at night."

"Been too hot to be sittin' in them springs," Jericho offered. "Boil you up like a potato. Not today though… it's downright cold!"

He spent the better part of an hour in the natural pool, marveling at the heat that soaked away his stiffness and felt so good. Jericho smoked and soaked while he gazed skyward, considering how negotiations might play out and what possibilities to be ready for. It was something he wasn't versed in, so he tried to stake out the most important points for him. When he finally felt like a boiled potato, he emerged with shriveled palms. He dressed and returned to his room where he strapped on his pistols and set his hat low. With a keen sense of the day's importance, he headed for town.

****

Governor Danforth stood in Barney's office looking at the big map. "You've put up all the cancellation notices?" he asked Barney who was sitting at his desk.

"Yep… done."

"Good. What about the auditor… Horace Sipe? Has he been skulking around?"

Barney frowned with puzzlement. "No… hasn't been by once. Haven't seen him around town either."

"Well, perhaps the little rodent scurried away when he saw the cancellation," Danforth said. He turned to Barney. "My sources tell me this Augusta range is mostly Indian Territory… troublesome and worthless in value for the foreseeable future."

"I think that's right," Barney agreed.

Danforth walked to the chair in front of Barney's desk and sat down. He leaned forward on his elbows and spoke in a quiet, deliberate tone. "My sources other than J.C. Biddle also tell me young Mister Buck has twenty-six thousand and five hundred dollars in the Carson City Bank. I want all of it! You sell him that land! If you have to throw in more adjoining land, do it, but get all of that money!"

"I don't think that will be necessary," Barney said. "Twenty-six, five is still a discount from the dollar twenty-five per acre that is a baseline benchmark for government land."

"Well, don't you let him get away! You understand?" Danforth pressed. "Get all the money!"

Barney nodded.

A knock came at the door just before Barney's clerk opened it and poked his head in. "Jericho Buck is here to see you, Mister Riley."

Barney looked to the wall clock. "He's quite a bit early," Barney said to the governor who nodded his approval. Barney looked back to his clerk. "Send him in."

Jericho entered a moment later as Governor Danforth and Barney stood waiting. "Hello young man… Mister Buck is it?" Danforth asked.

"Yes, sir, Jericho Buck," Jericho answered, extending his hand to shake.

"I'm Brad Danforth, governor of the Nevada Territory," Danforth said as he attempted to strangle Jericho's hand.

Jericho gave him the steel grip as his eyes widened with surprise. "It's an honor to make your acquaintance, sir."

"My honor as well," Danforth said. "I understand you wish to purchase a large tract of land in our territory. Nevada is the heart of the West… a special place where pioneers come to live freely and make their contributions to our growing nation. I thank you for picking Nevada and wish you well in your endeavors. If there is any way I can assist you in the future, please feel free to call on me."

"I'm much obliged, sir," Jericho said, almost speechless at the governor's seemingly genuine graciousness.

"I'll leave you and Mister Riley to your business. Goodbye," the governor said and then took his leave.

Jericho stood until Danforth left and then sat down in front of Barney. "Right nice man," Jericho said, still a bit stunned he'd met the governor.

"Yes," Barney agreed, adding nothing else. "The auction has officially been canceled. So now you make an offer and if I think it's in line with the fair value, I'll submit it to the governor for his approval."

"All right," Jericho said. "I reckon I'll start by just askin' what you would take for the land."

Barney appeared deep in thought for a moment. "Well, as I told you when you first came in, the customary price is one dollar and twenty-five cents per acre. However given that this land is in mountain wilderness that would not be considered prime, and given that it has not been surveyed, I believe we would be inclined to accept a lesser price… say a dollar and fifteen cents per acre."

"How much would that be?" Jericho asked, already knowing the answer.

Barney pondered, his lips moving in calculation.

"Twenty-six thousand, five hundred dollars?" Jericho asked with the tone of a rube who suspected he'd just won the door prize.

"Just a moment," Barney said as he grabbed a slip of paper and a pencil then swiftly began scribbling figures. "Why that's right!" he declared a moment later.

Jericho nodded his head, "I reckon you know exactly how much money I have… and you'd like me to spend it all?"

"That's correct, Mister Buck… on both counts."

"Well then," Jericho said as he stood up and walked to the big map. He pointed his finger at the township and then indicated the townships directly above and below. "For that price I also want half of each adjoining township north and south. That's a total of two townships… this whole one here… and half of this one, and half of this one," Jericho said, sliding his finger to each. "That would make the piece of land I want six miles wide, east to west, by twelve miles long, south to north. That's forty-six thousand and eighty acres… right?"

Barney frowned, "Well, yes, that's right… all except for the price. That's only sixty-two and a half cents per acre."

"Yes, but like you said, it ain't prime land. It sure ain't in prime location," Jericho countered.

"I'm sorry," said Barney, "I don't think you've offered enough."

Jericho abruptly stood up. "I'm sorry, too. I just found out about a chance to buy into a good freightin' business. I reckon I'll put my money in that. Thank you for makin' the choice clearer to me, Mister Riley. Much obliged."

Jericho began walking for the door.

Barney shot out of his chair. "Wait!" he called, panicked.

Jericho turned around.

"Please… come sit down," Barney implored.

Jericho sat back down and lit a smoke, waiting for Barney to say whatever it was he was going to say.

"Such is the nature of negotiations," said Barney. "Actually, Governor Danforth has authorized me to accept as low as half-price. We will sell the forty-six thousand and eighty acres you specified for twenty-six thousand, five hundred dollars. Do we have a deal?"

Jericho took a long drag on his cigarette in consideration and slowly exhaled in a slow stream of smoke that seemed to take half a minute to cease. Barney felt the slightest pang of nausea as he waited.

Jericho leaned forward and extended his hand to shake. "Yep, we have a deal."

"Excellent!" Barney declared jubilantly. "I'll have the paperwork all ready by tomorrow at… say noon?"

"That surely is fine," Jericho declared.

42

High noon arrived at the land office just as Jericho did. His horse was packed much lighter for his trip back now that the gold was gone.

"We're all set here," Barney said as Jericho sat down in front of his desk. "I followed your instructions and listed your name as it is on your letter of birth... Jericho Taylor Buck... and also put your wife's name on the quit claim deed... Wyanet Buck... and there are three original deeds, one for the county recorder and two for you as you requested. The governor will be here in a few more minutes to sign and stamp his seal on the deeds and the bill of sale, which also contains the legal description. You have the check?"

"Right here," Jericho said, pulling it from the top pocket of his new shirt.

"Good," Barney said. "We'll be surveying your land sometime within a year. But you have all that you need right now."

A half hour later, Jericho hand delivered one of the deeds to the county recorder who was eating lunch at his desk. He looked at the deed, his eyes paying respectful attention to Governor Danforth's signature and seal. "This will be officially filed into the record today," he said. "A notice of this will also be on file at the national land office in Washington, D.C. ... though that will take several months."

"Much obliged," Jericho said as he tipped his hat and then left with his remaining deeds and sales papers.

At one o'clock Jericho walked into the bank where J.C. Biddle ushered him into his office and closed the door.

"I'm sorry to see you have written a check for nearly all the funds you have on account," Biddle said, whimsically.

"Still have a hundred dollars in my account… right?"

"Yes, that's correct," Biddle answered.

"And you said I get a free safe-deposit box here if I keep at least a hundred dollars in your bank… right?"

"Yes, that, too, is correct."

"Well, I got some papers here I want'a keep in that box. And I'll tell ya somethin' else. It's damn likely I'll be puttin' more money in your bank over time… maybe a lot."

Biddle's face took on an expression of pleasant surprise. "Well, that's fine! Just fine!"

"I'll tell ya what's not fine," Jericho said. "Somebody in your bank told exactly how much I had in here, except for the hundred. Who do you reckon that is?"

Biddle looked shocked. "Why, that can't be!"

"It most certainly can be, because it happened. You got'a rat somewhere in here," Jericho declared matter of factly. "And I don't expect it better ever happen again."

Biddle stammered, "Uhh, of course not… I'll get to the bottom of it. I will not tolerate such things!"

Jericho smiled and extended his hand to shake Biddle's like nothing had happened. "Thanks for your help, Mister Biddle. Now if you can show me how my safe deposit box works, I'll put a few of these papers in for safekeeping and be on my way."

"Yes, of course. I'll show you and give you a key."

****

His deer-hide pack bags were light with just a few personals, some food, and a dozen dime novels. He mounted up and looked at his timepiece. It read nearly 2 o'clock. Six hours of daylight remained. Jericho would have preferred to leave early the next morning but he wasn't going to waste another minute. The well-being of Wyanet and the tribe plagued his mind. He put his horse to a trot up Main Street headed for the trail east out of town.

The two soldiers stood inside the sheriff's office. The older, tough one, Sergeant Gasper, was making his play to a deputy.

"Yes, the man we're looking for is called Jericho Buck. His mother lives in Fort Churchill. She's dying and wants to lay eyes on her son one more time. Do you know him or know where he is?"

"I know who he is," the deputy replied. "I'm guessin' he's gone now. He was staying at the Sierra Hotel but word is he checked out a couple days ago. Well, I'll be! There he goes now!" the deputy said as the rider passed the window.

Sergeant Gasper snapped toward the window to see the side of Jericho riding by. Gasper knew immediately it was the man they had braced several days earlier, before they'd continued on to Genoa. It was the man who had threatened to kill him and Corporal Dean.

"Thank you, deputy," Gasper said as he and the corporal moved quickly for the door.

Jericho didn't see the soldiers exiting the sheriff's office behind him. They stood staring a moment as he continued up Main Street.

"Ain't that the boy who said he was gonna kill us?" Corporal Dean asked.

"It sure in hell is," Gasper replied. "And the son of a bitch looks to be riding out of town. We'll follow behind. As soon as we're good'n clear, I'll put one in the back of his head."

"Ain't our orders to bring him back alive?" Dean queried. "You said Major Adams wants information from him."

Gasper looked at Dean with hate in his eyes. "That man said we'd be layin' dead in the dirt! That he'd be the one to kill us!

You brook that? He's the man we're lookin' for. We'll bring him in draped over his saddle! I'll say he made a move on us… and he will if we give him the chance!"

"You got a point there," Dean said. "As long as you can tell *how* to the major, we'll take him however you say."

The soldiers mounted up and put their horses to an easy trot up Main Street as Jericho turned east at the end of town. Jericho gave a quick glance back down Main Street and saw them, immediately knowing they were following him. He knew they'd be coming for him as soon as he cleared town. His mind raced. He had no rifle but remembered they both did. And he knew they'd use them to bring him down, shooting his horse or him as soon as they were out a ways where no one else would see. It came to him instantly. Jericho kicked his horse to a gallop. "Hyah! Hyah!" he called as he worked the animal to full speed.

Gasper and Dean didn't see Jericho had broken to a full gallop until they cleared the last building on the east side of Main Street. "He's runnin' now!" Gasper cried. They kicked their horses to a gallop and gave chase to Jericho who had already opened up a quarter-mile lead. Jericho's horse was fresh. Gasper and Dean had put fifteen miles on their mounts that morning coming from Genoa.

Jericho's lead continued to grow but he knew they'd keep after him. He guessed they couldn't get fresh mounts until Fort Churchill, which was forty miles ahead. He'd ride the pace again as if he'd taken up the run, all thirteen miles to the Dayton Pony Express Station where he'd tell them who he was and plead for a fresh horse. But he'd have to open up a ten-minute lead for it to work. "C'mon boy!" he called to his Indian pony as he paced him to make the distance with the best speed. The perilous afternoon heat of summer beat down upon him as he put all his skill and know-how into the ride for the Dayton station.

In a little under an hour, he saw the station ahead and took another look behind him. The soldiers were nowhere in sight. There was a small settlement a half mile northeast and he suddenly remembered the livery it had. "Damn!" he exclaimed to himself, knowing the soldiers might be able to requisition fresh horses there. Pony Express stations would not accommodate such a request. Jericho galloped into the yard at Dayton Station and flew off his mount, hitting the ground and hitching his horse to the rail in seconds.

Jericho walked into the station that looked so much like the others he'd seen and worked. Three men were sitting in rockers in the small parlor area where books occupied two shelves, and newspapers and catalogues were strewn on a table. They looked up, surprised at the sudden entrance.

"Howdy! My name's Jericho Buck. Is one of you men the Station Keeper?"

"That's me… Rob Schroeder. What can I do for you?" said the oldest man of medium build in his mid-thirties.

"Well, I used to take up the run on the Dry Creek to Cold Springs route… but ended up shot by some desperadoes and in the care of a Paiute tribe for a spell. I'm in great need of a fresh mount to get back to the gal I'm gonna marry. I believe she's in danger. Got a good, young mustang to swap. See if I can keep swappin' at all the stations between here and Cold Springs. You'll be gainin' a horse. I'm hopin' you'll say yes."

Rob started nodding slowly in recollection. "I heard about you… a lot of us have. Yeah… Jericho Buck… Pony Express rider healed up by Paiutes! Well, let's take a look at that mustang you got and get you a fresh horse!"

"Much obliged, Mister Schroeder!" Jericho said. "Not to be forward… but I'm in a dang fire hurry!"

Rob looked to the tender who was already getting out of his chair. "Brody, hotfoot and get 'im a good one."

"Yep," Brody answered and beat a path out the door.

Minutes later, Jericho had his tack and pack bags aboard his fresh mount. He swung up into the saddle and looked back west where he thought he detected faint dust on the horizon. "I can't thank ya enough! Best to ya! So long!"

43

Governor Danforth walked into Barney Riley's office looking hot under the collar. "I'll be damned!" he said. "I just found out the nature of the deposit to young Mister Buck's account! It was a check from our assayer Milton goddamned Summerdill!"

Barney looked bewildered a moment. "So? Buck said it was an inheritance from his grandfather?"

"Bullion? His grandfather in Texas left him gold bullion that he dragged all over creation before having it assayed here in Carson City?" Danforth asked, looking incredulous. "Not a chance!"

"No, that doesn't sound likely," Barney agreed. "But you yourself said he wouldn't have bought all that land... spent all that money when all he had to do was file a mining claim."

"That's the hell of it!" Danforth exclaimed. "I can't figure it, but something smells like rotten fish!"

Danforth walked to the map and stared at the circled land that Jericho had just bought. "So the intrepid Mister Buck just put his finger to a spot on the map... to hell and gone from anywhere else... and declared he wanted to buy it. I want that land surveyed! I want to know what's there. If he dug gold there and decided to buy miles of land thinking there'd be gold all over it, then I want to know! If he's got a mine there, he could be wrong about where it is on this map! A survey might show he was off by miles! Just pointing his finger at the map might have been like a blind man pitching horseshoes."

"That's certainly a good possibility," agreed Barney. "But I don't see how he would have had time to dig that amount of gold anyway. He said he rode for the Pony Express from Cold Springs to Dry Creek, and just explored that land on his time off, hunting and fishing."

"That's another thing!" Danforth barked. "Pony Express? I want somebody to verify that. But right now, I want that land surveyed!"

"It will take a long time," Barney said. "I'll have to put together a sizable crew… arrange some protection. That's Indian country. It wouldn't be completed till late fall… maybe December… maybe sooner, but not much."

"I'll send troops with them from Fort Churchill," Danforth said. "Get it going."

****

Jericho changed out horses at every Pony Express station between Carson City and Cold Springs, all twelve of them. He rode all afternoon and all night then galloped into the wind of a new day as he pulled his hat lower and squinted against the rising sun, humbled by the hospitality he'd received at each and every stop. As he rode the last legs toward Cold Springs, the brilliance of the Pony Express settled on him as if tempered by fire. In his yet short life, these were the greatest men he had ever known, not because they were educated gentlemen, but because they personified the very backbone of spirit, courage, and perseverance that forged the American West. Theirs was a stoic endeavor of men who streaked like meteors in wild pursuit, given to the land as part of the great landscape.

After eighteen hours and the better part of two hundred miles, Jericho galloped into the Cold Springs yard at 8 a.m. and gave his short greetings to Stan, Skinner, and Hags before quickly retiring to a bunk where he collapsed. Eleven hours later at 7 p.m. he rose and ate two plates of beef and biscuits, then poured a cup of scalding coffee and headed for a porch rocker. The puffer clouds drifted sweetly, their bellies painted orange and red with sunset; so fine and familiar it was as he lit a smoke and sipped his coffee. Jericho felt like he'd crawled through a snake pit with his adventures in Carson City. It made his current surroundings all the sweeter.

Stan came out the door with a cup of coffee and his pipe, having arisen from a nap. He sat down in another rocker and relit his pipe then looked over to Jericho. "I never heard of anybody ridin' that far that fast," he said. "You sure were all done when you got here! A cannon ball coming through the wall wouldn't have waked you."

"I don't hardly remember arrivin'," Jericho said.

"Well, I know it… that's why I didn't bother telling you then," said Stan. "But you should know now that there are soldiers looking for you. A company out of Fort Churchill of about fifty came through here maybe ten days ago, looking for your Paiute tribe. The Army major said they wanted to talk to these Paiutes about their means. And just before they got here, they heard you'd been healing up in a Paiute camp… so now they want to find you… have you show them where the Paiute camp is. They knew you were headed for Genoa. The major sent a letter back to the fort."

"Yeah, they had two of 'em lookin' for me back that way but I never made Genoa. Turned out Carson City's the capital now. They almost took me there but I played 'em false for a while… then they found out I was me. They chased me when I left Carson City. Least now I know why."

Jericho took a last drag of his smoke as he looked to the sunset once more, his face etched with grim recollection. "I played a lot'a folks false lately. I ain't proud of it… I didn't like doin' it, but it was the only way I could protect that tribe and my woman. I played you half false, too, Stan. Couldn't nobody else know until I did what I set out to do. But now it's done… and now I'll tell you."

As Stan listened with wide eyes and burning ears, Jericho told of the Paiute gold then speculated: "I reckon word got around that some Paiutes had bought a lot of goods and paid gold for 'em. That Army major must'a got wind. If he could find those Indians and their mines, he could just claim them mines and run them Indians out… or kill 'em. Not now. I bought all that land where they're camped and where the mines are. The chief gave me a heap'a gold to do it with. My wife-to-be's name is on the deed… and I had a will drawn up that leaves all to my wife and children. A lawyer told me Indians can't buy land or make land claims, but they can own land that's given to 'em by the rightful owner. It's all theirs now… the land and the gold."

Stan chuckled, "Guess you better get married quick and get to work on those children."

"Hell, I'd go tonight but I could never find my way in the dark. It's like a damn mystery… a regular secret passage gettin' into that basin. First light I'm off. Can I buy one'a your horses?"

"I almost forgot!" Stan said. "Your horse is in the barn. Willie sent him along with your saddle and saddlebags packed with your personals. Strung him from station to station… every other rider."

"Hot succotash!" Jericho sang. "Sent that note along a while back askin' if he could manage such. Forgot about it with all that's been whizzin' about." Jericho stood up with a smile. "Better go say hello to ole Buddy right now!"

44

Her work done for the morning, Wyanet sat alone by the river eating a meal of flatbread and brown trout as she daydreamed about her love, Jericho. Her eyes drifted to the other bank where Indian paintbrush cast its vibrant orange in contrast to purple lupine in an array of growth presently bathed in the noon sun. The sight of it warmed her heart as she swooned in thought of him. She finished her meal and moved to the water's edge where she washed her hands and splashed a bit of the water on her face. Then she turned back toward the camp and there he was, looking at her as he stood by the wickiup where he had lain healing for so many weeks. He began walking toward her. She broke to a run, her arms already extended in anticipation. Others in the camp were smiling and watching as Jericho and Wyanet reached each other and engulfed one another in a long hug, nuzzling their faces together and then taking to a passionate kiss.

After a long moment, she pulled back, cradling his face with her hands. Her eyes welled with tears that began to spill over. "My love, you are here! It is not a dream!"

He pulled her to him and held her tightly as he whispered in her ear, "It's our dream and it starts now."

****

A morning fog blanketing the river had burned off in the bright, autumn sun, showing crisp beauty in the change of colors. Grass of the long fields had yielded its green over to golden and auburn in complement to the falling leaves of the season, brightly tinted.

Wyanet sat on the porch of the cabin weaving the small blanket, the work of it perched on her abdomen which held the early swell of her first child. She had come out to cool herself from the cookstove and her present condition. From her vantage she could see the encampment of wickiups a half mile east across the river. And to the north of it, triangulated at another half mile, was the long, log building that was many times the size of her and Jericho's cabin. Like a machine of efficiency, twenty white men had built it in a month, complete with a stall barn and corral.

Late November's chill prompted her to return inside. A dim sound became apparent as she stood up. She tried to track the direction of it, but sound in the basin could ricochet and play tricks on the ears. The steady roll of it became faintly louder. She knew it was horses and immediately thought of Jericho who was across the river for a meeting at the log building. As she stared that way, she saw the twenty men file out of the building, all with rifles, and led by her husband.

Jericho watched the soldiers coming and then heard Paiutes yipping from behind him. He looked the other way to see the fifty Paiute warriors on the run, closing in support of his position. Paiute women and other men, including Growling Bear on a crutch, stood with rifles, assembled at the near edge of their encampment. They watched as their warriors sprinted toward the spot where Jericho stood with his men. Jericho turned back the other way and watched the Army Company of thirty soldiers and a half-dozen civilians closing from a quarter mile. "Stay here," he said to his men as he began walking out toward the approaching troops, attempting to head off any violence. His men began to fan out behind him. Willie, Hags, Stan, Hambone, Skinner, McCarter, Pooch, Huck, Purdy, Danny, Billy, Clyde, Sinkhole, Frank, Brandon,

Russ, Tombstone, Yerkey, Gabe, and Wayne, all of them former Pony Express employees who stood with their rifles at ease, pointed down.

Major Adams reined to a stop with his hand up and the command of "Halt!" Two sergeants reined up beside Adams. One of them was Sergeant Gasper whom Jericho had last seen in Carson City. Gasper glared at Jericho who paid him no mind.

"Are you Jericho Buck?" Adams asked.

"Yes, I am… and this is my land."

The major nodded. "Yes, I know. You pulled off quite a coup."

"All lawful and righteous," Jericho calmly replied. "What can I do for you?"

Adams waved his arm behind him to the right. "These men are surveyors… here to finish the survey of your land. We are with them to protect from any Indian attacks and ensure that they can complete their work. They only have a few more days to note the interior topography and characteristics of your land… isn't that correct, Mister Collins?"

The farthest man to the right dressed in civilian clothes spoke up: "Yes, that's right," Collins said. "We've located, staked, and pinned the four corners of your property which is twelve miles north to south, and six miles east to west. You might like to know that where this particular valley sits is… by my estimation… nearly dead center to those dimensions each direction."

A cheer went up from the men behind.

Jericho smiled, waiting till the whoops died down. "That's good to know, Mister Collins," Jericho said. "Much obliged."

Collins spoke again, "We have perhaps two or three days left… simply to see and describe the interior of those corners, the nature of the land to the degree that we can access it. As you already know, much of the interior is highly inaccessible except by small corridors to the north and south." Collins looked around for a moment in admiration. "A hidden paradise you have here," he concluded.

Another cheer went up from the men, which cued the Paiute warriors that they should cheer too. They joined in with wild whoops and high-pitched tongue rolls. Some of the soldiers in ranks smiled and laughed at the spontaneous joy of the moment.

"I can leave you with a rough sketch of your land's topography and your current proximity within when we've finished, if you like," Collins said, "and then an official version will be available to you in another month or so… in Carson City."

"Yes, please," Jericho said.

Major Adams spoke up. "Then I trust you have no objection to the completion of this work?"

"No, sir," Jericho replied happily. "In fact, if you'd like to camp here or nearby tonight, you are welcome to."

"Thank you, Mister Buck. That is most kind," Adams replied. "Though I believe we'll be camped a few miles south."

The men cheered one more time, joined by the Paiutes who would have to wait for the interpretation from Crow Talks before knowing what they had cheered for.

It had been Chief Leaping Elk's idea. When the Pony Express had disbanded in early October, Jericho had lamented its demise and mentioned that Willie of Dry Creek Station had once been a mine foreman. Leaping Elk had said they could use such expertise to realize the potential of their mines, and noted that additional men would mean some of the Paiute miners could return to hunting and other chores in support of the tribe. Leaping Elk suggested an overall ten-percent cut going forward to be divided for twenty Pony Express men that wanted to come for one year. Jericho had no problem filling that roster. In the previous year, the Paiutes had already mined a dozen 40-pound sacks before Jericho's trip to Carson City. And the yield was now increasing.

****

He held her to him as they looked out over the wondrous valley beyond. Winter was fast approaching. She kissed his neck. "My father likes our cabin. He says he may build one for himself, now that he has a permanent place he can return to."

Jericho nodded. "A cabin's warmer… more comfortable in winter."

"Yes," she agreed. "And the others will want to build cabins also! My father says they may move about less now… perhaps stay here where our children will grow strong."

"Our many children," said Jericho.

"Yes," she said contentedly. "And my father told me he no longer calls this place Swift River Valley."

"Yeah?" Jericho puzzled.

"Yes," she said holding him tighter. "He has named it The Valley of Brave Rider."

Printed in Great Britain
by Amazon

27391307R00157